S-Bahn 5:32

Stories

BEN ROSENTHAL

Adelaide Books
New York / Lisbon
2021

S-BAHN 5:32

A collection of short stories

By Ben Rosenthal

Copyright © by Ben Rosenthal

Cover design © 2021 Adelaide Books

Published by Adelaide Books, New York / Lisbon
adelaidebooks.org

Editor-in-Chief
Stevan V. Nikolic

For any information, please address Adelaide Books
at info@adelaidebooks.org

or write to:

Adelaide Books
244 Fifth Ave. Suite D27
New York, NY, 10001

ISBN: 978-1-955196-19-2

Printed in the United States of America

S-BAHN 5:32

To H.L., Q.F.B., and K.G.

Contents

Mara

The cable man said the leafcutter must have climbed the roof and done something stupid; some misdirected end run around the powerlines, and in taking his shears to the hanging palm, cut the line that ran four hundred and eighty-nine HD channels (excluding premiums) into the posh den of Bunny Weidman's ranch home. Mara went into the guesthouse and retrieved the only ladder she could find. She presented it to the repairman, whose coverall nametag read Narek. He was a darkish-colored Armenian, thick, potbellied, his face oddly rotund, like an infant's.

"Be an hour, think," he said. "I will run a new line, clip this to the siding with a clip. Then we'll resend the signal from Central."

"Okay," said Mara. "I'll tell Doctor Weidman that's what you're doing."

She rounded the house where Tommy Rebel was shining his hotrod rims. Her lipstick was on his neck and it looked like part of his tattoo. He looked up, squinting. About twelve feet under the pitched roof, on the deck overlooking the swimming pool where Bunny Weidman sat reading about the sports cars he would happily lend to his fetching tenant, was Stan Weidman, still in his bathrobe, pantomiming golf strokes, sipping at his warm morning coffee.

"You know," said Tommy, eying Stan. "Once they fix that line that prick is going to a feature of this place."

"Who are you to complain?"

"Who are *you*? Do you want me to get started on that?"

"Right on," said Mara. "You just wrench."

She walked away, noting the color splash of Tommy's new bull rider tattoo as he bent to shine a rim.

Narek set the ladder up and began climbing.

She had to remind herself that this was real, for Mara McNamara was a runaway. New Jersey had held a receding claim on her but now and then it would sting her like a prank-calling ex. She had, at the age of eighteen, asserted her position with her mother fundamentally. It was the culmination of a verbal sparring that began when her father fled the manor to skirt chase his way across Monmouth County with a trunkful of widgets he could sell. He'd phone them from Day's Inns and Econolodges, Red Roofs and Marriots as far south as Cherry Hill, never saying what the trunk held or what exactly was the gambit. In the coming months, Joe McNamara would alight in rural Tennessee with a cosmetician from Moldova by his side. Somehow Mara was seen as the cause of his leaving, having flouted her mom's edicts, having "dabbled" in white Incan substances, but really, having done nothing more than be her daughter. At long last, there in the linoleum, she and her mother, a former majorette in Parsippany whose try at hawking Mary Kay to homemakers came to a lot of handwringing when HQ got wind of just what kind of whack spiels the housewives were getting, had it all out in a plate hurling contest. But it wasn't the back and forth about dad or even the crashing ceramic sounds that were so liberating to mom and daughter; it was the airing out of something words, and even plate hurling, could only begin to address.

The Lindo Baby was resettled. It was all down to Mom.

That was indisputable.

So Mara tore out, fled to the depot, a striking brow gash from one of her mother's side-armed tosses a permanent trademark on her face.

A westbound Trailways out of Elizabethtown rode her across the Great Divide. At the end of I-40 she would cannibalize her pipe dreams in the fast lane, LA style. Failure was written into its nuclei, her nuclei. That was the plan. If one is to cry Uncle, why not do so in a warmer place? The solar rays of LA were nothing like the spuming greys that hung over the rooftops of Bayonne's tidy and judgmental Tudor tracks.

She thought she'd "act".

Thus weekly improv group sessions in which she played the ditz (less present wit required) allowed her to explore her range. She auditioned for a small one-act opposite a declining daytime soap star and summarily "went up" on her chosen "sides." Did she really care whether she was a medium between words on a page and eyes that were only pinned on her décolleté? Did she care about anything? Acting was a religion to some people as likewise religion was acting to most. The secular choice was to fade, do nothing; not even temp, waste away backdating insurance claims in a dental office, or sire more kids. The trick was to find a pool and wake up beside it at sixty-five, half keeled over on Bloody Maries and breaded kale, lounging until the mortuary claimed you.

To that effect, she now cohabitated in a craftsman split ranch owned by the semiretired urologist, Arnold "Bunny" Weidman, and had to ritually deflect his no-go golf pro of an offspring, Stan, who would come around and beg his father's scrip pad while wearing the wraparound sunglasses that cinched his scanty locks into a ducktail. Mara thought a guy like this didn't need to open his mouth to be an asshole. What he wanted was usually painkillers, sometimes a bit more zip. On one of his visits he saw Mara binning compostables near the guesthouse and became a solid fixture for a week. When nothing amorous came to pass, he took his scrips and removed himself back to the links around Alameda, where biotech wunderkinds were sealing deals near the water hazards and would pay through the nose for his golfing knack. He was back again this weekend, on the fiend, and Mara missed the spatial fluidity, the good spans when she only waited on Bunny Weidman, slipping a dustpan under broom hairs and sometimes running errands in his sky-blue Kharman Ghia. The unmarriable physician was eyeing her like a caged dog on those errand drives, his eyes seizing on her midriff and her soft manipulating of the wheel. He was a fiddle she could play, whether it would be a jig or a symphony was up to her. For now, eschewing his company, she would try and take those drives alone. She would buy tacos *el pastor* above the Tujunga Wash and then stare at the fly-buzzing water, the stalled trough of diverted river sludge that began as rainwater above. She would eat tacos and watch trespassing coyotes holding their sunset battle royals in the channel mud. Sometimes she would drive to overlooks which gave her a less impeded survey of the balding molehills, the dried San Gabriel Mountains, their brush kindling wildfire distress signals to her place among the chaparral. She would greet these distress signals. She would live in them.

Narek was hammering in a new line and beating away fronds from the nearby palm. His banging was spaced, more like an inebriated door-knocking than a hammering of the utility type.

Mara sat by the pool and modeled her silver pedicure for the urologist, letting her feet slap the surface of the water. He admired her from his chair but made no motions. Up on the roof deck Stan in the paisley bathrobe vaped and peeked out indifferently at the chlorinated lagoon with its bright rim of ersatz sea coral, at the seamless nothing-going-on down there and amid the nothing saw the muscular ax-thumping roustabout Mara went to bed with swimming breaststrokes. Mara let the straps fall on her bikini top. Bunny Weidman looked over his *Road & Track,* doggedly unenthused behind his mag. Mara looked over the landscaping, observing where she'd fetched up. She noted at once the atavistic plant life a bladder doctor could trick out his spread with, the Japanese lantern skiffs in the waterless fishpond cut in handsomely by the sandstone walkway. There were Bose subwoofers tacked to Palo Verde trees so primordial noises could accompany morning tai chi. A birdfeeder proffered suet to scrub jays. A plasma screen fireplace blinked.

She fell in and out of sleep now; at the moments she would wake up, she would look at Tommy, another whack across the chops from her own hand. Why Tommy, who played dank rooms and slashed through feedback-heavy, only nominally ironic country punk? When he wasn't fouling the air with his Rickenbacker, he was showering Mara with the bright stubble shavings of his true love. He wanted to shotgun it in the desert with her to some outpost wedding chapel but Mara wondered seriously if she would ever return alive. She had seen him level a bandmate with a bike lock for doing nothing more than break tempo on a power-chord sandblaster indistinguishable all the other noise he ever made. He drove a refurbished black Packard with flame trails to his gigs and his arm read *Lucy, You Got Some Splainin To Do,* the inking courtesy of the El Sereno tattoo shop he co-ran with an quasi-remediated arsonist from Gardenia. He was not a violent guy, just you know it, and he believed Israel downed the Twin Towers; furry, iniquitous Shin Bet had placed covert calls to Zionist fellow travelers awaiting the high sign from Tel Aviv in the Sky Lobby. "Clear out. Incoming. Zein gazunt."

Tommy thought this Bunny Weidman was bound to die early. A porridge of unaired thoughts was surely stewing in his body, mostly regarding his bum son Stan. And really, one only had to look at his bedtable: a murderer's row of anticoagulants, Benefibers, Prilosecs in seven day squares.

"I won't pimp you," Tommy said to Mara once. "But you'n give him eyeful here and there. Flash those headlights in clear lace. Guy's got a sweet spot, you know?"

"I don't want to use him any more than I am," she said. "He's sad."

"He's a profiteer," said Tommy. "Know your pharma."

Now her man was fake-ruddering in the water, wetting down those stupid tats. She reapplied her Coppertone and closed her eyes again. The hammering from the cable man had stopped awhile back, her mind had traced that.

"Hey, Stan," yelled Tommy, buoyant on a duck raft. "Nice robe."

"I'm glad you admire it," Stan replied nasally from the deck. "Is that a bullrider on your carotid artery?"

"Sure as day, brother."

Tommy spun into the depths off the raft, kicking up a lot of spray. When he came up again he peered at the top gable.

"Doctor Weidman," he said, after a moment. "That guy is still up on the roof."

Mara opened her eyes.

"What?" said the doctor.

"The high speed guy from the cable company."

Weidman lowered his *Road & Track*.

"Hmm," he said, as though having spotted a rare bird.

"He's just *sitting* there," said Tommy.

"Maybe taking a break?"

"But Doctor Weidman," said Tommy, scratching his new bullrider. "The line is *in*. The guy like finished it an hour ago. "

Stan went over to the gable first. From the pool, they saw him talking to the cable man, his head shaking back and forth, hands flexed into the pockets of his robe. The cable man seemed to be dispensing wordless kernels, like an Indian baba would, his movements spare and precise, his mouth impenetrable. Stan shrugged at the man and walked back over to the pool, shaking his head.

"He's not talking," he said.

"What do you mean, he's not talking?" said Tommy, slicking his hair back with force.

"He's just *sitting* there." Stan shrugged.

"Does he seem dehydrated?" asked Bunny.

"No, dad, he seems fine. He just won't talk or move."

"What if he's having a stroke?" said Mara.

"Nah, that's not it," said Stan. "He's just, I dunno, he's like *in* some place. You know, a zone. I don't think he's happy."

The four of them walked over under the gable.

Bunny smiled up at the man.

"How's it goin', buddy?" he said through a beatific smile.

The man said nothing.

"Mister," said Mara. "Why don't you want to come down? Are you okay?"

Narek shrugged his shoulders, his mouth furling in glum ticks.

"The hell is that?" said Tommy. "He *shrugs?*"

Mara placed a hand on his shoulder and squeezed.

Bunny Weidman took a second, smiled at Narek like a realtor and said, "I'll bet that system is running famously. You sure do know your wires. Have they resent the signal? We real get antsy in this household without our weekday lineup. So thank you, man. But much as I hate to add this, we're going to have to call some people in authority if you won't take those splicers there and, you know, *come down.*"

Narek shrugged again. Stan half-giggled into the cloth of his robe.

Tommy bit his own hand and said, "Where's the ladder?" Mara pointed at the roof. Narek had pulled the ladder up the gable slope and there it rested.

"You don't have another one?" said Tommy. Weidman shook his head.

"Listen, guy," said Tommy. You did the work, now get into the van that you came in. I'm not gonna say it twice."

Narek grunted but said no more. He looked even glummer now.

Stan said, "At least tell me the cable works. I mean at least tell me that."

Weidman Senior shook his head, walked inside, clicked on the remote and gestured in the affirmative. Stan puffed out some air.

Mara stared at Narek on the gable. Tommy jazzed his eyes around. There were no lintels or footholds he could see, no landing on which to hoist himself up to where the Armenian was sitting. It was sheer under the top and even the split portion on the lower side was unclimbable.

"Shit. Ain't *this* a bitch," said Tommy.

"We could wait him out?" said Stan.

"I don't wanna wait him out!"

Mara thought Tommy was working too hard to convince the elder Weidman he was an ally, a loyal lieutenant who stood for the peace of the ranch and deserved the perks of this ranch. Finally, his temper could be trained on something beyond noise. But it was agitating everybody.

Bunny Weidman stepped back onto the deck through the sliding door. He shook some horse pills out of a tinted phial and downed them with some wheatgrass slurry Stan had left burbling in the blender. Narek sat with his ample fundament right on the pitch of the gable roof and he looked like something in a storybook.

They had gone back to the pool to wait him out but it just wasn't working. Tommy seemed to be doing anger revs; the sort of knuckle-cracking foreplay of a man who doesn't want to spend his wad before he can work up a full torrent. Mara knew Weidman had brooked Stan and Stan's misgivings about launching himself into anything with solid rigor, so he could, for awhile, brook Narek. Mara worried about Narek. She told them not to call the police. It was for her they were refraining. This was power, she guessed. They were being courtly.

But the man wasn't moving and try as they might to stretch this impasse into a war of attrition, there was the question of liability remaining. He might slide off the roof and impale on the lattice. The dumb old hulking sulker might just heatstroke and sue.

Tommy passed under the roof where Narek was sitting and messily eating a Snickers bar.

"Live it up, faggot," said Tommy.

"Don't talk like that," Mara said, walking behind him. "He's not in a good way."

"I hope you like eating mice, asshole, because you're gonna be out of a job faster than you can spit."

Bunny Weidman had put his clothes on (kakis, squared-toed henna slippers, a paisley shirt identical in color to his son's bathrobe) and planted himself next to them.

"Maybe we should spray him with the sprinkler water?" he said.

"Electrolytes," said Stan, pantomiming a 9-iron swing.

"I'm going to the neighbor's, get a ladder," said Tommy to Narek. "And when I come back, I suggest you ditch the roof, man. Doc doesn't have time for this. Maybe Stan does but doc doesn't. Mara's got scripts she's gotta read. Mara's face here is gonna be in lights. Everyone has got dreams, Bluto, and we can't just wait for you to Zen out up there before we hit the ground running? You effing register me?!"

The man maybe did or didn't smile a tiny bit, and remained stationary on the gable. He was sitting what used to be called Indian Style but was now called Criss-Cross-Apple-Sauce.

Stan said, "You think at least it would be hurting his buttocks."

Weidman said, "All right, we've got to call the black and tans."

Stan said, "What if he's suicidal?"

Tommy said: "Good. I wish he'd jump."

"Why don't you just play your music?" said Stan. "He'll roll right off." Tommy quick- faked a smile and then socked Stan in the jaw and the latter went down just that quickly. He lip was fat upon rising, and before they knew it he had gone right back down again.

Narek on the roof shook his head back and forth in parochial condemnation.

"You hit him!" said Mara. She socked Tommy in the side. "What are you taking these days?"

"I'm a mess," said Tommy. "I'm displacing shit. Hence the force of my sound. Have you noticed how hard my music's getting?"

Bunny Weidman bent down to his son Stan.

"You all right?"

"Lip is, I dunno."

"Teeth?"

Stan wiggled them: all clear. Bunny pulled out his cellphone and walked a few steps away.

"Who you calling?" asked Tommy.

"The black and tans," said Weidman, almost casually.

"On him or me?" said Tommy, pointing at the roof.

"Both."

It was only a matter of minutes before the police and the fire department were there. Tommy got cuffed. The Weidmans, thinking only of Mara, implored them to let him remain on the scene, but two tall men led him down the Japanese rock garden to their cruiser. The pitched roof was just low enough that one didn't have to raise their voice but pretty quick the marshal seized the chance, producing a handheld loudspeaker to talk the Armenian down. The firemen were loath to go up there because the man was big and, owing to his sprawled arsenal of weighted wires, could potentially be a threat.

Where had this Armenian been, Mara wondered? What was his distraction? His, his *deal,* as Tommy would say. He was sitting Criss-Cross on the roof tile, barely meditative, and though the Palo trees were losing leaves to the propeller wind of a banking news copter, his sparse hairs were barely flicking. She could swear he was looking at her, through her. He seemed dumb and wise at once, the way babies did, the way they silently judged you. The boy within him was here, surfacing. Did he know the Lindo Baby or was the Lindo baby *his eyes* in *his head?* "Que lindo," she mouthed to Narek, but he said nothing in return. Why would he? The Spanish salon girls in Bayonne, those tousling mamacitas next door, when she'd wheeled the baby by, had always said "Que lindo" and "frio" when it was too cold and she hadn't the reserves of motherly finesse to bundle the little one up against its wishes. Her mother eventually offered to watch the child when Mara was too stunned, too slung out, too *working*, but the mother took palmfuls of Ambiens and soon collapsed in a leaf pile hallucinating. The child, wet from the leaves, was found walking in circles around the mother, this fulminating halfwit speechifying about cosmetics to a breathalyzer and a badge. She had not taken her wallet with her, had sought no friends beyond the promotion of her Mary Kay, so nobody knew who she was or to whom the child belonged. There was a marauding cruise in a squad car to poll residents of the housing tracts but eventually they took the little unnamed child to the precinct, pro forma. Calls were made, hours fizzled, and quickly ACS stepped in because time had lapsed. By the time Mara got home from the Vital Dent the boy had been "placed". They couldn't wait forever. There was a warring courtroom but it was only a little warring. Mara was not flush, only seventeen, and the Mastersons lived in Montvale, which was more suitable for a boy of these years; eventually visitations would dwindle and it was decided the child fared best in an atmosphere of "consistency". The last time she saw him, the time that *mattered*, he was simply playing on the Jungle Jim, calling out regimental orders to the step sibs. He gave her a quick hug, his face turned to the side, when she went away. A stoplight at a jug handle, an onramp, and she was zipping along Route 4 in no time. Raindrops.

Que lindo? The cable man wasn't going anywhere, all Criss-Cross Applesauce and no-no. Mara had Stan planting a hand on one shoulder and the senior Bunny Weidman on the other, imploring her to please step back, using the cop's own talk. The propeller was blurring everything. She wouldn't move.

The Armenian smiled with his eyes. His lids, when he did it, made a kind of nascent flutter and it was clear, very clear, this was a place like many other places she had been and would be and could never call home; there would be no place like that for this mother.

The Wolves

And then the world becomes a little quieter. Libor has shaken off the rifle cracks and the soldiers have laughed themselves silly, done firing fragmentation rounds to drown out the drumrolls of the Rads guns. Libor has whistled them down. Silenced.

He walks to the tree line, radiocollars hooked to his waist, the metal echoing like tambourines with the forward push of his bowed trotters against the snow. He has a jar of wolf urine hooked to his tool sash for baiting traps. The radiocollars with their locators are bound to lead anywhere the remaining wolves would be.

Behind his back, the soldiers smirk, hock strips of mucous, rechamber their guns. Two weeks of exposure, snare drum sounds from the Rontgen counters, and for what?

Libor smiles at the sight of the forest that has no business being there, arbors that have spread fancifully outward in a vacuum.

"Do you suppose we have them all?" I ask him.

"As many as we'll get today," he says.

The young soldiers crack their numb wrists and set to work placing collars, trying hard not to stare at the hulk of Chernobyl across the marsh.

By 3 PM, Libor has united his primal confederacy within a garrison of stretched wire. He has haltered his wolves, tagged the ailing for radiotherapy, some of the more malformed to be billeted in "rehab" dens. Upon recovery, every wolf on the leeside of the Dnieper River is to be radio-tracked, each pup counted in a ledger, the locks of their pelage run under slides.

Trapped, the men sit flat on their haunches, eating chicken skin off a hay bed and downing Staropramens courtesy of Libor's stash. These men smirk at me. I understand: My figure is no friend to faith; an aged hobble, a bulbous nose at the tip of which deflated capillaries have massed into a strange rosette.

There is a whimper. An omega with mange lesions is scratching at its underbody sores. Libor bends down and shines his penlight.

"Poor bitch," he says. "Twenty years ago I'd've caused her such misery myself."

A young soldier shakes his head. *We should shoot her*, says his smile.

The soldiers are accustomed to winters, patrolling the barren oblasts near Belarus in subzero times, but the wolves reduce them in some way.

They simply can't fathom why they are doing this.

Why has the commander returned, hellbent on packing his corral? The naval scientist was infamous in the preceding years for his brash style in one thing: culling. When the wolves came back in '96, ten years after the abandonment of the zone, Libor had commanded a killing squad, a kind of Einsatzgruppen for flushing envenomed canines. The story goes that Libor had special hand-wear made by a glover in Kyiv, the pig's-hide running up in perfect contour to the elbow, like peeled skin rethreaded to the fascia underneath, and that he used these gloves for "reducing" the wolves in irradiated zones. The gloves were his killing costume. He had the regal lethality of his training commanders have, and compelled lackeys to search out the contaminated predators. Indeed the wolves came back duly haltered and beset with abnormal pains. They experienced unusual dysplasias, mirrored the aplastic cell lagging of human beings. The men went to work; shooting with kidlike fervor. Libor led.

It was prolificacy.

They couldn't just torch the piled yearlings for the quantity of cesium to fill the air. Libor had them buried on the fly, the animals submerged and packed twelve-deep like protohistoric artifacts in vast trenches.

But Nature survived him. The wolves returned.

Now, twenty years since, he has, too: a feral tracker, keeping the wolves alive, working to preserve them in number. I am as confounded as the soldiers are.

We hear a scream from the paddock.

A fumbling greenhorn is attempting to salve the wolf with the sore gut. The thing whimpers, snaps, rears back to slide clean of its halter; tries a miracle swing of its tongue to lick at the incensed node of flesh. The greenhorn holds on to the writhing pelt, his face stamped with failure. Libor pushes him away. The greenhorn swipes mucous off with the flat of his hand, spitting.

All of the sudden, as Libor is trapping its muzzle so to buckle the halter down, the wolf spins, as if springing its cervical hinge, and bites, driving a bloody rent into his hand. Libor's face compresses, activating crow's feet as deep as coin slots. I bend to check the cut, already noting the shallowness, when I look up and see the creature jump the wire fence and bolt to the forest.

The greenhorn, his pig-nose popping snot out, raises his gun. Libor backhands the gun barrel, using the forehand swing of the same arm to send the private hurtling to the snow.

"That isn't a tranquilizer gun, you nitwit!" yells Libor.

When we turn back to the woods, the wolf is gone.

"Mika," he says, sucking at the wound on his hand. "We're going to leave these hatchlings to their fizz."

"I'm sorry, sir?"

"The wolf is sick! We'll have to retrieve it."

"Why me?"

"You were an original liquidator, were you not?"

I nod, looking at the carapace of Chernobyl across the marsh.

"Another pilgrim," he says.

I am, I will admit it. I had been a liquidator, which did not mean corralling wolves but carting away poison soil and dropping in dolomite sacks to where the zirconium fuel rods fractured, helping to round up confounded citizens and pack them into the municipal buses out of town, but I am heartened Libor thinks me a searching candidate; he was the reason I have requested this detail; for leaving Rostov and the enviable comfort of First Rank.

As the wind snaps our coat collars, Libor expands his smile. "Another pilgrim," he repeats.

Libor unfolds his fallout map, charting our path through red-shaded areas; wildlife clusters where a runaway lupine might be. Depending on its hunting pattern, we might encounter a vacated Pripyat, all ours. I fear it. I have been out of the area since '86, after the forced march of the Pripyatans to safer corners where the Rontgen density did not make the Dosimeters go ape. The land bounding the core, uncradled by the State that had cleared out the forests for farming workers in the Motherland's collectivist frenzy, has seen animal life assert its right of return. The town is a crazed terrarium. As for humans, they have remained humbly scarce here, and nothing has been touched. Each half-buried teacup is a tabernacle; each child's doll, shaken loose from their grip in the tumble of a panicked herding, remains unaltered on its little patch of earth.

"It wasn't radiocollared," I say as we set off, watching as Libor belts on a sedative gun. "How will we ever find it?"

"I can howl," says Libor. "I have summoned some."

Libor has, in his fashion, become a wolf; in some prelingual manner he can dialogue almost caressingly with the packs. It is evident in him now. When the detail began he had a pornographic beard but now he is shorn and in aspect of chin is sorely wanting. Somehow a four-fathom cleft has stove its way into the nullity; my eyes look to his, then automatically run to the cleft: a triangle, as seamlessly tapering as a wolf's face.

We have to cross the ice into where the marked soapstone of a village will notify us that humans once lived here. Libor goes to one knee, cups his hands around his mouth, releasing a feral warble that begins its ride through the surrounding lindens and ends in a raking volley from the marsh, a howl that ebbs and returns, like an accordion.

He rises in the angular motion of certitude.

"It didn't go to the city," he says. "Near enough. We'll have to pass through it."

My face betrays me, and he pats me on the shoulder.

We tread some narrow defiles and slide rump-first onto some frozen scrub, a finger of scaly land where the Dnieper forks into the significantly more contaminated Pripyat. We are waved through the checkpoint where two soldiers strain for warmth inside the high, galvanized iron coils of a watchtower.

Winds filtered through from vacant box-buildings across the Dnieper scrape their rouging faces to the quick. They are there to spot horse poachers, fences who traffic in metal scrap, "free spirits" chancing the becquerels.

We enter the empty city from the East. Amid the obscene vegetation, snow-caked, a dust that is almost fur. The dolls are present, as I might've guessed. One, in overalls, lies akimbo on a stump near a rust-bloodied monkey bars. Another lies on its side, a dark-haired stripling, dust packed in the bow of her lips. There is a toppled crossing sign, a green Lada a shade of green lighter where the oxidized metal led to verdigris.

I have come very far afield from my comfort as Captain First Rank, if only to ask the gloved culler a dangerous hanging question, and here, in the reliquary, I go forth.

"What brought you back here?" I say. "To preserve the wolves?"

Libor says nothing, walks a few strides ahead of me down the street. When I catch up to him we walk parallel, silent, until he swerves towards me and bumps me almost flirtatiously, then stops in front of me.

"Here is one for you," he says, snapping a hand off my chest. "Two squirrels are on a date in a restaurant. It's a human restaurant. The male is ordering for the female, as is his pleasure, very chivalric animal. He asks the waiter about the special. He says 'We'd like to share your special. What is your special?' 'The special is trout in a yogurt sauce,' says the waiter. Squirrel asks the waiter, 'Is there dill in the yogurt sauce?' The waiter says, 'Yes. There is dill in the yogurt sauce.' The squirrel says, 'I can't stomach it. Raises Cain in me. No dill.' The waiter says, 'It's already in the mixture. We can't remove the dill from the mixture.' The squirrel says, 'Fine, no trout, then.' Now, looking at the menu again, the squirrel says, 'We'll have the braised beef and noodles.' Waiter says, 'Of course.' The squirrel then asks, 'Is the beef from a Red

Gorabov head of cattle?' The waiter says, 'I don't think so. I'm not sure.' The squirrel asks the waiter to go back into the kitchen and ask the chef the source of the beef. The waiter does this. Comes back, says, 'The chef isn't aware of what breed of cattle produced the noodle beef.' The squirrel says, 'Pity that. I adore Red Gorabov beef cuts, my wife Vasilisa just the same. We'll pass on the beef.' 'Okay,' says the waiter. 'What might I get you in lieu?' Squirrel 'hmmms' a little and says, 'Yes! We'd like the Selisian-style pheasant dumplings.' Folds the menu up. The waiter says, 'Good choice.' Writes in his little pad snappily, sets to go. 'Ah,' says the squirrel, his hand up. And he asks if they contain ground chives. The waiter sinks and says, 'Yes.' The squirrel says, 'I find the addition of ground chives too much of an Asiatic note, a touch which is fine in your Uyghur dishes, your provincial West Asian consommés, but here, I find it registers fatal on the tongue; anomalous.' The waiter says, 'Once again, the chives are already wedded to the ground pheasant. We cannot undo it.' The squirrel says, 'Can I request a new batch of ground pheasant? My wife and I will gladly wait the while.' The waiter says, 'I'm sorry; it's too late. All our dumpling meat is prepared in the morning.' The squirrel says, 'I figured as much. Well,'—and now he peruses the menu again—'What about the pork hocks in beer?' The waiter scrambles to write it in his pad, says 'Great!' and grabs their menus, begins walking away; snappy, happy waiter. But then the squirrel says 'Wait.' Waiter sighs, turns around, says, 'And now?' Squirrel says, 'Are those hocks deboned?' 'Waiter says, 'No, and I can't debone them.' Squirrel says, 'What are the chances someone else does? Can I get them deboned?' Waiter says, 'I don't know. I don't think so. No.' Squirrel says, 'Can you check?' Waiter says, 'I think they're very busy.' Squirrel says, 'It'll only take a second.' 'They're very busy,' repeats the waiter. Squirrel says, 'Oh, I don't think so. If you'd do me the favor of going and asking, I'd be so pleased.' The waiter sighs, 'Fine.' Squirrel says, 'Thank you.' Waiter goes off. Minute or so passes and the waiter comes back, says, 'We can make an exception.' 'Wonderful,' says the squirrel. Waiter writes the order again and begins walking to the kitchen. Then the squirrel's arm comes up. 'Just one more thing,' he says. Waiter stops dead, takes a mortal second, turns, leaden, positively leaden. Squirrel says, 'Can we have the hocks with a side salad?' 'Of course,' says the waiter, beginning to sprint away. *'But,'* says the squirrel, 'can we have red leaf lettuce instead of the standard kohlrabi?' Waiter says, 'We don't have red leaf.' Squirrel says, 'Fine, but we'd like extra fennel in the salad.' Waiter says, 'Fine. Done.' Squirrel says, 'And if you please, could you mince the endive and put it in an anchovy sauce?' Silence. 'You want the endive minced with anchovy sauce,' says the waiter, incredulously. 'Yes," says the squirrel. 'My wife likes it that way. Would you make sure before we order it?'. Waiter shakes his head. 'I can't go to the kitchen again.' Squirrel says, 'It'll only take a minute.' 'Yes, yes, yes!' says the waiter lurchingly. 'Fine! We can mince the endive and put it in anchovy sauce.' 'I don't believe you,' says the squirrel. 'I'd like it confirmed if you don't mind. It's not that I don't trust you, you're quite the server, I'd just like to know if the endive can be minced in anchovy sauce before we proceed. From, if you will, kitchen sources.' The waiter says, 'I have other tables, if you don't mind, sir. *If you don't mind.'* 'Oh they'll wait,' says the squirrel. 'They know what your job is.' The waiter sinks, his shoulders sort of die in the air, and he goes back to the kitchen, comes back with a handwritten note from the chef which says indeed they will mince the endive and put it in anchovy sauce. The squirrel reads the note approvingly and says, 'Fine. It's settled. My wife and I will have the pork hocks in beer.' The waiter exhales a beautiful, rapturous breath, the greatest exhalation of his days, and begins heading back to the kitchen when the squirrel says, 'You know, I think we'll cancel the hocks and just have a bowl of nuts.' 'Nuts?' says the waiter. 'Yep. That's it. Just nuts. Nice big howl of nuts. Nuts will do.' Waiter stands there, silent. The squirrel smiles as wide as the day is long, thinking of nuts; the throbbing of a native appetite in his gut."

I shrug.

He exhales.

"I was made a waiter by the State," he says. "I ran to the kitchens thinking I could better the nature of Nature. I thought it insufficient as it was."

I shrug again.

"Think of rams," he says. "They need horns because some other animal has talons. Well there would be no need for horns if their adversaries did not brandish those riving claws. None of these predator scrums bears an Empyrean footprint and so, I thought, let us devise laboratories; let us create a kingdom of noncombatants who dwell among the forests in synergy. Only a human could rain peace on the animal kingdom. Then the power plant; the updraft that killed it."

"You were going to engineer animals from scratch?"

He shakes his head.

"I had *faith*. I thought we could be an example to them. We are the only species that does not accept death, which is the stance one should prefer. Eventually we could eclipse the warfare ethic; our science would render acceptance of death unfashionable.

"If we couldn't accept our own death, we wouldn't accept anyone else's," I say.

He nods. He puffs some air out.

"You stay real within yourself, loyal to the spirit of Man and then without even the faintest renunciation you wake up godless. Your Man-God has failed you."

"Is that when you began wearing your gloves?"

He starts at these words, his cold breath joining the wind against me.

"When did you hear about those?" he says, his voice strangely sad, a hangman's voice.

"Lore among the initiated. We all knew."

"I've never been good with disappointment," he says. "Someone had to pay. The nonhuman accepts death. The wolves were dying. And I couldn't kill my countrymen. So it was the wolves." He shakes his head, rubbing his wounded hand and repeats, lower this time, "So it was the wolves."

You will not sympathize with Libor. Understand. He is military.

He is government.

I am military.

I am government.

Everyone knows we hid what happened. Then our air turned up in Norwegian reindeer, curling like fugitive eels in their blood. The reindeer became bellwethers of the drift.

And to be sure our neighbors have had reindeer trouble, but I believe there is much they do not know that I know. I know I was once a conscript medic, in a helicopter that spun above the smoking reactor core, the propeller lulling me, when my pilot, a certain Yuri, looked over at me and dropped a lick of drool that unspooled from his lips like a measure of yarn. He began crying and told me to kiss his wife, his mother, and to do my best to become him, to parrot his gestures when I met his kids. "Be me," he said, more urgently and farcically with each jounce over the smoking core. He was crying like he'd waited years to tell me, but I had only met him once before.

I awoke burning, seared in a jangle of engine wires only feet from the smoking reactor. For hours men were loath to come get me; eventually I screamed "Brothers!" enough that the anticontamination suits began alighting on the rim of the core. I lived in a bubble for a month, a reinforced egg among neonatal monitoring tools, a sort of sterile chrysalis where a mobile of sucking hoses wheezed and rattled, demanding a rebirth, gratitude.

"The nuclear magnetism froze your controls," said my colonel, standing over my little bubble. "Did the same to your pilot. Expired." So I would have to mimic for his kids. I had lived, healed clean save for the enduring rosette. Why I was pardoned I do not know. I haven't done much asking around to the Fates, have never probed the Four Winds for answers, they who listen with an open mouth, not ears.

I never did find his family. They were resettled: ostensibly nowhere, which puts them everywhere, much too thriving to repel with a stolen conscience.

The street of the little town, its name chalked on a hard rind of monzonite, has the air of a soundstage or say, a fairgrounds where a ride has gone monstrously haywire. Down on one knee, Libor raises his head and howls. The baying sounds accusatory, ringing off the iron rails near the shunting portion where trains no longer run. High above the station sits the old school, some of the windows plucked out. Libor points. I look up. There is the indelible sense that the wolf, wounded, has followed something unnamable to its birthing ground. Libor pries the door open and we head inside.

On the wall, the flapping of exemplary papers, and upstairs are some caustic barks. We walk through the halls, painted green on the first floor, unfaded baby blue on the second, the stairs leading up to it all snow and radon. In the hall, Libor slows his gait just a little as we hear snarling in a classroom, the door marked Kindergarten in colored paper scraps. He walks in, waving me over from the door. I'm drawn to the cubbies, where old rucksacks rest in cramped space, and in one, a blonde doll sits as if on a proscenium. Across the room the wolf cowers in the corner with a snapping jaw. It backs in a few inches and retracts its head, whimpering. It wants acceptance of something and Libor is not going to give it; the closest thing he will proffer is the sedating barrel of his gun, raising it, and the soft plug of the tranc against its body makes the wolf ours again to take.

And I stand, in this room, lifting the doll off its stage.

Here in the cubbyholes, kids' dolls still nest; peated by the dank of infinity. The dolls have no breasts, no organs, but their living likenesses who never got to read the books on the shelves, volumes that stand smirking, these likenesses have commanded that we forget and let the animals have their way, for these children can never be as animals again.

Somehow the doll, hair turned a shade darker and dusty in the flat palm of my hand, sees behind it and regrets not having words that might get its secret to the kids, who are no longer children, far away, in distant oblasts.

We are headed back to the camp. Libor leading his wolf on a sled from the gymnasium storage, the dash runners braised with a phosphorous light, easily seen if one wants to, the wolf's long tail fanning the air though it's sleeping. There is laughter across the Pripyat from the unproctored ranks in the camp, playing like hoary field rodents, the closest thing we have to humans until the job is done. A little ways across the river ice, the wolf opens its left eye, looks up at Libor and I know what it wants: It is asking for relinquishment, but Libor, looking ahead, offers only the promise of birth.

He is angry.

I am grateful.

It is snowing and it will snow till it doesn't.

Monolith

Today was the coldest day of the year but spring was there in situ; undercurrents of renewal in the freeze. I stayed in, where I'm remaining, on the tenth floor. This building maintains me, the way an insidious murder plot maintains the crack gumshoe. Lincoln Center lets out its sweater-vested denizens down the block, the Hudson looms on my starboard, every day a fishy zephyr enfilading from the windstorm of Freedom Place. Hate rings. Spring is sprung. Hope burns like a tire fire.

The certified envelope came this morning, demanding signature. Inside it, pursuance of an "Objectional conduct termination of the proprietary lease" of yours truly. I won't deny I have earned this. I have not played well with the Co-op.

Maybe it was about take your pick.

The building was originally artist housing for quasi-failures in the nonpaying medium of their choice, one of whom was my grandfather, a commie violinist and all-around dingbat in the School of Life (shock treatments, aborted tenure in the Boston Pops, stroke). His son, a Reagan democrat by the name of Dear Dad (nee Jed Klingman), died here, on this selfsame rutted vermillion shag rug (eighty percent carpet coverage a requirement of aforesaid lease), cause: glioblastoma. A year later, my mother, Dasha Klingman (nee Koplowitz), "passed", consequent to blowout aneurysm. Latest among the forgotten: my dear cat, *aliva sholem* – although, really, only possibly.

This building is a Jewish flytrap.

There are so many death notices they have to send out for new paper (2/20 – Lita Wurtzel, 3/10 – Merv Stein, 3/13 – Judith Stein, 3/15 – Gladys Erinprice. 3/20 – Myrtle Pincus, 3/24 Larry "The Luau" Dinnerstein, who took up the ukulele at seventy-five and died plucking *An American in Paris* to captives in the first-floor rec room). Once the units "clear up" and the realtors can flip them over, it's up to Tessie Maisel and her goons at a coop board to handpick the yuppie who overpays. One-bedrooms clear five-hundred grand before maintenance. Two bedrooms and you might as well stick a broom in your ass and fall backward.

I am a forward faller. So sue me, which is I guess in a way what they did.

I think I may know why the letter.

Last Tuesday morning, the fifth anniversary of my father's death, I cranked "The Horst Wessel Song" while attending to some overdue housekeeping. I found the martial strains really put the gusto in my Dyson vac. I blitzkrieged the linoleum spotless. I scoured the countertop schnell and rescoured the countertop schneller. I feather-dusted the whole place from A to Z and felt myself damn *volkisch* when I did it. Old Adolph's banner number, the Horst Wessel Song is proof positive that the worst regimes have the finest anthems – it may rate a close second to the Soviet's for aural grandeur but the race menace in the origins is precisely the straw that stirs the drink – you can really see those gatecrashers at the Reichschancellory waiting to romper-stomp Ernst Rohm's men, unscabbard those Long

Knives and have at it. You can really see those swaying brau brawlers hoisting their spilling tankards to the verse; drug-crazed Fokker pilots dooming the Warthegau and hailing unmerciful Wotan as their tailgunners rake the vermin Poles. Mostly, I could see Tessie Maisel in her shower cap, wondering what in the fuck was going on, Chloris Shupack in 3E lurching for thick earplugs, bowels unleashed by the subwoofers.

For maximum verisimilitude, I copped an old Rhinelander's scratchy 45 from some sicko of a war collector in Far Rockaway. Since then I've received nine calls from this guy to "hang out." He has time, having been canned from his shop-teaching gig, some infraction involving "familiarities" with sophomore students.

No doubt, it was a leavening day, the anthem an encomium, of sorts.

As the music played, I waited, grabbed for grandpa's old Fleischman's firewater from the rosewood wet bar. *You have been a bad boy, boychik.* You have sinned. They all want to die in peace, the thud of the embolic stroker hitting the polypropylene rugs above is considerately muted so to not interfere with your reruns. The reruns do not interfere with your stroke. The Horst Wessel punched through that Maginot Line something wicked.

And so by 10 AM I was getting a lot of broomsticks. Someone was pounding on the door.

I waited for word from the co-op's chief wiccan; wondering what shape her burning wrath made out of her wilting features; whether red rose from the almost pellucid cast of her face.

We have a history, destined to repeat itself.

When I took over the apartment five years back (the first thing I ever owned), I knew the flytrap would claim me. Maisel,

Tessie, of 10B, was on me from the start, stumping for her live-in clone, her one genetic spittle of her loins. For weeks, she angled, intimated, then one day handed me two tickets for a show in Teaneck.

"Across the bridge?" I said.

"Little Anthony and the Imperials – Doo Wop group. I'd like you take Dorie."

"All right," I said. "I'll only go if you knock down a dividing wall and give me the neighboring unit."

"Why?" she asked.

"Lebensraum."

That tore it, as they say.

I do recognize that, by living here, I am preserving the Jewish quota; as surely as New Canaan is to Episcopal, our crimson monolith is to Hadassah League. FDR, the three-termer, is their Jesus. I tell them FDR almost singlehandedly forestalled the Jewish rescue; thousands of kinder swarming the gangplanks to flee to our haven cities from the piers, the bulging transport cruisers making their fateful U-turns back into the lion's mouth of infamy, care of the Jewphobes at the Department of State. Look up your Breckenridge Long. And then the camps: We had P40 Warhawks divebombing oil refineries a mile away from the crematory stacks, aerial reconnaissance ready so our flyboys could bomb the rails, but they did not. Oh but give me my venerable Delano till hell cools. Give me my mezuzah and Lo Mein. My neocon chopped liver sandwiches.

Give me my carpet coverage.

Give me death.

I have barely even mentioned my missing cat.

My dear Abyssinian purebred, Zampano, swallowed. It happened two years ago and here is how it did: The elevators do weekend Sabbath runs, opening and closing on each floor automatically so the pious can bypass some actionable sinning. As I was airing out the stove into the hallway he got out while my head was turned and hopped on an elevator, the door shutting just as I lurched to board. I saw the Up arrow light and raced up the stairway to meet him a floor above, but the elevator evidently skipped it. I ran up three flights but when door A opened there was no one there. I watched the upward track of elevator B as the numbers blinked on the lighted panel. I could only guess where he'd get off, who would take him in. I spent a week going floor to floor, rang every bell, got only shrugs and (I will presume) prevarications. I came with no probable cause, really, and could only fisheye a few single gals whose eyes were suspiciously watery (I looked for sniffles, scratching posts from my vantage from the door, sniffing for the cleansing mist of HEPAS). Nothing turned up. My "Missing Cat" signs kept getting pasted over by death notices. Zampano is somewhere up there, or down, I am sure, shanghaied among the homogenized Jewlies, warming to an unfamiliar litter, the feel of new caressing fingers on his ruff. Sometimes I hear meowing through the vents, furtive echoes; an occasional plaintive purr. When I try and track it to its source, the noise vanishes.

This afternoon, Gillespie, the building manager, comes in shrugging, Fischbein, self-appointed cleric of the monolith and a legit, ordained rabbi, steps in behind him.

"You shouldn't have played the Horst Wessel song, chief," says Gillespie. "It's not good cricket." He is sitting on his hand to slow the shakes – Parkinson's.

"The woman upstairs from you," says Fischbein. "Silla Greenblatt. Do you know there are numbers on her arm? One of millions!" He is really torqued, fumed, *tsetrogn*. "Belsen, kid. A labor camp was her forwarding address. Ten years old. Put *that* in your corncob and smoke it."

"My cat was commandeered," I say.

"Your cat?"

"No forwarding address." Silence.

"Next time I'll play the Soviet one," I say, by way of atonement. "Will that be better?"

"Hey, kid: The septuagenarian anticommunist in 10B doesn't want to hear operatic Leninism any more than the Hillel cantor in 10C wants an earful of Horst Wessel, *ferstay?*" the rabbi says. Fischbein, it should be said, is the son of a welterweight boxer from some small iron tract under the menacing black trusses of the Pulaski Skyway in New Jersey; and although he rebelled as a pacifist bears his father's unfiltered parlance. "Now before I get madder than you see here," he says, "I'll tell you a thing that's important for your future in this place."

"I have no future in this place."

"Eh, that's maybe negotiable," he says, wagging his hand back and forth.

"How?"

"Maisel – I have this from the horse's mouth – is going to forgive you the lump of your sniping shit if you take her daughter to Little Anthony and the Imperials."

"They're back?" I say.

"Did they ever go away?" says the rabbi. "They seem to come to Teaneck like the bugs come in spring. Now you got a play here. Go and she'll call off her proverbial rotters, take you back."

"I prefer Alsatians," I say, "to rotters."

The rabbi sighs. "Lenny: See Anthony, you're golden. No see Anthony and she runs your fat little saddle to the ditch."

"The Salvation Army bell for you," says Gillespie.

He gives me a cozy wink – he's had his own dwelling nixed by Tessie Maisel and the board. He figured thirty years of troubleshooting their radiators would stand him in good stead, land him a unit and a deed. He suspects it's down to ethnic disharmony; and of course, well, probably. He's as Irish as Semtex in a Jag. On the other hand, friendship with me hasn't earned him much favor.

"Wrench in Lenny here?" says Darryl. "Too much time on his hands. Needs to get cracking on the want ads."

Boffo, Darryl: But not having a job is a full-time job, and there's no security; at any time you may be fired and have to go back to work. As a preventive measure, I've put away a lot of my mortuary lucre, abstained from market risks, earmarked enough of my inheritance for interest so I can ride out my timetable purely on the sums I have stashed in the bank.

"I'm a pariah, Fischbein," I say.

"You're a fat lump," he says. "Degraded schlepper. You look dredged. I know some prairie varmint that wouldn't trade faces with you to land themselves a winter's worth of seeds, but the girl seems fixed on you. Now I don't know why Tessie doesn't truck in some other fat fuck with a similar balding pattern who would steal Hers Nibs away and presumably just feel 'chuffed'. But your family was liked here, and Tessie sees hope for you. Dorie sees hope for you."

I think about Dorie, a walking shower cap, always a little wet in the nose. There is a significant chance that she has never had a man on top of her who didn't trip.

"I'd rather be an orphan in Belsen," I say.

"You know," says the rabbi, "It's easy for you to sit here in all this luxury and spout this jokey muck, this *scurrility*. Let me tell you, partner: It wouldn't be so easy were you a Pole in Lvov oh long about '33," – now he jabs a finger out, real thunderbolt of the Baal Shem Tov. "You better just thank your luckies FDR won the war for you."

Gillespie and I walk along Freedom Place, named for poor Goodman and Schwerner, desegregators, both, Freedom Riders murdered by the South: Jewish braves: deep-sixed in one body of murk and now memorialized beside another oozing river two-thousand ideological kilometers to the north, and yet, our orangutan of a fearless boy king, so cozy with Dixie and the would-be lynch mob circuit, bestrides their eponymous street in the form of a spiritless (and equally eponymous) pile of rivets that fetches him two mil a room.

And the rabbi says jokes.

For Darryl, the wind makes walking hard.

"We need love," he says. "Lenny needs love. Gillespie needs love."

Gillespie doesn't need love; he needs a neuromuscular miracle. But he now and then beds chicks and his tremors miraculously subside. The last one he took home was a "sporting" woman, sporting rayon stilettos and crab lice that sprang like Olympians to his dong. It isn't exactly a coming down in the world for Darryl. When he was little he tested so poorly his parents sent him to the Glendenning Academy in Connecticut, a special needs boarding school, grades Five through Twelve. Darryl was in fact the sort of wordless brain trust who bores easily taking tests. Savvy, he took the When in Rome approach and ran the table on the senior class, nailing every third coed whose parietal deficit landed them among the knotty pines and prefabricated rock grottos of the "learning sanctuary." Now, festinating in an SRO in Sunnyside, he socket-wrenches A/Cs, remembers his jaded antics, and feels a little swinish about it all. For where his Parkinson's is concerned, he's resolved to giving Nature its restitution.

We stare into the wind, eating apple turnovers from the morning snack cart. The river shivers, the redbrick mausoleum looms.

"Look at this," he says, noting his shaking hand. "What a mess."

"You need comfort," I say.

"Couple," he says forcefully. "Marry."

He knows I won't. Knows I've seen the toll. I don't even want to marry someone I'll love to the end of time, because who wants the end of time? It's the last port in a nightmare cruise, and even if that port is the Cote d'Azur, oiled breasts on sunny bodies to a far horizon while along the autoroute a fledgling out of the Cannes *scene* tongues you to infinity in a gullwing Benz, I don't want to ever dock that ship.

Darryl backs against a railing, the building in back of him, obscuring the water.

"You won't like this, Lenny," he says, leaning against a railing. "But you're about stalking up to the age where shit happens. It'll roll you like a trashcan down a mudslide. I never got to even try skiing."

Dear, this smarts. Guys like Darryl, heavy with the genes of Viking rapists, are not supposed to die. The dead know when to dig in, to signal "lay off" to the bushytailed who would overpower them with hope. So out in their metaphorical backyards they shovel their metaphorical holes and think of their progeny's bequests. Not Darryl; he may only bequeath a barstool in a humble ceremony.

He turns towards the water. We look like we're rehearsing a play. Sensitive longshoreman. Doe-eyed wharf girl at stake.

"Go to the Imperials," he says.

I think of Dorie, rating her on the Jewish spectrum. We don't have faces that scream the Golden Ratio like our Scotts-Irish rugged friends do, or the rose-cheeked specimens out of Andover who seem hellbent to sucker-fuck our girls. I have often wanted to produce a coffee table book called *Jews Who Are Better Looking Than Me.* It would be the one coffee table book that could not double as a door stopper. You'd have Kirk Douglas. John Garfield, Lauren Bacall, then …? Seems the aqualine of our brethren stopped surfacing around the time that Harding ruled. In other words, Dorie might rate more than passable if graded on the Jewish curve. Objectively, biochemically, she is kind. She has learned to blow her nose and seems to be fond of primping for me before her premeditated run-ins in the hall. It wouldn't be all self-preservation either. Sex is worthy. I've lucked into it before; it happens to anyone, and, as people seem overly wont to say, (strongly indicative not only of death wishes but of an overarching paranoia as regards wheelmen of the MTA), *I could get hit by a bus tomorrow.*

As for being turfed out by a rightful termination, it is not a little thing. I would have to produce income. I could never do what Darryl does. I see job fairs, rideshares, myself in the "gig" economy, using my E-commerce portal to command my warlock rain hell on the avatars of aging multiplayers sitting equally fucked in their own listless sliver of Routertown, USA.

"Where do I sign up?" I say.

Darryl smiles. It is nice to see.

The Imperials are a happily desiccated bunch, the whole squadron outfitted in eye-popping, silver lame suits. The people here seem rescued from a cryogenic internment, some hissing cylinder out near White Sands, frenetic with brainwave monitors.

The floor is wobbling under them. The amp sounds horrible, the work of a local roadie probably tossed from a bandshell in Asbury Park. Now and then the mic punks on the vocalist (Little, Anthony), who still smiles when his words go untraveled.

We stand in the middle of the floor, able to make out subtle fissures in the grinning of the quartet, small flaggings in their finger snaps. Dorie has already leaned over and said four times she is "On Cloud Nine." There are frequent breaks, presumably so the band can make bathroom sorties. "Goin' Out of My Head" fizzles into "Better Use Your Head". Why no space between head songs? Dorie claps the hardest at "Hurt". Telling: It is not their finest number.

It is, in its own way, a lovely scene; one I do not feel like shitting on because up on the bandstand these guys, these Imperials, their mouths pearly and their aged girth bulging out of their blazers of silver fleck, were no doubt back-scoring make-out sessions in the front seats of road racers years before nonearning clods like yours truly, overeducated in the finer points of irony, killed the streetlamp serenade forever. It is good to be back in a place where crimes were so odious you wouldn't touch them, just fiddled sweet-nothings Nero-style.

Still, take the Doo out of Wop and you have got yourself a room full of them. And though I thought I only thought this, evidently I said it, too.

"Don't ruin this one," she says. "I love this one."

It is "Tears on My Pillow", and there is something of a killing charm in the helium tenor of Little Anthony as he sings *"You don't remember me/but I remember you..."* I remember me, plugged into my first first-run Walkman on an actual pillow listening to this song when I was eight. There had been screaming in the living room. My mother had been having an affair with the man she'd met at Lincoln Center; he had kept the books for Nightingale School. He was on the board of the City Ballet and had "contacts" among the dancers, a revolving stable of marionettes who solemnly resisted his advances to the final grope. Mom took them. Mom was no dancer. I didn't know most of this at the time, just knew when I removed the headphones I could hear a slap, then another. "Jesus, Jed, stop hitting yourself!" "I can't," I heard from my father.

The amps blow out with unearthly whistle that sends the septuagenarians to the floor. (They must be having autonomic flashbacks to the duck and cover drills of their youth). The bandshell castoff mumbles and leaves, coming back in with giant tools, cursing creatively into the dead amp's nylon dust screen. Little Anthony does an honorable job of announcing the cessation of schlock. Genuine disappointment from Dorie, young among the pre-Boomers heading home in their pensive economy cars, those white-walled Bel Airs in the rearview of recorded time.

"I want an ice cream," she says.

"Ice cream?"

"Don't look stupid at me. I know a place."

In a mirrored diner, Dorie eats her ice cream; just a little girl, shoveling rivers of hot sludge over molehills of Rum Raisin. She reaches across the table with the spoon and holds it to my mouth. This is the moment of commitment, I see. I can let it hang there, let a blooming gob of syrup drop onto the sea-colored fool's-grain of the table, force her into sheepish retreat. But I don't. I take the full dollop. It tastes too good, too redolent of childhood, a gastronomic time warp too rich with pre-shattered promise. I must reverse,

"No one this excited about ice cream could be anything other than a virgin," I say.

She draws back and her smile goes straight.

"You know, you're really stupid," she says.

"But right."

"No, not right," she says, learning forward. "I have had sex with a lot of people. My mother doesn't know this. My mother still showers in a shower cap. But I *have* had sex. I have even had gonorrhea. *Len.* I give head, good head, and I'm a pretty good bet to swallow if the guy isn't a complete shitheel and wines and dines me before he drops his pants. I know what is out there on the internet and I make sure that I do that very nicely. I know from rough stuff. But am I happy about it? I am *very* happy about it. Do I want some constant nuzzling? I do want this, Lenny. I don't like saps and I hate guys who are convinced they know what's in me. You think you're so smart and that's the shonda, you, what is it, self-loathing bore. You are only another person of the building. I know people'd give their eyeteeth to sit where you live hurting lonely people, one of whom will be yourself if you don't rot by the age of forty."

So there it is: an erection. You can't beat a good martial scolding; it is somehow the essence of American pride.

In the cab she says, "I usually use this place."

The Metuchen Econolodge. Its lights are a shamed dim yellow. Unlikely we'd run into a stray Imperial in the halls here. In fact, there is no hall; all access to paradise achieved from without. There is a transactional flavor to the way she card-keys the room, in the way she walks in and flicks up the light switches. She seems to have been in this room before, pats the pillows; shuts the drapes. Fingers loose a scrunchie from her hair. She sits on the bed and takes first her blouse off, then her bra; like a lot of homely women, she is shapely in places that the average judging person will never see. Holding the breasts, I kiss her, and she backs off a foot or two down the bed, then punches forward with her jaw and crashes like a semitruck into me, biting my gums, yanking hard on my lower lip with her front teeth.

Lying up in bed afterward, staring at the stucco frieze that is the motel ceiling, the stilled ceiling fan dusty from the rising of human particles, she says:

"I hate you, Lenny. I really hate you."

"Why?" I say. "Because of the building?"

"Not that," she says.

"Why, then?"

She takes a moment looking up.

"I hate you because you fucked me," she says, her voice not angry or sad. "Somehow I didn't think you would."

"I hate you too," I say.

"Well, anyway," she says, "you're safe. You went with me. I'll make sure mom rips up the termination letter. You can stay."

She rolls over, her face away from me.

"Thank you kindly," I say, thinking that tomorrow it will feel more like relief.

I've stepped out to wait for Darryl, the fish wind off the river dices me: I haven't slept a wink since the Dorie night. I rub my nose now. The smell of the subway carries. Vapors compete; fish and tunnel.

So this is home. This is where the world wants me. A legacy. An unsevered bloodline. Like mom, pops, gramps, grandfather with his shock treatments. He sawed his little Hoffman Maestro as elegant as cruising swans; then, off-key, in perfect tune with the contrapuntal mania of his head. Stroked out mid-sob in the bathroom, a beautiful turd half-traveled from the aperture of his rear. My father, in his time, began smelling things that weren't there – odd remoulades, cedar wood, hoisin sauce. We found him drinking out of the koi pond at a Chinese restaurant, and knew we were in for a round of "tests". After that, it was a skater's compulsory; each bracket turn of degeneration hit square off the leading edge. Changing his diaper, my mother held him by the chin and in a baby-voice said, "We never fucked on our honeymoon, did we, and now you've got a helpless hard-on, my little bean counter." Eventually he slept and for the four hours a day he was awake he asked if I could smell that smell; finally, the smell was a real thing, and it was the inside of his skull rotting through the defile of his nostrils.

On his sickbed, seconds from the now-conceivable, he clasped my hand and said, "When life becomes smaller than the experiences, you're in trouble." My mother told me he was demented, but I knew that he was not. The building had folded in on him. Rabbi Fischbein came in, said a rhubarb of lamentations. His hands, eczema-specked, flicked my father's eyes shut.

The southern exposure made shiva a hot affair: these "mourners", lined up like Moscow breadliners in Jobst compression hos. Most came with meatballs from the Food Emporium and fixed smiles of "God laughs." *We have been here. We have always been here.* Smile like you mean it, Tessie.

The radiator hissed for months. Darryl hammered it, but the valve was "out of true". My mother sat, her mouth tracing a life's chronology that was too vivid, too stark: Young – Jed – Old. She read her Marie Claire, watched technicolor Gene Kelly prancing with his rain-repeller on the Sanyo rotary, and then slid off into Neverland just as easy as you please. I got the apartment, the natural deed transfer: a "legacy".

And that is what a legacy is; a building that fell on your long ago.

By the coffee cart across the street, a cop is conversing with the Arab vendor, the siren of his vehicle ablink. The vendor is pointing in the direction of the building and then collapses in a gestural demonstration of events. He shrugs. The cop nods. My hand shakes from the cold. I'm distracted by the sound of an ambulance rolling up to the drive. Out from the automatic doors the rabbi is holding Gillespie by the arms and the doorman Ronnie is holding Gillespie by the boots. His eyes are half-closed in a way you don't see on stoners, nor on the desperately unslept.

"Shir la ma alos, eso aynai el he horim…" the Rabbi is saying; something he'd said to dad something he'd said to dad before the lid-flicking. The paramedics quickly spell the residents, slamming Darryl on the stretcher. I notice a bright burn gash on the side of his forehead, blistering juicily in the open air. They climb in the back and bump in the stretcher: Moishe's Moving Company. The men are yarmulked, from the Hatzalah, a Jewish volunteer force, a Jewish volunteer force. As the door closes, the rabbi is still talking.

"…la mot rag lecho, al yonum shom 'recho …"

"He's not Jewish," I say.

"It's okay," says Ronnie. "Let it be, man -"

"He's Irish."

"Lenny, please."

The ambulance drives away. The men watch it go, as though parents had driven away with a gifted child who had mistakenly enrolled in their remedial summer program.

"What happened?" I say.

Ronnie shakes his head.

"He was cranking some wingnut in the boiler room. His shakes. Jerked right into the boiler. Head went on it and his body was still jerking that way; he couldn't pull out of it. He comes stumbling down the hall in the middle of a heart attack."

"Screaming," says Fischbein, the rabbi. "I know that screaming."

And it happens without a second thought. I hit him square in his bearded kisser. He doesn't go down, simply tap dances sideways a few wobbles from the blow. The boxer's son. He bears his teeth and charges me and my hand goes up halfheartedly, not even close, and the pain from the thick paddle of his hand is dull and sharp at the same time. Mostly, it is real, and conclusive.

I go down to the ground, but I don't know why. Maybe that's just what you do. Ronnie comes right over to me, bending down.

"Lenny," he says.

I want to say something but my mouth is stilled even though the cheek was where he hit me. My eyes are burning. He genuinely cares, the fool. I can't say it, but I think it into his eyes:

Can I leave now? Do you think I can? Do you think they will let me go?"

The Best Worst Perfect

Somebody, it might have been his grade schoolteacher, once said that the dangerous thing about Lortel was that Lortel wasn't dangerous at all, maybe just a touch too rife with unrequited kindness to be liked. Imagine a redneck standup minus the cornpone yuks. Imagine the boll weevil of ambition burrowing through aisles of corn, a bauble of righteous love shining like a hell gem for boots to tramp. Lortel would be the weevil that tried to become the corn.

Oh, but that was wrong, too.

Lortel wanted people to be what they were, and he wanted to see it in action. He needed to see them milk their particular voodoo to feel he had a fighting chance. He demanded excellence; astronomical prowess as a lightshow, indominable finesse. To wit: In Saint Thomas he entered the summer mansion of an NBA point guard named Reg Viers, aka The Clutch Man, tied up the Clutch Man's children in the bedroom and took the children's little Fischer Price hoop set and planted it on the kitchen floor. He told Reg he had to sink fifty foul shots in succession by day's end or there'd be two foul shots of an altogether different magnitude to report from the children's bedroom. After Viers sunk and missed all day, finishing out the with a rim-rider that whinnied off the metal onto the floor, Lortel went into the bedroom, gun cocked, and simply untied the kids; fleeing out the window and into the street. After picking up the unloaded weapon Viers hugged his children, sobbed out a life's worth of gratitude, and called for the island gendarmes, who tracked Lortel negotiating over a pair of gimcrack Ray Ban shades a mile away on the seawalk. He served five years, the Crown judge decrying the decline of American morals when he chucked a jolly Lortel in the klink. Viers, for his part, had trouble hitting foul shots after that, and. no longer harmonious with his crunchtime moniker, retired at the age of thirty-one.

In Pittsburgh, newly liberated, his passport snatched, living with his aunt Desiree in Esplen, Lortel far from renounced his unnerving ways. A week after shipping back he boarded an empty bus at two in the morning and forced the driver at gun-point to demonstrate three-point turns. Satisfied by the wheel-man's artistry, Lortel ran off into the night. "Fucker nailed that last one cold," he noted in his moleskine scrapbook, "Just beau-tiful." (Since the Viers trip Lortel had taken to writing these formal entries, noting at which points the skills of the shang-haied departed from their given rep).

Oh, but the bus had a dash-mounted camera.

Lortel preferred Allenwood Correctional to the subterra-nean lodgings of his previous jail, the oily stink of the jacaranda withering through the ceiling vent. He emerged after a year of admiring the bench presses of his cellmate, noting the even plant of his upper traps as the cast iron barbells rose in density.

And, notwithstanding his PO, who was certainly a fly on stink, life was good so long as there was talent out there.

The night something of an acrid mist fell over Lortel's aspi-rations he was watching Gwen Sohn pirouette at the urging of his loaded gun. He had tracked the supple dancer from her Barre and Basic movement class to her walkup in Venetia. She, mistress of The Pittsburgh Ballet Theater, was a sort of promenading egret for the pleasure of gentle widowers in the loge. Lortel had never become rapt at the masters before, only technically driven to adjudge their wares. But the flourish of this Sohn en pointe was no mere compulsory marvel; it socked him where it hurt. He felt it *beautiful;* not as craft, but as a thing that *is* and that will not be something else, so unitary that even witnessing it from a distance causes pain. Lortel was suddenly unable to hover at the right distance, gauge his place in the firmament of extraordinary beings.

I'm not *beautiful,* he thought.

I must become beautiful, he also thought.

But he couldn't steal a face, and, owing to his years, which were not old but simply unpopulated with the burning drive towards his own decisive mastery of a form, found that remolding himself as anything more than a rehabbed convict was a pipe dream on amphetamines.

Crying made him cry harder, so he laughed.

Laughter isn't beautiful, he thought, unless an infant does it.

"I want to be an infant!" he screamed.

"Shut the fuck up," yelled Aunt Desiree from the other room. "You are one and that's the problem."

It was the eczemic Wally Udall who came by that day, looking for a syringe in the bedsprings, weaponry. (Lortel kept his across Esplen hidden in City Park, its strange crenels harmonious with the crags of untouched rock). Udall was the one man Lortel did not wish to prosper at his profession. He had been hard, a miser, his eyes not bright, not beautiful.

"You look bummed," said Udall, raising the mattress as Lortel sat in his chair.

"You know I ain't using, man. Never did that; I ain't that kind."

"Not just drugs I'm looking for. You could have a winning lottery stub."

Udall searched the closets. He interrupted the noon soaps of Desiree's, wiggled loose the already uneven baseboards, did a five-over all barbarous on the chipping wainscot. To Lortel, the old pudsucker's love handles were kind of like the undead's hue.

"This is nice, Jesse. No no-nos" said Udall. But the oddest thing then, as a car sprayed sludge from a foaming bilge puddle outside and a broom fell stingingly in the hall, a disruption: Udall began to cry, the folds beneath his eyes spitting out gelatinous tears, prolific as sparks from an open hearth. Lortel crossed to him and heard himself say, "I get you", though as lives went the men were a galaxy apart.

He had never seen someone this fat sobbing. It was an image. And, emotional, Lortel was stentorian-prone.

"Sure, you do feel gripped by Churchill's 'Black dog' of depression," he said, his register a fathom dropped. "Would that we could scamper to a pasture of May and upon return we could leave that buzzard groping for a *raison* to walk the Earth."

"You called it a dog, and then you called it a bird," said Udall.

"That's me," said Lortel. "Always a hair off mastery."

"And it isn't any dog of depression, or a buzzard of such," said Udall.

"I'm not beautiful," said the other.

Udall turned to Jesse James and said, "What?"

Of course it was not Udall's standard hankering for the continual upward climb that created this twitch of inadequacy, or that he was bound to check the bedsprings of the planet's Lortels instead of reclining on a sapphire beach. It was not just the malcontents he was helping strive towards illusory prowess that saddled his sinking morale. It was the simple instance of watching his son's dinosaur film. In this movie, he learned that raptors had "peripheral awareness". This allowed them a panoramic sight. He imagined these raptors should have lived forever, that this sight should have led to the dreamlike and suspended frisson of joy that attended Cretacean dominance. But even they were destroyed, eaten by fucks with longer teeth and a greater economy of stride, and you could play "Taps" for the theropods as well; casualties of a galactic sandblasting begun in the Outer Reaches. So Lortel's hand on his shoulder, the charmingly challenged high-tone words that emitted from the hole below his mustache, would not begin to remedy his morale.

Maybe it was meeting Lortel that first planted this idea of inadequacy? He couldn't put all the blame on the Jurassic, the toddler's almost congenital lust for primordial lizards whose mouths he'd imagined stuffed with the entrails of early man. Dissatisfaction creates a shadow self with a much higher standard than the entity that answers to your name. His specifications could not be denied or embellished: Weight: 280, height 5'10. Glucose: 153. His wife, he decided, was part of a lineal conspiracy to have him farting the same sausage for the duration of his connubial life. His father had done that, got wed to a pork encaser from Simnas, Lithuania, and punked out a day shy of sixty, his chest all plaque. Udall was fifty-four.

Indeed the "change of life" baby had done its job, retiring the idea of retirement. Yet here, not his child, but this redneck Lortel, was guiding him almost telepathically to his car. This freak with his raw umber hair and swank, cosmically godawful way of talking, this freak like the ferryman of the Styx rowing him to his Buick Regal.

Udall was destined to meet him, he knew. Lortel must've known it, too.

It wasn't the all-in spirit of a war reporter that had him living in a world of Lortels. He had fucked up his life, dropped out of college; but since he lived in this world, he couldn't help but let it shape him. The harder he fought against it shaping him in its image, the more it drove him away from plastic tyrannosaurs, the safety of Lithuanian sausages.

The seat squealed against his weight as they climbed into his car. Neither knew where they were heading.

"I can't be beautiful," said Lortel as Udall drove the ramp onto the highway. "Just isn't happening. You know a latecomer like me has ever managed a snowball's chance of surpassing God's gift raffle? Nobody ever done me a cradle dance. And I'm a *good fucking contributor* to the commonweal as you will find in a repeat felon!"

"I don't disagree, Jesse," Udall said, in a provisional tone that promised a new clause in the sentence that never came. Before the dinosaur film, Udall would have found that clause, a preemptive caveat to guide his unruly charge.

"I wish I could make you the best PO in the world. I could make *you* beautiful," said Lortel.

"No one's doin' that," said Udall.

"I sure wish I *could.*"

"I know."

"I mean I sure wish you'd let me."

"Yeah, yeah."

"Sure can't say I wouldn't hold you at the point of a gun to *make* you let me. Come on, man."

Udall let his lips pucker and he didn't look at the man in the passenger seat.

"Do you have that weapon?" he said, the exhaustion in his voice both real and strategic.

"I do. I do, Mr. Udall."

"I won't ask where it is."

"There you go," said Lortel with genuine surprise, "not letting me make you the best PO in all the *Trois Rivieres*. That is beaucoup pigheaded, man! If you'd let me I would lead you like a modern Hannibal to my Wesson which, I should offer, is stashed over the municipal hills someplace. I'd forgo the Life of Riley for Allenwood just to see you grinning in the annals."

"Annals of what?"

"Parole officing!"

Udall just drove. The city receded like an undertow in back of them. After a moment, Lortel said, "And I don't need you to tell me them annals ain't a thing."

"You're not stupid," said Udall. "That's what you're telling me."

"Yeah but I ain't no Niels Bohr neither."

"Who's that?"

"I don't know," said Lortel. "Maybe I'd have to be Niels Bohr to tell you."

But where they were going was still open. Neither could go back to Pittsburgh proper knowing what they knew; there was no point living a lie if you couldn't be perfect. Once you thought that you would be skating on a slush pond up a mighty mountain slope just to try and get your bearing. When both tried to think what was perfect they found they were at odds to pin it down; they just knew they … weren't.

Looking straight ahead, Udall saw the road: a little pocked ribbon through the blue spruce when, suddenly, as though guided by some obscene force, his head at the tip of a robotic arm that moved his neck at a demon's whim, he turned to Lortel in the passenger seat.

"If I loved my son, he'd be perfect," said Udall.

Lortel nodded, but was struck dumb. He wanted to be stentorian, but this was a perfect comment, and he could add nothing, nothing but nothing at all. It was not a perfection either one of them liked, because they both understood it. They could touch it like a hot stovetop. Udall had never asked about Lortel's father. He could see that the boy looked drawn.

"No one is perfect," said Lortel finally. "Unless they be loved perfectly."

"You stamp that nugget on a Hallmark," said Udall, "and you won't be robbing nobody to make your nut."

Whatever messianic trouble Lortel might have been hatching for the other side of this trip, no one could find any harm in skipping rocks. So they took a turn to French Creek and the two went down to the water, left the car in the shade of the mercurial hemlocks. Lortel flicked stones just a little above the water by employing some sidearm windage he might have learned anyplace on Earth. (Udall knew he was an army brat, and, despite his jerkwater affect, spoke at least five words in eleven different tongues). The hydroplaning of the stones was a fine thing, the water ruptures as dainty as piano plinks.

Udall thought a perfect man, an eternal man, would be skipping perfect rocks with his child. He could only look to his right see the wiry Lortel, his townie hair and tin-pot viscount mustache. He thought the little man's mustache came complimentary with the purchase of '76 Ford Comet.

But he sure could skip river stones.

"I can't do that," said Udall, watching him. "I've created life that won't follow me. I'm not at one with it. I'm not at one with *me*."

Lortel winged a stone that danced nearly to the bank of the creek. He turned, surprised.

There was a boy walking towards them. Udall wasn't sure he was real until Lortel said, "Damn if it ain't Opie gone feral."

The boy had a lot of sun on his face, but wasn't squinting. He was perfectly freckled. He had no shoes on.

"You wanna skip some rocks with us?" said Lortel.

"I don't skip rocks," said the boy. "I float 'em."

He said this perfectly, movielike. He held his hands up before the men. The boy had taken a large leaf and beveled it at the points into a shapely aft and hull, the small craft as fragile as origami. He took the rock from Lortel's hand and sat it right in the middle of this craft, bent to the water and set it down, where it glided with only a gentle wobble down the creek.

All Udall thought was that if it was a little later in the day the water could act as an elongating mirror, rendering his hipline less fat. Lortel wanted to grab the boy and squeeze him until all the winsome life became his own, but neither could move. They would stand there all day, watching the space where the boy had been standing long after he was gone. They would have liked to ride the wake trail of the leaf down the creek current, and if the creek had been longer, it would ride them along its ripples for years, depositing them at the pool of a waterfall, polished as ancient stones.

Bunkbeds

Nobody ever thought my mother was a common bird. She was known to hoot loudly at town football when the high-school games took up our autumn Saturdays, even though she had no son in these games. She chaperoned for prom in spring and, in fall, when the Halloween rabble launched Barbasol fusillades at the revelers in cul-de-sacs, she was there to provide cover for the tweens. But no boy of hers existed to trick-or-treat. Everyone tried to hide pity and so her strangeness was greeted as there, no more anomalous than wood on trees or screams by a dowager on *The Price is Right*. I had been born with a twin named Reginald who passed away months from our difficult birth, thus I was wheeled in a twin pram all over Schenectady till mercifully, I turned three. Growing up I slept on the bottom bunk of a fine wooden bunkbed with no one sleeping above the springs. The mattress had been made a shrine and there were new stuffed animals, of a sophistication commensurate with the chronology of "Reggie's" milestones, every birthday.

My father acted like all this was standard to the grieving process. In fact, his familiar refrain, when challenged by me or anyone, was, "It's a process." The process, such as it was, never did work itself out, but my mother held down jobs without enduring hitches and headed up nonprofits while, failing to thrive as a gumball wholesaler, my father met only a surfeit of useless orbs. A destiny to tipple caught him up, and he died at the age of fifty, low on a long list of candidates to receive a liver that didn't crackle like firewood when pinched. By then I was sixteen. After the tearless funeral I leant my head on the bunkbed where a Goodwill-purchased track trophy was set down in place of mohair wolves.

Reggie, meet Daddy.

My mother was beaming from the door.

I reached thirty as a woman in Massachusetts, a setter, a husband, an herbicided strip of grass separating us from the Wahls. The unhoused poor got houses on account of the work my husband did. Little tots in Roxbury saw fresh fields instead of asphalt in summer, ran paper routes instead of rock baggies around the low rises to addle-heads. I became a social worker. *The solutions are easy, and only the problems are hard.*

Jed and I tried restlessly to sire kids, the former buying Letrozole combos and leaving them on the nightstand for when I returned tired from a day of difficult sessions, and it was only in my forties the Stork alit. The in vitro did its trick with relish and the kid came out as … twins. We named them Alex and Reese, never establishing Reese in our voices when his name was said. Nothing was entirely natural and nor, we thought, should it be. We were older, had lived more than half our lives unparenting, and layettes were a foreign body in our home. Reese proved himself the real spanner. He was not bright, and Alex was. He had a frat-boy's galumphing carriage early while Alex minced around the playset like a kid at Harrow School. Reese kicked Jed on the regular, spat on his palms and wiped them everywhere. Reese cussed. Reese insisted on the top bunk and rained Skittles from those wet palms torrentially down on a sleeping Alex and we would dash into the bedroom and yell. When Reese found he would not receive spankings for his flourishes, because, as Jed said, "We are not that kind", he escalated his warfare against us, applying more aggressive rhetoric in countering our reprimands.

"Where did you get those Skittles?!" I said after a one of his downpours.

"From up in your asshole, mommy," Reese said, almost equitably.

Now Alex, who evidently had become a confederate after witnessing the scolding of his sib, had taken to laughing at these rejoinders. Jed shook his head in such a way that I knew the meaning right off: We should've stopped at one, but we never had the chance to.

Reese flunked so reliably at school we found ourselves grateful for the consistency, until he began selling clay penises he had molded under the radar in Ms. Hasakawa's Tuesday art class to a group of Albanian kids in from the Korab mountains on a school exchange, the school having dispatched six or so untamable troublemakers from Grade Five to Tirana hoping they would take to the country and remain. Now: If an Adriatic politesse is a thing, it was not in these tweens; when not quiet they were all found lowing like bovines in-season on the Jungle Jim, a taunting way of addressing the tiara-headed girls they were doubtless sweet on without knowing it. Reese did not get money in return for his gonad art, as they reciprocated only with chocolate milk. He gained a lot of weight on that and now cavities were on his baby teeth like poppyseeds: a great shame for us and we couldn't wait to redeem ourselves when the first set dropped. Coleen Wahl phoned us one day and said he had cornered her tabby by the rainspout, it was cowering in abject terror while he waved around one of his clay manhoods like a fan-dancer and she had never seen Mr. Grumble's ears pinned this far back.

"It doesn't even look like a cat anymore!" she screamed over the phone.

When we got over there and punched the air with his name the cat shot off into the road, barely escaping eternity at the wheels of an 80s' Jeep Wagoneer maxing out its degraded power brakes, its rusty tow hitch swung out very close to the hedgerow Ben Wahl died pruning when an embolism took him a year to the day.

My mother called from outside her Crown Victoria, a car she couldn't part with and perhaps the only car she knew how to drive. She was right in the town center at the Lukoil gassing up, and she was panicked.

"I'm lost!" she cried. "I'm just lost. No one in this state drives at an acceptable rate. I think I missed the interchange just to escape their grilles, Peg. I really do."

"Mother. Calm."

"*You* calm."

"If you'd used the Mapquest like Jed suggested-"

"They were chasing me like I was one of your Salem Witches!"

When Jed drove down to the station so she could follow him home, he found her in the gas mart scoffing at the Yemeni manager who was sneaking licks off his fingers to sop up the Yodel cream from his nails.

"I think 45 has it right," she said. "I don't care what anybody says."

She had proposed visiting the previous Saturday, a "freshening" drive from upstate New York. Jed, deep into rehearsals for Alex's school play, had asked me to dissuade her, but we could only stall so much. She was always rude to Jed and I, enamored solely of our offspring, and we dodged her intrusions into our world, where an unhappy dichotomy between the boys had created a systemic unity more rooted in a desire for shape than in any real connection, and if a more loving home was to remain in the realm of fantasy, there was, within our walls, a kind of jailhouse dependency we could count on; any new cellmate would disrupt the balance here. Mother had not seen the twins since a year before. That time, Reese had stomped on her instep and ran giggling down the hall upon greeting her. She thought it was just too darling when he laughed. Later in the visit, she pinched his drawn cheeks like our boy had cherub cheeks. He swatted her away like she was a wasp.

"I'm grandma," she would say, bending to him condescendingly.

"I know," was all he would say back.

When she entered the house this time, Reese wasn't even present. Alex was, and he made sure to run up into her arms, but she bridled at the moment he was close and he nearly collided with the door behind her.

Alex had advanced in his schooling. He was at Reading Level N and made Eco Student of the Month in January, Math Student of the Month the following month. These commendations were relayed to her straight away and were met with perfunctory nodding before Judith turned with lynxish precision on her heels and made haste to the hall, her head craning around in what we knew was a search for Reese.

It was already noon Saturday. My mother had suggested the trip with some urgency but now that she was here, she had settled into her working state of elliptical hostility and swanning entrances worthy of Hyannis Port. She seemed far less picky with our dinners, and I was forced to revisit the circulars after her uncharacteristic scarfing of the fridge. Jed always made sure to be scarce when mother was around, but he was so scarce this time it hovered over us in our iron chairs Judith said resembled patio furniture.

"I know Jed hates me," she said over her half-caff at the kitchen table. "And who can blame him. I'm formidable."

"You are," I said.

"I don't beat around the bush. I've lost too much to do that."

"Yes, mother."

"But I've pulled up into untrodden country hale, ready to mine ore from the valleys."

"Right."

"I made a lot of good come of our pledges for Mandela's release."

"You did do that."

"Who in Western New York did more than I?"

"So what is it you are doing now?"

"I clean the parsonage. Jack Rance sees I have two nickels I can rub to buy basics."

"That keeps you busy?"

"I really do think Jed should be present at this table. I really do think that."

"He likes to sneak work in. You remember what that was like? Half of his time he spends peddling his own ass for the MASSGrant, or the cheapskates EHS deals with in allotting funds."

"45 has done more for the urban poor than you blind do-gooders ever could for all the earmarking radicals want out of our treasury."

It was alarming and inexplicable. Mother had only ever been insane regarding Reggie. She had labored for righteous causes, often in lieu of attending to my emotional needs. Now Neanderthals had washed her brain clean with such efficiency I could only put it down to dementia. Micro-strokes seemed to account for the phenomenon nationwide—that was the charitable view anyway.

Presently, Jed entered in an oddly rumpled dress shirt under a loose-fitting white sport coat, the effect that of a Don Johnson fresh out of a lean-to out in the woods.

"Whaddoya think of these duds?" he said. "Colleen is spring cleaning Ben's things."

"You're wearing Ben Wahl's clothes?" I said.

"He's wearing the clothes of a dead man," said my mother, although how she knew Ben had died was a puzzle.

"They don't fit you, honey," I said.

"The treadmill paid off," he said, looking at his reflection in the window. "I'm in fine fettle and Ben is dead."

"That's the spirit," I said.

"Never guess," said Jed, "Yesterday. That truck on Pineview that sells oversweet Korean tacos in the rice buns? There was a guy in the line wearing rags, he had on this silk scarf that appeared to have been through the Argonne, and soiled wing-tips under slacks with urine spots running down the split seams in torrents. A fucking beret like a trash lid on his head. Do you remember the inimitable Vaughn DeHaan?"

"No," I said.

"My acting teacher when I took the Method class? Yes? No? Well, you didn't play it from the heart, whatever role you were playing, and he'd fume like Krakatoa till your head rung. I was playing Pollo in a snippet of *A Hatful of Rain* and when he saw no inner life in me, *marone!* I still get a jolt from his shellacking."

"I see."

"But Peg," he said, now whispering. "I think it was *him.*"

"The man in the rags at the stand?"

"But it *couldn't* be him."

"Why not?"

"I mean Val Swersky told me he died."

"Val Swersky?"

"My scene partner."

"You've kept up with her?"

"The thing is," said Jed, pacing, "it was like one of those computer programs that age you with whatever photoshopping voodoo Macs use, or maybe he had a long lost tw-" Jed tensed his shoulders and looked fleetingly at Judith, who raised her head in defiance.

"Go on," she said. "Say it."

I couldn't help but roll my eyes. Drama was the subject and drama was never far.

"Now I'm just sorry all over the place," he said, sitting down and smirking.

The white jacket smelled horrible. My mother winced and drew her head toward the window. Jed looked at my mother, leaned back and propped his leg up on the table.

"What do you think the Albanians are doing with the clay dicks?" he said.

"Watch your tongue," I said, knowing this crassness was for my mother's benefit.

"The Albanians?" she said.

"Reese is in trouble these days, Judith," said Jed, "for creating clay penises and 'selling' them to exchange students."

"From Albania?"

"Yes," said Jed, as though that affirmative was the capstone on everything. He was playing with different notions of himself in the tones he chose, I could see it. This was a facet both new and not in Jed. He'd been through all three schools The Group Theater had splintered into upon its dissolution in the 1930s. He had studied straight Strasburg at Braintree, then Meisner's mirror exercises across the Charles, and then Stella Adler on our side of the Charles, hers a kind of fusion technique that split the merits of the former egoists without having to tow around the legacy of their brimstone tempers, and all schools failed him in the end. He was bitter but did not know it, and perhaps I was glad of this.

"How old are these Albanians?" said Judith.

"Ten, I think," said Jed.

"Well, I suppose," said my mother, stuttering, "Albanian children have a right to be puerile. War was their first education."

"There's something ponderous about them," said Jed. "Like their blood is thicker, too thick for their veins. It makes them slow and it makes them pervy."

"At least they're not running speed up from Matamoros," said my mother. "Or wallowing in tunnels feet from the Alamo."

Jed looked at me and we had our first simpatico moment in months. That look lasted until he began picking at Ben Wahl's collar, smiling obscurely.

Old Argus, our setter, came into the kitchen and sat staring at its full bowl.

"Why is it not eating?" said Judith.

"He does that," said Jed. "It's like he sees dead people in the bowl. He kind of breathes them away like a little process and then he digs in."

"You've always burnt a hole in your pocket on whatsis-name," said Judith.

"Argus," said Jed, keeping a poker face.

"Pets," she said, shaking her head. "I hope the pound police relieve me of my felines." She tickled at her cup nervously with her fingers, shifting in her chair. "One thing that flummoxes this girl is clumping litter. $12.95 a box and one poop out from the smallest fuzzball and heavens! That is a solid block you can dump out in one run and wonder what ghost blew through your money!"

"You could use some cash, you're saying," "said Jed, flatly."

Mother paused, her expression pleasant. "Yes," she said, as if just snapping to the thought. "I could."

"How much?"

None of us would say it but it was blackmail money; guaranteeing she would stay due west of us; and since our combined income was barely enough to support our current clutter, we were able to draw on her inconsideration as a working spark to make this extortion work. I could see Jed's mind working, wondering of forbearances on his student loans, earmarking his dad's ungenerous loan to the cause instead of the thirty-year mortgage, when Alex came running in.

"I drew this, grandma!" he said, holding up a marker sketch of a Nepalese Yeti holding his twin Reese by the head. I'd never seen him so proud of a sketch.

"Yes," said Judith, wiping her mouth and turning her head back towards the hall, where Reese was trying to jam the swing arm of an old-fashioned brushed alloy Tonka into an unplated socket in the wall, producing from the hardhat some lisping rattles clearly meant to mimic death.

"Aren't you going to do something about that?!" said Judith.

"The socket's dead," said Jed, mayo on his chin.

"What if it comes alive. Things come alive!"

Jed, his mouth full, turned to her abruptly.

"Whaddoya mean 'things come alive'?"

"Watch your children," said Judith, curtly.

She got up, wiped her mouth discreetly with a napkin, and went into the hall, where she attempted to pull Reese from his peril by the outlet. He shot an arm up at her to brush her back.

"Reese, dear."

He rose and walked bandy-legged down the hall, his little hands working to balance the Tonka truck, and slammed his bedroom door. Inside came more death rattles.

Judith waited a moment, then took furtive steps towards the door, stopping only several yards from where his room began. She didn't move, just stood there, and only thought the better of knocking when she was snapped from her trance by a thud inside, something obviously thrown with force against the door, as though warding off an alien presence.

School had gotten out early that day. One of the Albanian nationals had drained an entire bottle of Grecian Formula into his mouth in the cafeteria after calling the students over to watch. His compatriots continued to clap as the child spiraled down to the floor like soft serve from a spigot. He recovered in the ICU woozy and a bit hurt that attention-seeking landed him in this sterile hoosegow, far, far away from his mountain brethren who would now make the seamy cow noises at the tiara girls without aid of his alto for harmony, but worse than that was the hair-dye stench sweeping up from his stunned tract in waves. The principal had sent the students home to "process" what they'd seen but elected not to cancel that night's event. When my mother heard about the boy she insisted on going to the hospital. Alex had the school play whose staging was arranged by Jed, and roping in my mother proved a hard sell once she was aware how much our attendance meant to him. The play was *Twelfth Night* set postgame at a bar across from Fenway Park, Alex having the role of Duke Orsino, and the pentametric dialogue was rendered modern by the white-washing pen of a lifer from the Board of Ed, who consulted with Jed as the kids did heroic work moving to his brusque commands and keeping stride as his tongue lashings became more and more unhinged as they dropped lines; Jed was un-bound in theaters. In the end everyone would have to concede the viewing experience would have been more fun, or at least more novelly interesting, had the play been mounted as per folio, the meager ages of the players beside the point. It seemed like everyone was there. Colleen Wahl, childless, was standing off to the side like one too nervous to be trapped in the con-fines of a chair, as if even a minor miscue could kill her. Val Swersky brought three friends who all seemed single, swiveling heads at every semi-eligible male, even the toupeed claims ad-juster whose wife died of pancreatitis not a week before. Val had stayed young the way artists tend to, whether successful or not. There was a good shot that pottery would be her thing. Judith became more and more fixated on the little Albanian with the locks-darkening potion still tunneling through his gut, and at the little reception afterward she would speak of nothing else. Jed put his arm around Alex and the boy looked up at his grandmother as if his childish gazing would awe her, but she was able to do no more than smile almost quizzically at the Duke. It was only when Reese, who had been outside doing God knows what in the hall, came in with a jealous smirk, that she dropped any talk of the ailing Balkan.

At the very moment Judith was pressing me as to why Jed had not cast Reese as at least a token participant I saw Jed speaking oozingly to Colleen Wahl, who seemed to have made efforts to fly her widowhood at least as appearance went. The word "pert" came to mind. Everything was just as if an adrenaline needle had been run into her hide, turning the girl as firm as polymer, and when Jed turned and saw I was looking he did not present a natural face.

"Why not Malvolio?" rattled Judith, carrot dip on her upper lip. "You could've found him something even like holding props."

"Oh Jesus, mother, shut up."

Jed was wearing an unfamiliar shirt, something of festive polyester that seemed like it could catch fire twenty yards from a stove. It was jammed into slacks and the crotch was too roomy, and even the blind could see his hair had changed. It now hung lankly in a left side part, not to the right, like I had trained it, as though he had come back from the dead as a funhouse iteration, just a little shifted from the man I knew.

I drove mother and the kids home while Jed went out to a late dinner with the bowdlerizer from the Board of Ed and to renew some ancient pleasantries with Val, perhaps soak up some animal glances from her companions. I had not liked the bowdlerizer, who struck me as an erotomanic stalker, dogging Jed's heels, the latter feeling pumped as the potbellied nuisance rained undue plaudits on his "blocking", my husband's crotch appearing as attractive as a salmon to a bear. That his name was Devin Blount only irked me even more. I hated the name Devin, it brought to mind a kneecapping linebacker from Andover, the sort of dead eyed prom date rapist whose ancestral standing among the minted powers his measureless sociopathy. This Devin, though, was unctuous and not a little silly when he spoke; a chubby fop who chirped from his adenoids. I tried to forget the evening, unconsoled by Alex's mature portrayal, as he really nailed the Duke, meaning he was as boringly declamatory as befitted the traditional style.

Reese and Alex punched and jawed at each other in the backseat while mother noted street signs, shuddering at the number of closed warehouses, the distant orchards a cobalt nothing that loomed behind them, the window opened enough that the apple scent came through, but it was a mixed scent of seedlings and gravel as we approached little A-frames across the railyard. The windows of one had been boarded up against a vista of salvage yards to the west, while on the eastern exposure only cream-colored waste tanks remained visible. Judith shook her head at the sites in rhythm, the razor wires working as if channels to relay signals only she could hear.

"That boy in back of me," she said, "needs a role in your life."

"Which one?" I said.

But I knew it was not Alex who sat behind her.

I had given up on any notion of putting the kids to bed. They wouldn't oblige me without daddy. I let them go at it with each other in the hall while my mother placed herself in the kitchen chair to gather herself up. The gaiety of the afterparty seemed to both of us unsettlingly preordained. Someone had made a decision. An agenda would have to play out; the kids were only pretextual in the game.

The boys had set out anime cards all the rage these days; the two outbid dimmer kids for the ones with the elaborate dragons on them. Now it was a dispute over one particular firebreather drawn up in screaming indigo that had the boys trading punches in the hall. I heard a sigh in the kitchen, felt the combat boil up in me and had a stray thought that become too familiar much too quickly to not have a bearing on my world.

I got up and crossed the narrow lane to the Wahl's, past the fateful hedgerow and recyclables in olive drab bins on the walk. My assumption that the door would not be locked proved solid, and I walked through the hall to sounds I knew but one sound I sure didn't: the pitched, almost ermine voice of a man yelling with theatrical relish, "Sebastian! Heel! You're giving Olivia a hip flexor!" I stepped forward and in the frame of the open door I saw the forbidden tableau: Jed and Colleen, congressing as is standard, and Blount sitting without cladding on a low seat and with his hand on his rather spriggish wad. Of course, a fit would not be misplaced here, and so I allowed this vision some real estate: This was happening.

I screamed with the sense of impulse Jed had tried to revive in himself in all of his acting schools. A sharp cry in unison came from the players, Blount's voice overpowering theirs, and Jed pulled out ungracefully from Colleen Wahl. With less impulse than before, I turned and hustled down the hall; Jed tater-sack racing after me in the act of placing on his pants, and as I stepped out onto the lawn, he tried to grab my shoulder.

"Listen," he said. "This looks worse than it is."

"What!?" I said, spinning to face him.

His pants were on now but his chest was bare, sweat or spit glistening on it.

"It really is," he said. "It's not so crazy. None of it is."

I shook my head incredulously and made for our house. I could hear his bare feet slapping the cheap tiles behind me. When he caught me up in the living room, I sighed and turned again, suddenly spent with the relief of knowing.

"It's okay," he said boyishly. "It's not me. I'm a ghost. It's just a part. We're all just playing one anyway. Right? You, too. You can't mistake it for real."

Another scream cut the air, this time Reese's. When I turned the corner into the hall my mother was standing over him, attempting to touch his shoulder. Alex looked at us imploringly, his eyes somewhat terrified.

"Reese, darling," said Judith.

"No! Off me! Off!" He hands were fists at his sides.

"He was being too rough with you!" she said.

"You are not my mother! You're my mother's mother. You just pretend you're my mother!"

"Darling," said Judith.

"You're going to die alone," said Reese. "You think you can die with us but you're just old and you're going to die alone where you live! In the shit land, you ugly old killer!"

"Hey!" yelled Jed, beginning to storm forward and only stopping when he saw a slight spasm shake my mother, but it was one that seemed to gird her in place. She remained half bent, and walking a little forward it became clear the spasms were silent sobs, and though the thing to do would have been move to her and to bless her with a silent touch, or a small token gesture to free her from the gaze of the boy, we let her remain in the space between him and us, with an eye towards letting it play out.

Travels with Jerry

Watchdog

At four PM, the Mughal sun is cut by the crossing partitions, but the outlines of business travelers set stark against the high windowpanes of the Shalimar dance in the spears that get through. They move their forks and enterprise sternly over Motorolas, animating pipe dreams, making mincemeat of pipe dreams. The track lights remind us we are not in Peshawar. Men in fitted tunics hand me Johnny Walker Blacks. Bond traders in pinstripes yell close it! Cricket batsmen and fire-breathing muftis share Saag Paneers, debating bioethics versus the arm of God. Courtly waiters – prim as manor valets – bend to smoking men. They do not scowl like the northeastern frontier's blue marchers, the jack-steppers in tight tunics, or the policemen we cannot trust.

I check the time. I check the faces. The man is not here.

I am a Finlayson Watchdog, part of a covey of nonworking marines, "watchdogging" the industrial titans, shadowing arms men as they transact with busy emirs, or simply sightsee the wider environs. We recon threats to motorcades; post up undercover bird's eyes and snatch intel from all over; we succor "moles" and rogue ISI ops. We quarry aimless rattles across our wires. We fire when fired upon, and that can get messy. When an unplanned murder takes place, we dandy up in finery and face the band, eating crow pie for a panel of senators. No one among us has seen jail.

My man is in town to hawk arms, to glad-hand the foreign ministers and triggermen at the Lahore Expo awaiting his genial pitches. I have suggested Data Durbar and the Shalimar Hotel. Here, among buildings drawn on the unimaginative German lines that stifle a rigorous plotting, we can interact minimally with Islamic Lahore, and those who would doom him.

I am getting antsy when a clatter stuns. Largo, nine minutes late, arrives. He is wearing a Turnbull & Asser untucked over a dhoti of cotton pleats, his feet shod in Milanese sandals.

"Right," he says, gripping my hand. "You must be the man. My god, you're as sexless as a can of beets!"

"Thank you."

"Bloody horror show on the ride here. They was galloping hairpin turns in a Senny. Around the tenth switchback we was tearing through and the eighth fucking mandrill we'd pulverized, I was all but prostrate as a vicar!"

He snaps his fingers and a waiter bends to our table.

"Gin. Flagonful. Don't tarry," says Largo.

"What kind of gin, sir?"

"Bug off, any kind, bug off."

At a table by the window, an ancient diner, a westerner, his mouth collapsed and grim, his skin verdigris, sets his eyes on Largo.

"The fuck are you looking at," says Largo to the man. "Back to your ponce!"

The man steers his glance away, cracks his papadams, stuffing in tremulous mouthfuls. Only now do I realize the man is missing a leg

"Mister Largo," I say. "We have intelligence out of the frontier. Lashkar is planning something coordinated. Here."

"What you want from me end? I got appointments. Think I got time for tick-tack? I got three towelheads in from Sharm want me to front them Supacats and toss in a hundred glider winches free of charge. A Royal Jordanian AF is angling to Jew me down on some Cobham drogues. I got multinational shareholders on my cock."

"All right. My turn to talk."

"Whoa now," he says, rearing back. "I'll slick your hair back with your own lymph, you dirty Jew!"

"I'm Episcopalian."

"Say, what's it like to get brissed? Knew this bloke out of the Brill building wrote me some charters, Syd Lerner. I asked him. He said he didn't remember."

"Mister Largo, you are a confirmed target in Lahore."

The westerner at the window looks our way.

"Something you'd like to say to me, you nosy shite?" says Largo to the man. "I'll spatchcock you au jus like the hobbling old squab you are."

The man shakes his head and crunches some more crisps. The arm that does not crack the crisps is outsized; a prosthesis. It is unsettling. There is so much to unsettle me here. Since hooking up with the Watchdog Group, I have established open channels to a range of top arms men. Ammo dealers are what are known in the guns trade as "contacts", and if recent history is any guide, they are perishable – at least when I am guarding them. There was Wally Ajax – a plankhouse backwater no-name out of Saskatchewan – dead; there was Guy May the Bogotá kingpin and rifle-runner lackey, likewise suspiciously expired; Sam Snell the Manitoba Jewfish with his head shot away in Bagram; there was the bad apple Welshman Vic Royce with his acid trip meets-Andalusia stencil-mustache, pulverized with the rest of his car last February when his motorcade slinked a tripwire across Bahawalpur Road. Now the leader's torch has been passed to a man of song.

Largo checks the quartz-powered hands of his Aquaracer, sighs and clamps his right hand on my shirt while with his left hand he stirs his drink.

"Right you are. Have at it, Yank. Spill me itinerary."

I produce a touchscreen organizer on which is stored our recourse plans.

"Safe bet me friend'll want to hear this," says Largo.

He points to the eavesdropper at the window.

"Let's leave him be," I say. "Why bother?"

"He'll need to be privy," says Largo. "He's me assistant."

"Your assistant?"

"Finch," says Largo, signaling the old man. "Bloody millstone but I don't travel anywhere without him."

Garden Path to the Shalimar Gardens

In the taxi on the way to the expo, Largo keeps rolling the window down; hocking phlegm gobs out the window with exuberance.

Please let this not be my seventh.

You see, Jerry Largo is a kind of legend in the underworld arms trade. He was a songbird at the Palladium in London, handsomer than Alain Delon and richer than the House of Saud. His face had a blazing ruggedness between his muttonchops; his pants ran in a modish taper above his gleaming plus-fours; his mop top screened his eyes like a pleasing awning (piercing but narrow-set, like cuts). All of this costuming paid off when he hammered through love ballads with the backing of choral singers whose unison was like the parting of the clouds. He won eponymous top-billing on the *Dick Rangoon* TV show which dominated Wednesdays on Channel Four, blowing away turtle-necked saboteurs with silver-painted ray guns to instrumental renditions of his own songs. He was all set to chase Tom Jones back to Wales after his tenth chart-topper, but a dark wolf reared and he became known for chugging Pernods, firing Italian revolvers at the clotted friezes of the moon ("I'm going to knock off Aldrin's Yank flag, just you watch me!") and menacing all cleavage nearby. He tossed crystal chandeliers off the terraces of hotels and creamed his Royal Enfield on the Zillertals. He once nearly killed a woman with a cocktail fork. He is rumored to have solidified Dusty Springfield's sexual preference as a lesbian.

None of that worked to humble my "contract".

Largo was speeding the M-4 and cratered his Quattroporte, mangling the backseat passenger, a whore-mongering parliamentarian whose femurs snapped like twigs, after which the singer fled the country. Meanwhile, Paris gendarmes raided his mansion in Neuilly-sur-Seine, scattering clothesless ingénues onto the flowerbeds of his miniature Tuleries. Inside the chateau they found a decaying chauffeur; he'd been upright in a Hepplewhite five days while the lissome aspirants were down on the rug doing amorous theatrics to Serge Gainsbourg songs, writhing against a revolving roster of strays from the Quartier Latin while a chest wound puddled around the mosaic of squirming limbs. No one could say why the driver was dead or who shot him; but a studbox of Phenobarbitals and cut coke found in Largo's sterling armoire was enough to suggest the latter had been deep in the fray. They called for a tarring inquest. Nothing stuck, but the moral fester was on the man, and he went, as the saying goes, to "ground". Years of incommunicado passed; silence tempered by occasional unannounced Hokkaido tour dates; a halfhearted comeback working supper rooms on the west coast of Florida – alligator wetland Shan-gri-las where bottle-blond pole dancers-turned mermaids submerged in froglike poses behind reinforced glass while on the other side a deflated Largo blustered strenuously through a medley of his forgotten songs. This was not the bright elusive butterfly of love. His got back rashes from the lawn chair straps and no one he ever bedded rated ink in *The Sunday Times*. It was an old Tory buddy of Maggie Thatcher who pried him away from this slaughter – no headlining or Aston Mark IIIs in carnelian dropping him off snockered to a packed concert stage. It was anonymous work and regimes would fall. Good men led down the garden path by modal absolutism (the brave and cheerless adherents to the word of Marx, St. Francis, Eugene Debbs) would swallow their balaclavas and feed the fish. He informed his unflappable valet of his career change, and Finch, ever Finch, shrugged, murmured, and mail-ordered a Kevlar vest.

Largo turned me and said, "Scout, how'd you get to mothering scalawags like me?"

Well.

Need I tell him that I recall well the flameless ration heaters, the shelf life of dehydrated fricassees and the calorie charts that said nutrition was "a force multiplier", that I remember ditch-digging long nights and getting depomedrone for my collarbone in a skidding Humvee while our Stallion copters whisked the Mosul sands like a bowl of eggs. And some other collected things:

The 1st Marine Expeditionary, my "unit", me on loan from a supply battalion, finally out of the Green Zone and stuck with the First of the First, and what a stunning wing of merry rabble these jarheads were. They called themselves the Gein Berets, after Ed Gein, the serial killer whose ultimate project was the sewing of a "meat helmet" from the viscera of the folks nearby.

While they went out on "runs" I only dug, jammed poles into dunes. I only drove a sand-bleached RV filled to the backdoor flaps with heated C-rations. I only watched the flurry of metal in motion as it left in a slow-going convoy from the base. So much for adventure tales, heroics to replay to friends. I was a housekeeper. One day I got plastered with the Noncom Sayers, a bottle of Buchanan's scotch Jack Hulse brought in spent by the chime of noon and then Hulsie got to rambling about his dozen undiscovered homicides in Peshawar. He described the fire-breathing Pashtuns, the rice in wicker vats, dead animals floating in the alkaline rivers. We raided the base commissary and I had more scotch. I woke up with my hand inside my skivvies, a bandaged wad over the bell-end of my crank.

My bunkmate Janeway was laughing over the bed as I woke up.

"Welcome," he said. "You earned your wings."

I touched the gauze. Some of the blood was not dry.

"Now you can set to raw dogging port whores without a bag on," Hulse said. Then he put on a little seafaring accent. "You're an honorary koyk now, meboy."

I hobbled into the sandbags and slunk there. In the weeks after I had to stifle erotic thoughts should such entertaining rip the sutures. If I imagined a bathing beauty, the pain of the pared spot would end me. So I kept it all ugly, thought of hunchbacks Frenching dead lepers in a mucus pit.

"That man hates wood more than termites," said Sergeant Hulse, when he heard what I was up against.

So it was that and dull chatter, until one day they came in with the stretcher and I was getting sprayed by my bunkmate Janeway's carotid, white as calamari spuming squalls of pressurized arterial blood; the heart confused by the novel aperture, trying poignantly to meet that natural freedom on its own terms, pumping out more barrels to meet demand. I didn't want to tell Mister Largo that.

Nor tell him at the precise juncture of when I wasn't making sense because my words could not stop the reel of arteries, ventricles, force multipliers, sutures, spumes and squalls, and when the officers, commiserating pleasantly in their kakis, voices breathy with the seasoned prowess of desk jocks, prescribed me anti-seizure meds as a stopgap against the inevitable wish, I was spun out of inertia by the thought that one foot in front of the other meant more than anything not going back. Contracting seemed a fair fit, and sounded better than Section 8. Why the subcontinent? It felt like the most visually sumptuous place to expel blood memories without reeling from the squalor of a dishonorable discharge.

The blood, however, has continued flowing. Largo is no kind of tourniquet.

Reprise

A fluted eyesore of steel and glass, the Expo Center is less a Sikh watchtower than it might be a Bauhaus sham. Yet it receives us, and the trade show unfurls without incident. Largo, however, takes time to inform the Interior Minister of Yemen that, as of today, he is slated to reprise his songbook at the Shalimar Babu Room West, a furiously-appointed dinner theater that rims the steel capstone of our hotel.

"Don't do this," I say. "Please, Mister Largo."

"It's done. What, you don't think Pakistan deserves me?"

"I'm not sure you deserve Pakistan."

He claps a hand on my shoulder.

"Be an advert for me munitions sales."

"You can do that *here.*"

"Nah, this is boring."

"I like boring. I can live with boring."

"Hey," says Largo. "You remember that scene in *Citizen Kane* where that weird prairie dog bites Orson Welles' hand off?"

"No."

"You're mood is a little like that scene."

A noise surfaces; I ready my guard as Largo seems tetched: Finch is on the floor by the credenza fifty feet in back of us, jackknifing, as though in a seizure of the hip.

"Oh my fuck …," says Largo. 'The plonker forgot his leg!"

English Land

We lunch late on the terrace and greet the enveloping haze. Finch sits on the veranda, his long legs crossed and his yacht-sized weather-beaten Oxford tapping two-fours in the midair while the flapping emptiness of his other leg veers with the slight breeze toward the mountains. Doves barnstorm the parapets – Finch (no flincher) remains stock still by an armless mountain lion coated in a sunny remoulade of bird-spew. Largo cracks into his papadams and spills wheat germ in his mango Lassi.

A mufti eating *gobi* looks at us. I shrug. Largo's impiety is dicey.

"Excuse me," says a voice. There is a diner standing over our table. He wears a dhoti, his gentle dewlaps stained with lush age spots. "You are Dick Rangoon?"

"Jerry Largo," says the singer. "But Dick was me tele alter man."

"We are very happy to see you here, Mister Rangoon. We have watched your show for decades."

"Boffo! Syndication. Perpetuity! Keep a man forever twenty-nine!"

"Please, sir. Can you say your famous line?" The diner is fey with excitement.

"Eh?" says Largo.

"That you say in every episode."

Largo rolls his eyes and girds himself up to do the favor. Suddenly animated, he cocks his head at a steep angle and says, *"Getting a little torpid there, Jane."*

The dhoti man immediately guffaws and claps his hands together. Then, almost too quickly, he stops.

"I have a daughter," he says. "May I show you a picture?"

"'Right you are," says Largo.

The dhoti man produces a small cylinder and airs it out on Largo's face and the latter tumbles hip-first to the roof deck; wheezes out some "bloody gods". I would have already tackled the man but I am too stunned that he is still standing there, wasting time; precious time. I am burdened by the fullness of his smile. There is a pen in his hand.

He is waiting for an autograph.

Mermaids

Largo, chuffed, emerges clean-shaven from the loo, dabbing his pallid sheen with a washcloth emblazoned with a Bosporan moon. His mouth attempts some declining notes and furls in an O as he preps for his latest renaissance.

"Hey, Finch," he says, "Why don't you tape your dick to your navel, stand at the urinal and see if the piss reaches your own chin."

Finch, working his charcoals on the sketchpad and tilting perilously in an ormolu rocking chair, says, "Oh I shouldn't like to try that on, sir."

Largo turns to me, says. "He writes children's books, you know."

"I didn't," I say.

"Hey, Finchie," says Largo. "Get Dick Feynman to fly out with his bongos and talk to me about Space."

"I believe Mr. Feynman is dead, sir," said Finch, still not looking up.

"Dead? How long?"

"Oh, getting on about twenty-five years, sir."

"Mm. Never got the skinny on his particle bits. That zagging voodoo atoms do, Scout. Them cathodes and all that. Feynman, he were supposed to *knew*. Decoded the unknowable. Man were a Jew, just like you."

"Uh huh," I say.

"Dead," says Largo.

"Yes, sir," says Finch.

"Innit a thing innit," says Largo, his laugh jittery, and thin. He sits down and his hand is a gnarled slab on the bedpost. Then he burps, rolls down his diaphanous compression stockings and cools his heels on the jute rug, sighing, heavy in his bones as he sits.

"What's wrong?" I say.

"Seems it's … closing in."

"What is?"

"Phone call from the States earlier," he says. "Me ex-wife croaked." Were a suicide.

"Sally?" says Finch with a start, looking up from his charcoals.

"I'm sorry," I say.

"She was a Weeki Wachee mermaid," says Largo, "Swam an 85,000-gallon Ray Bay Aquarium underwater fishtailing these fantail whirls over polystyrene Atlantis figurines. She was always fast-tracking for some dismal investment. I bankrolled this gambit where divers were going to excavate hydrothermal vent shrimp to serve to the octogenarians gumming their Early Bird Specials at the mermaid show."

He stares at the jute, his head slightly shaking.

"Sometimes do wonder, Finchie. Am I ready to go the way of her? Assume I'm going up."

"No, sir. Please, sir."

"Have to say, sometimes me answer is yes. Lennon is there. George. Newley. Bowie. Syd Barrett. Might play a good set there among them cherubims. Finchie, you'd dish yourself with me just so's you might go and catch a look at barmy Syd."

I have lost six, but never to themselves.

Largo sighs long and rises, then pulls down his pants, underwear and all, palming his ample scrotum as though he were packing clay.

"What the ... heck are you doing?" I say.

"'Knew a lady manager who could read your lifeline in your dillsack. She said me sack lines was a telltale that had me hovering just this side of eternal life." He inspects it.

"Nope," he says, sighing. "Still vivid, them. Hoping the lines might say 'iffy'."

Largo pulls his pants up, goes to a portable dispensary; a septet of squares in clear plastic containing a week's worth of dopamine stabilizers. He chugs a few, and motions at Finch.

"No clairvoyant could read this old gaffer, eh? Finch has the testicles of a man who spent his life riding a stucco horse. I can say from experience. He were in his glory when I met him. One of Clyde Rankin's Coronation Day fuck-on-the-rug marathons. Rankin pay em to stand there, be like this de Sade mascot. He were singing and crying Vera Lynn in orphan kid's culottes and like wearing this diamond stud collar! Him in this wheezing falsetto butchering memorial English torch songs, and them long tall starlets taking rug burns on their mantis gams – eh? – they what ain't paying the old nutter no mind!"

Gunshots rock our window. There is an arcing stream of clear chunks falling at our hands and feet, of all us having rolled down to the carpet upon the blast. Jolted, I push Largo's head down to the floor – it strikes me that a bruise might affect his appearance for the show – and I let his head go. I wriggle across the floor and steal a glance at the street. Below, a man in a woven topi lies prone under a lobby guard's boot. The guard waves over some fellow law. A faint sound of a police siren is audible.

"Last night on earth!" says Largo under me. "Make Altamont look like an Eton tearoom."

North Stars and Manservants

Countdown to twenty-one hundred hours. The traditional sisal low chair I am sitting on aches and my watchdogging hours are soporific, but Largo snores like a prewar furnace and sleep is phantasmal at best. Why am I not frightened? Why is he is not frightened?

In the adjoining room, I find Finch at his pencils.

"Working on your children's books?"

"Yes, sir."

"You want to show me?"

Finch's face shrinks with the force of one suddenly reconsidering his very grip on the world.

"Yes, sir," he says timidly.

I pull up a sisal chair and sit next to him. He opens a sketchbook.

"This one, see, is about a sheep," he says. "Poor sheep. This one thinks he's a cat, and like wants so to elbow his sheep's head into a tabby's window space, oh but the unsmiling shepherd, not-nice shepherd, says no, you are a sheep. You'll stay grazing – am, is, is this all right, sir?"

I nod.

"See," he says. "My first stab – unpublished, oh they didn't touch it, yes. Our sheep dressed up like a cat and these day school badgers came across him by the lake. 'You're a bounder,' they say. 'Sheep in a cat's pullover and painted-on whiskers.' Well, just like the badgers in the book, the publishers, oh the publishers had no fun of a sheep pretending to be a cat by slapping on a tabby-looking jumper. They did not want a sheep to be a cat. Am I running on a bit too chatty, sir?"

I wait too many seconds before shaking my head "no".

He closes the sketchbook. "I've said a mouthful now, sir."

"You didn't. Really. I don't mind."

"I've said quite enough, sir. I suppose I shall turn in. Get you anything, sir?"

"No."

"I must rest up before tomorrow. Big night," he says, now sprightly with toothy cheer. "We'll see Mister Largo, right you are. We'll see him sing! A right reprise!"

Shalimar Nights

At the top of Durbar Shalimar, the Shalimar Babu Room waits. The stage is a riser of bejeweled footlights; overhead of us the strictest panoramic windowpanes granting guests a nighttime bird's eye slice of the Anti-West. After the MC's introduction, Largo strolls on sly in Winklepickers and a tapered sharkskin fixed with high lapels. His tie is an electric eel pointing phallusward.

Claps greet Largo, suited in trademark blue. The other Watchdogs, there at my invitation, pass around conspiratorial glances. On the chance I survive the show, I know a murmuring lakeside in Ohio awaits.

On a six-note horn blast followed by a mandrill-scream of prerecorded sitars Largo swings like a monsoon into the number, the Walker Brothers' "The Sun Ain't Gonna Shine Anymore". In front of him a lounge dancer swivels in a salwar kameez. At the close of the first chorus, the building shakes. Finch smokes ruefully at a small table near the front, and does not regard the girl. His eyes are arrows into the bull's-eye of Largo's four-in-hand.

I eye the crowd and I am pleased to see genuine appreciation. The man can still do it, his baritone seared only slightly by a hoarseness of his ravaged cords. He now sings Jacques Brel *en anglais,* a riff on Scott Walker's "Jackie" – but his bloated frame can't hack the swagger required, dragging four beats behind the poetry.

Then he stops.

The backing players, hastily assembled from a local Fab Four cover band, plays through seven bars before petering to a few cymbal crashes from the six-foot Ringo Starr. Largo sways. The gin has caught him up, I think, but then, there are no gins on stage. I have to consider phenobarbital. Which waiter had supplied him his preshow cocktail? Had we adequately vetted the helpmeets?

Largo sputters into the mike, looping it up to his face once again. "Do you shites know the story of when I shagged your tinseltown sweetheart at the World's Fair Unisphere?"

The room trembles in silence.

"I'm talking to the Red White and Blues in the back. You Watchdoggers!" He swallows the non-response and ups the ante. "'64, yeah, year our mop top hordes unseated your Old King Presley, and the label Decca, bless their hearts, signed me. Was peachy-keen on me, your Natalie Wood. Little Natalie. A spitfire."

"Oh for God's – not Natalie Wood," says an American from in back, and he storms out.

"Natalie Fucking Wood, I said it!" screams Largo to the door. "Shagged her atop the Unisphere ball. I had her rolled down and face-planting off that dome when I brought her to climax!"

The room hushes because of course.

"What are you doing, Jerry?" I whisper. Finch's head is down and he is tapping his prosthesis.

After a silence, an imam in back, his hand fingering a ceramic dishful of ripened medjools, says, "Sir. We do not speak ill of the dead."

"Ah, you want to get fucked, you dirty slag?" says Largo. "Don't surprise me a *bit* it wouldn't to think when she was underwater in that little dinghy, sucking minnow piss in her dying spasms and screaming hosannas to the harborrmaster, wouldn't surprise me a little if she thought of Jerry Largo balling her little minge atop that titanium shell. And if you ask me, I think her drowning *was* murder.

Boos begin their travel through the room. A young man in tarbush sidearms some annis bits from his little saucer.

"You are here to entertain us," he yells.

"I am here to arm you barmy plotters against yourselves," Largo says. "I am here to make sure your dick swamp of an English remnant don't ever forget Lord Mountbatten. I'm here to smash revolts so some other revolution can pay me more than I get playing half-empty gigs at the Albert Hall. I don't like you people. I bloody dagger your cornholes in me dreams! You stain-faces just chomp on that."

Finch raises his chin finally.

"Jerry," he says.

"This is despicable," says a Watchdog, although I know this man is more of a bigot than Largo on his worst day.

When the fusillade rocks the eyebeams from over the mountains, Finch's metal prosthesis flares blue and switchblades up at a right angle to the table, and by George he is Julie Andrews about to sail the South End's roofs on a twittering parasol.

The sprinklers have flooded the coatroom. A Watchdog seals the doors.

Outside, Lashkar e Taiba torches the cricket stadium and the leering crowd thins out to a smattering of Punjabis and downcast Finlayson Watchdogs who gaze on in gloomy silence at the spectacle, waiting.

There is an electric zing of sulfur, a brief, silent light, and my eardrums implode; a high whine descends into the sound of horse hooves on gravel. Waving through the hanks of thick smoke, through the sharp-suited bodyguards, my countrymen, I can find Largo socked in the fleering rubble near the stage. Another infusion of light and then it is dark again. A bomb in the basement, no doubt, ravaging the generator.

I use my phone light. Most have fled, just a few coughers slicked in red and hanging on for whoever may come, good or bad.

Finch is in the corner, on his stomach, his prosthesis bent under him setting his body in an offset pose against the floor. He would look peaceful to anyone here, anyone at all, save Jerry, who sits backed against the stage, holding the mike to his chest, occasionally making it bobble.

We wait. Hours pass and gunshots ring from without, flat, scattering sputter sounds that cacophonous bombing won't muffle. The noise is methodical, making a ping pong skitter down the lush rugs of the hall and only when a gunman stops to convene a cellphone session, or prolong some poor beggar's little life, do the chamber rounds commit themselves to silence. There is the distinct sound of a baby crying from a faraway suite, or perhaps it is near us. Nobody is disposed to quiet it.

The Watchdogs still in the back have their guns out, but I haven't unholstered mine. The perpetrators are thorough, but the hotel is large, and the constabulary is audible from below. Now will be the time for gunfighting.

And it passes, and the only thing heard are the knocks of rescue, hopelessly far away. Jerry kicks away a few stray bodies and gathers up his valet; a scrawny pieta in the burly arms of the Babu Room's first and final showman. Finch's eyes blink in provisional affirmation that, even if he has only minutes, he will take them in his housemaster's quarters. We carry him down an unblocked stairwell, heading to where our suite awaits.

Pink Elephants

Down on our floor our room is pristine but there are faint hints of bomb smoke. Largo sits in the kitchen, his jacket ditched and his collar undone, a Chesterfield cigarette notched feyly in the wedge between his fingers while a few feet down the wall Finch stares into a private space; shearing off the vague wools of his life.

The medics have not gotten into the building and can't. Finch's light-swarmed visions will export him to the higher reaches before medical heroics can intervene. Minutes before Jerry had sat with him, bespeaking the merits of the afterlife (Bowie-Barret, Newley reading his sheep book to all of the Blitz's dead children), and, when Finch utters a sharp sound and his wattle ruffles, we know he has entered the private space. Largo tilts his head and smiles with his mouth closed, emitting a short, barely audible chuckle.

We sit in quiet, and the quiet suits. The light through the window slowly changes. Perhaps an hour has passed while we sit here.

"I ever tell you," says Largo at long last, sipping tea, "how Finch got this gammy half-arm and the bum flank he's got on him?"

"No," I say, envying the tea.

"Was on account of a stray mine when the boy were five year' old. He were running through Eastbourne sands maybe a year after VE and the mine-sweeps hadn't cleared a Hawkins mine from under. BAF lay these Hawkinses to blow krauts out of the subbies when Adolph give the go-sign to Op Sea Lion, but Adolph never give it; shit-cans the boat raids and goes full-tilt with Meister Braun's screaming rocketry and a rain of ordnance commonly known as the Blitz. So, war's over and little Finch running dilly circles and hopping round the dunes in like, full frolic – *swabaaam* – mine blew the foot a mile high and it rolled out with the flotsam into the waves. Lifeguards got a trawler out and his bloody trotter's midway to Normandy! Was only a moment later when they'd come out of the shocks they saw the paw was gone too. But *keep calm and carry on,* eh? And there wasn't any way mum or dad or some bleeding heart archbishop bawling out his grimy little psalms could convince that slumping beanpole the war was over and done."

"And you hired him? Even without the limbs."

Largo shakes his head, smiles dimly, his eyes moistened at the fringes.

"I did."

He sips now, lowers his head and stares at a little plate of tea cakes.

"It shouldn'ta' been him, Scout," says Largo. "It were supposed to be me."

What else could a man do but nod?

Our wall mural, held over from when Hindus ruled the town, reveals a blue elephant sinking its trunk among the Pippals; but when the gelled fuchsias of the track lights shimmer down onto the painted scene, this elephant, eternal under the sacred sky of murals, appears to us in a shade of pink.

"My favorite mammal, pink elephants," says Largo. He holds up the bottle.

I drink.

"Scout," he says. "If this was *Casablanca* or something like it, I'd say I was short a valet. It would be the kind of codswallop you Yankees choke on."

"So don't," I say. "Don't say it."

And he doesn't. We walk out to a battered Lahore, leaving the Shalimar in smoke. The smoke does its office and follows us, catches us up, and sets us free to walk on.

Origin Story

Cleg's mother Sara Hainsey, passing a windmill and roofless granary six full miles out of Hays, looked over at her nine-year old snapping Bazooka on the passenger side and launched into a recitation of memory; a memory of a memory, it must be said. The land was so unlike it was now, she told him, with the sprouting of stucco mini malls and the overpowering Montgomery Ward over there. Kansas was no summer romance in her grandmother's day. It was on this same flat space the woman and her father watched the tumbling Black Blizzard like a wall of beclouded marshmallows screaming through the hickory from the south. The Dust Bowl, '36. Five years of murdering silicosis in the farmlands reduced her pool of friends. Coils of brown dust uprooted miles of bluestem prairie; timber cascades and sagebrush flickers in the cellophane air. The silos creaked and splintered in the cracking windstorms. The roiling sand particle-enervated metal molecules created electric arcs of blue that went fizzing up the rooftrees and the windmills poled into the groundwater to irrigate the rain-starved fields. A man in pinstripes was dynamiting pastures to instigate rainwater clouds. He left town after impregnating her cousin in a fugue of ether-bred somnolence. Some anemic perennials battered their way up through the dead grass, but vermin from underground ravaged them. Then there was the Jackrabbit Day; the drubbing of forty-thousand running blacktails who nipped at her grandmother's calliopsis, the eel-screams of the bludgeoned land bats fleering up the smokescreen prairie, the electrified savagery of the God-fearing brash in the sulfurous haze; laughing and sucking on their brined tumbleweeds and clodhopping like maniacal jackal dancers.

But though that all happened, it did not happen to Sara's grandmother or any member of Sara's clan, snowbound and Polish in North Tanawanda, New York. Sara had told him she was Kansan, born a half-Kaw from which it would inhere he was a quarter Kaw. Young Cleg could not know her accent although he knew other kids in the Kansas motels had said she sounded like no kind of Kansan they'd ever met.

… and then onto the numberless motor lodges. Sara drove in circles through Kansas, stopping when the white lines began replicating, the mileposts turning a blurry cream hue. They cycled around the Dillingham Freeway to the turnpikes and hay, then back through the iron clench of Wichita, the aviation hub with its numerous beached Learjets, the skinless airfoils of the Cessnas lying sun-streaked in early pupate. From the highway at night, the ground-lit COR-TEN steel sculpture of a watchdog Indian "Keeper of the Plains", shone inside fire rings.

Presently, they were settled in Lenexa, in a road motel. Things had become ritual quickly. Cleg would pore over the dogeared Andean Horn Frog dissertation left behind by a Texas A & M student who had eloped with an NCAA-sanctioned football star. Leaning against the soda machine, her almond hair untied, she'd flirted with Cleg but he didn't know it. After she left, he kept her dissertation in the top drawer where the Bible would be. The paper detailed humid spores that seemed to mirror the pestilences warned of within the Holy Book. Already superstitious, he scrambled hard for the leather-bound, rain-bent Gideon's he'd swiped from the last motel and put it atop the paper stack, frightened, but then, thinking of the student's leg hiked up against the Hire's dispenser, he put the dissertation on top of the Holy book.

"If I was writing a paper on some Andean frog," said Sara while watching him read it, "I'd've eloped with a roid head too."

Before they fell sleep, Cleg would ask her what they were driving for, following twister paths through exsanguinated sorghum fields, the winnowing combine hulks at their edges Holocene therapods to Cleg. Emboldened by the act of questioning, he felt his groin harden, and she would promise to tell him later. But the money for the motor lodges was running out. If they got to California, where she said they were originally going, its bounty would welcome them next. Fanciful Atlantian sea beasts, and great loads of unspent cordwood to heat them in the solitude of the mountain winter.

One night Sara brought to the motel a man who was bald but whose healthy sideburns ran thick down the curve of his jaw. "Call me Mick," he said. "*I* sure do." Later in life Cleg would know he looked like a defeated barrister. The young Cleg only saw what was in front of him. The man had been a doctor but had lost his license. Now he was bound for Hollywood, he said; 110-pages of Velo-bound goldmine in his threadbare briefcase pocket, a verifiable "blockbuster" to revitalize all of Hollywood.

"Son," Mick said as they sat on the bed in the motel room. "Do you read science fiction? At your age, I read science fiction. And the most bankable subgenre is Time Travel. The reasons are wishing to escape the present and to inhabit the closest reality has for fantasy life, which is to live out of the scope of your fear, which is dictated by Time, to crease yourself off in a near-familiar corner of the swerve. I will commence my hard sell in earnest."

"What?" said Cleg.

"My elevator pitch."

"He's never heard of that," said Sara, exhaling her a cigarette.

The man caught his face in the mirror, pulled at the grim frizz of his remaining hair, and shook his head, then looked at Cleg, suddenly brightening.

"Oh. Son, this is industry prattle," said Mick. "The plot: A man, not so different from me, wants to inhabit the 50s, not to change history per se, or say get his picture snapped with the estimable Doc King as he weathers his race trials in Bama but just *be,* just inhale the decade, sniff the poodle skirts, you get me? So he blazes through the quantum in his pod and lands in the sweet spot of his desired time. He's one happy sumbuck in the land of Ward Cleaver, lapping lint balls up from the dustpan of the aproned honey Donna Reed. He does wonders here in the boom years. He deploys his modern acumen. In my script he utilizes some modern swim techniques to helm an Olympic champion. He falls in love with a chiquita who is this Olympian from north Ohio and who can't resist him after he guides her in Melbourne to a medal win. Her futuristically aerodynamic wetsuit sends our indominable aquatarian racing laps ahead of her Swedish rival – also a lover and they both have a thing for the coach. But then something happens. He gets cancer. He didn't foresee this. He hadn't factored in the possibility. His momentary relief at the histology and the diagnosis of Prostate Stage One, eminently treatable in our modern age, is supplanted by mystification at the lack of oncological knowhow on the part of these Midcentury types. What do you mean you don't have brachytherapy? Can't you fucknuggets try and mount an external beam? Where is the ice guy to come in with a cryoablation freezer rap and convince me we can deuce this with a nuclear winter? To make a short story shorter he watched Stage One become Stage Two become Three, helpless to find a module back to his time of protonic remedies. Instead he's left to witness these oncogenetic termites route a path from the backside of his piss ducts to the front side of his brain until the last drop of cognizance is gone. The Olympians go off for a little lezzing, but our benighted time jumper suffers the hardhearted ontological motherfucking of his life."

"The lesbian Swede," said Sara. "Can I play her?"

"No," said the man. "I got an unknown quantity in mind."

"Why not me?"

"Because I want everything to be in the future. I don't want anything settled."

"Fine, you bastard," she said. "But why would I ever pay twelve cents for that bummer of a cancer flick?"

"You want a happy ending, go get a Bangkok massage," said Mick. "Jesus, who listens?! Am I just talking to myself?!" He stormed into the bathroom and slammed the door. Sara shrugged and put out her cigarette.

While Cleg slept on the cot the manager brought in Mick slept in the bed with Sara. When the lights were off Cleg heard "close your eyes", like a thrown voice in the dark, his mother's voice. The flutter of the neon outside gave their entangling shape in spite of Cleg holding out against seeing them. Mick seemed to be holding Sara in a stirrups pose, and he was telling her to call him Owen.

"Mommy," Cleg whispered.

There was no answer; only the low, piggish grunts from the screenwriter and then, minutes later, the voiceless shifting of the covers as one or both of them fell to sleeping.

In the morning, while she tended to the cuticles of her foot with a nail file and Mick bought coffee, Cleg asked his mother "Why?" He wanted to know how she could do that.

"What?" she said.

"You were *with* him," said Cleg.

"You're lying," she said. "I wasn't."

"Come on!" said Cleg. "*You're* lying."

"We would never do that," she said. "Not with you in the room."

"Then why did you say 'Close your eyes'?"

"Who said 'close your eyes'?"

"You."

"Pff. You hear what your mind tells you."

"I *saw* you."

"Nope," said Sara. "You saw what you must've wanted to see in your head."

She blew a powder of filings off her big toe.

"There," she said. "Now don't go thinking that's fairy dust, you degenerate tall tale-teller."

The screenwriter drove off westbound, seeming like a man in flight. Cleg watched his mother hug him by his car from the motel window. The hatchback was soon seen ramping just barely in Cleg's eyeline onto the elevated road. His car didn't sound good when he drove off. Sara came in, ruffled and pale.

"You okay?" asked Cleg.

"Yep," she said, hanging a smile on her face. "But I have a surprise for you: We are going to flee the state."

"I can't wait!"

"*It* can't wait," said Sara. "You think Mount Shasta lasts forever? There are forest fires out there as steady as the morning paper!"

Cleg watched her driving, her posture unaltered in the new terrain. Before Kansas and their continual loop around the Kiowa, there were a hundred days in Memphis, some more chancing inns in the belly of the exurbal prairie, each state line a nail in the geographical coffin of the Originator, the Story Man, who had written Cleg into the backseat after writing him into the womb. Sara never mentioned him by name, but that only gave him stature. Cleg, who could see, read, heal, and burn like the collaborative offal his body essentially was, could thank this unnamable slayer for the pain of this ruling thought: His stinks rose from his failure to trust his mother.

But nothing Sara said about the man was ever the same.

The Story Man couldn't counter; he was elsewhere, Pittsburgh probably, so he couldn't tell Cleg any more about Sara than Sara wished him to know. Cleg couldn't know it but Sara bought plane tickets so she could cop seats at airport bars. There she could meet the lowly unlovables who "puddle-jumped" the sprawling cornfields on commuter planes; the outbound swaghawkers with rank marriages that worked as a kind of collateral to shape their lives, men prone to jocularity and regret, sartorial mismatching. If they were not loaded – and most were not–they were open to escapades, sudden flurries of affirmation, away from the ingrained self-scrutiny of home. She was sure they had all been driven quietly batty. They would happily table their flights for a day's stay at a Sheraton, never planning on more, ahead of her stratagems each time. She thought she could hook money from them this way, draw from the extramarital largesse; avail herself of their gratitude. She was, physically, a damn sight better than the "best they could do" and they should've known that. But her superiority frightened them, rendered her exceptional in the way that a Ligurian holiday would appear to an Amish clan. You would have to get back from that to not become a peacock. They needed God, to pray to the housewife-in-muumuu if there was going to be sex on the road.

She could never give them children to make them forget their own. And suddenly but not, like a lesion turned colorful one day, she was too old to reproduce.

It would be her and Cleg and that was all he knew, but for one fact to remain unspoken: She was exhausted, and he had a lot of life left in front of him.

Barakokos. They'd made it to the cabins safe, a "lodge" that contained a mesquite pit, its dead neon gasping for wattage through the knobcone pines. California didn't have range. They had seen wilder skies in Topeka, a more flagrant generosity of ponderosas in Casper, Wyoming than here where the trees were close-set.

Barakokos, the owner, had died just a month back. His daughters were chunky, perfunctory, gave them the cabin keys. Sara told Cleg there had been murders here, not on this cabin ground, but in another one nearby, many years back. One of the daughters overheard her and volubly disputed the severity of the crimes.

The door closed. Within two months a skunk and a coyote had gotten in. There was piss on the Horn Frog Dissertation. Cleg wondered what kind of urine it was.

"Bear urine," said Sara.

Cleaning the cabin, one of the daughters had moved her bowels and neglected to flush. Sara insisted it was the bear again.

"There's no *bear!*" Cleg insisted. "They poop in the woods."

"In California everything is different," she said.

At night Sara would play cards with the daughters, who touched each other a lot, folded their bulk towards each other the way Sara did with the Screenwriter. Cleg at first thought they looked alike but the more they behaved he began to wonder if they were related at all. Sara insisted sisterhood was like that. She would laugh with them, play cards late at night while Cleg lay in bed, lose at cards until one day she beat them at cards. One of the sisters didn't talk to her for a week after that, but the other hung around too much, cleaning their room thrice a day, refolding their garments; slighted kindness like a lightshow on her face.

"Get up," Sara said. "We're leaving."

It was cold and frost had run streaks across the Corolla, the hard blue of the night too hard and he felt a muddy mood ring forming around his thoughts. Sara hit the ignition and the car combed the gravel rumbling in a low gear past the unlit neon sign, past the mocking pines, quiet as a soapbox racer. Lights were off in the sisters' cabin.

"We're going to Los Angeles," she said halfway to the city of the same name. Cleg hadn't asked, hadn't dared to, watching the bright grids of chamomile flowers wave at them in Visalia as they drove on. He looked at her in the light and noticed scratches around her eye.

"We're out of money," she said. "The bitch stole it. Whole fucking shoebox."

"Is that why you -?"

She ran a finger along her eye scratches. "I talked to her."

They were quiet.

"We're broke?" he said, after a moment had gone and they were past the chamomile.

"We're broke."

Cleg didn't believe her, but it was the first time she had ever told him the truth.

Sara held onto the paper scrap. She looked at it once again, making sure they were where they belonged in Culver City. Gum wrappers lined the verandah runner, on which a little terrier suspended in a pandemonium of funnel cloud was repeated as a pattern of rhombuses. Culver City was where *The Wizard of Oz* was shot.

Sara scoffed. "Sam Cooke died with his pants around his ankles in a place like this," she said.

"Who's Sam Cooke?" said Cleg.

"The inventor of the Cuisinart," said Sara, knocking.

No one answered but she turned the knob and they walked in. What was overpowering was not the light through the mold-stained blinds or the scatter of the ambitious pages on the rug, or the full sink clogged to the rim with blackish coffee; it was the feeling that something had so recently been, and now was not. The briefcase flap was open like a tongue on the desk chair. The Velo binder was in scraps and dried mottles of red splotching stained all over the pages.

Sara sighed and simply called the police.

There was evidence of morbidity in the apartment; a note that apologized to the maid staff for having to be the ones to find him, a note stating regret that the chemotherapy had not "performed". Forensically they were mystified however. They just couldn't ferret him *out*. There was no body. They were left to guess at the reasons. Cold feet. Deception. He had maybe reconsidered ending things in a fringe hotel, an antiheroic Hollywood death he would know was trodden ground.

Police and detectives were loitering busily and had no issue with Sara and Cleg being there. They swabbed things and dusted; sampled their own expressions in front of the novel woman.

"It doesn't wash," said one of them.

"Is he dead?" said Cleg.

Sara gave a laconic nod but the detective shrugged his shoulders. The other detective, younger, his face fine hewn but also rough, like the star of an action movie, held up some vitamin chelation in a tinted jar.

"If he isn't dead," the man said, grinning out of one side of his mouth, "he sure deserves to be, falling for this line of shit."

Sara and Cleg felt the sand cold below them, small slings of it accosting their faces now and then when the wind blew. The water was not any color really, nothing Cleg could put on a palette, nothing that would propel a fantasy; nothing amenable to the notions of a westbound oaf. A surfer slid off the shore down the beach, lone and unaccommodating, tiny.

Sara unruffled Cleg's hair, pulling loose strands over his ears. There was no use saying they'd made it. In truth, she had always known where they were was not going to change until his father finally came and took him away from her, which

would happen of course, physically or not, say, when the preoc-
cupations of the Originator ran fallow or Cleg began tracking
life as the thing which fell between the cracks. For now, she and
Cleg could conceive what was in front of them, let the wind
sling it forward. She could tell him this was not the ocean he
was looking at, and once more, he could believe her.

A Friend of the Zoo

Errol Condon's office is not a bright affair. Lead animal sculptures barely restrain his paper stacks and the ceiling freaks out in a swoop of parrot mobiles. Old pinups of Giant Pandas – pandas who no longer exist or have been repatriated to Sichuan – festoon his wall panels. There is Frank the Wildebeest and Lonnie the lion curator who died of angina pectoris, there giving a thumbs-up in his safari tans under the pre-renovation Monorail. There's one of Jamie Marquez who managed the sea lion sanctuary. Jamie is a married woman – and who'd of believed it, Errol thinks. Bo Hendricks smiles and he ran the elephants. Now he's 6 by 8 and lives above a cheeping radiator as an immortalized raker of dung. A lot of vivid snapshots of a Bronx past contained – Italians, the borough prez chummy in a porkpie handshaking some natty union guys, Craig Nettles in a batting stance from '77 when the Pinstripes took the Bronx back from the Son of Sam. Condon is Bronx bred, harrowed by memories. One can find him on Arthur Avenue, teasing caramel ambrosia from his marron glace, wishing the neighborhood young again.

Errol Condon leaves his office and knows he will snoop on one of his volunteer docents.

There is a line forming, contouring to the triple-pane glass which separates the great apes in their crouches from the viewing hordes. Edith Frankel is looming. She wears a logo identifier like a laminated pendulum around her neck – "Volunteer Docent"; below that, the typical grinning passport shot – and a statement of who she is underneath it.

The gorillas are grooming each other, and it is a heartening sight, their quarried rocks a nice spot to animate some primeval theatrics and the standing crowd melts, the general thinking being, "They are just like us, but nicer." Something about their motions suggest robots in a slow reckoning that, contrary to their wiring, they can now feel. There are a lot of peering children in today. Edith is always there for questions. Eight decades, jaw dewlaps and edemous wrists and ankles don't stop her. She stalks up on a viewing huddle.

"Do you have a question for me?" she says.

"How long do the gorillas live?" asks a winsome little boy.

"Now with these gorillas, maybe to fifty or sixty," says Edith. "With the breeds in Africa and the rainforests, about half that. We take care of them here, clean their teeth, scrub their gums; groom them for tick-borne diseases. When they're in for that kind of top treatment, they last."

"So when they lose their teeth they –"

"They can't eat, that's right. They starve."

The boy's father interjects, "You would think evolution would provide for longer life. I mean if they can be kept alive by simple teeth-cleaning you would think Nature would find a way to have them do it."

"Nature doesn't ask anything of us but that we fuck," says Edith. "So we can you know, reproduce the organisms. Once these hairy females reach menopause, they're good for pretty much nothing."

She taps the glass and makes a neck-slitting motion at the ape. The crowd is in mild-gasp, but the child ventures forward.

"What is menopause?"

"When a woman can't have any more babies," answers Edith.

"But when does it happen?"

"Often around forty."

"My mother is forty-one," says the child.

"Yeah, well. You can pretty much throw her off the fire escape at this point."

The child clubs his own face with his mitten.

"Come on, sweetie, she's just a crazy old woman," his father says, shuttling him away.

Edith moves further down the viewing glass, where stylish Brazilians look on.

"God they are have so much coarse fur," says a woman.

"Not so much," says Edith. "You ever see a hairy Jew on the beach? Makes these things look like Yul Brynner. Now Marvin Rifkind, spent a month of Sundays going through my Norman's estate, had me down in Pompano to go through the assets. We took a day just laying out and reading *The Winds of War*, and I almost cried but that's another story. But this man's chest – you could disappear in it like some poor fuck in Vietnam."

"Miss," says a stunning Brazilian with a wild black mane. "Where are the Emperor Tamarins? The little monkeys, my son wants to see them."

"Do I look like I know from Tamarins?!" screams Edith. "Go back to Ipanema and shave your box!"

The Brazilians clear out in an oxygen vacuum.

Go, Edith, go, whispers Errol. Don't let them out. Take it to the Bastille.

Edith sidles up to a family from Detroit. "Do you know gorillas learn?" she says. "I was no good at math but I was a special ace at literature. I went to Hunter College for one year with my friend Bernice."

"That so." says the father, looking straight ahead at the animals.

"Bernice got around, very popular. Now that Judy Symcowitz – a railroader of a *lot* of men, a real pump – used to rope me into Mah Jong and wouldn't you know it those gossipers, those unconscionable yentas in Crotona Park were always chewing on this notion I was this slut! Well let me tell *you* something! I was not. Bernice Krumholtz is the one. Oh she was so glamorous; yeah, spent a weekend with some cousin of Henry Cabot Lodge, yeah. But she settled. I'll tell you, that Neapolitan peasant that she married never had a hard-on she didn't coddle. She babied that fucking thing like it had colic!"

Heads swivel. A stroller is motored away like an ambulance. A mother holding a young one in a papoose skips off.

Just entered, a family of Bainbridge Avenue Irish stare warmly at the mandrills on display. A marmoset teases fate and ambles down a sprouted copse to a where a silverback knuckles on bowlegs towards the family, thinking their paleness strange: There are no soccer jerseys in the western lowlands. The gorilla delivers a Congo snuffle. Edith hears the brogues, the clover chuckles, and insinuates herself near the clan.

"Do you have any questions for me?"

A large grey ape rubbing his breastbone sensually in front of them bears his gums to the Irishman's sheer delight.

"Yes," he answers, a cuddly pad of red hair atop his face as wide as a pumpkin. "Such expressions. How do they do it?"

"It's the Sagittal crest," says Edith. "Runs like a black fin over the skull and powers the facial muscles."

"Really?"

"They have to chew a lot of tough meats. I never used a tenderizer. My husband hated my meat, and I didn't like his either!"

"Ah," says the Irishman, confused.

The Dutchman returns his gaze to the ape.

"I hear they have the ability of knowledge," he says.

"Yes, some do," says Edith. "The Koko makes family bonds. Even signs and can imagine a past and future. They like to look at each other when they screw."

"Hmm," he says. He looks at the nametag, bewildered. "You uh, you *work* here?"

"You know these are the *real* urban gorillas here," says Edith suddenly turning to a platinum headed Dutchwoman in back of the Irishman.

"Yes," says the woman.

"I don't know why they call them 'Urban Gorillas'," says Edith with honest consternation. "I mean they called that Patty Hearst one, and she was no gorilla. She was an attractive woman! Not quite a beauty, I'll say, but you know, you know, attractive. And with that gun, you know, the picture with that Tommy gun she was modeling up against the cobra flag, she was even *more* attractive!"

"I think the spelling is g-u-e-r-r-i-l-l-a, Miss," injects a smiling Dutchman wearing wraparound, orange-tinted specs. "It is a Spanish word. It is a fighter."

"Well, whatever it is, she was more attractive with the gun than without. You fuck."

"I beg your pardon?"

"What are you, swimming the freestyle? You look like a walleye in those things!"

"Why are you harassing him?" says an old woman, her accent strikingly London toff.

"Hey," says Edith to the woman, all of a sudden reverting to a schoolgirl. "You sound like the PBS people who narrate those *Masterpiece* shows. The ones where the whole house sips tea and a horseman strips some married twat down to her garters and fucks her into Pluto on a four-poster while the husband with the mustache plans World War One."

"You don't say."

Edith shrugs. Errol bites happily into an apple. The Congo chamber, a multi-buffer zone of rug and glass, feels hushed and bustling simultaneously. The silverback pounds its chest. Its brother, a yard above on the maximally landscaped copse, models a pink erection, presenting it as a stemmed tulip to an Ecuadorian girl, who cowers behind her father.

Edith says to the tiny man concealing his daughter, "Milton Berle was supposed to have a huge cock he liked to show to people when they were dressing in their changing rooms. Now *that* was scary."

The Ecuadorian, uncomprehending, grunts.

"He was a very funny man," says Edith. She bends and pinches the little girl's cheek and picks at the ribbon in her hair, straightening it. Errol smiles, lets his abdomen stick out. Roar, baby, he whispers, roar.

Another morning in the hopper. Errol goes back to his office. He answers twenty-two email complaints, assuring the insulted he will address the situation comprehensively. He drinks his Instant coffee and lets the heat of the brew tickle the coils of his throat. He is enjoying this gig for the first time in ages, at least since Sharfstein began his tenure.

Errol has been a zoo man twenty-five years and has shepherded the volunteer program for all the zoo's primate displays

– Jungleworld, Madagascar, the Congo Gorilla Forest with its legions of tailless gibbons in perpetual knuckle-drag, and, of course, the Baboon Reserve. The program is neither boondoggle nor moneybags but it is near to a lasting source of pride. He has seventy-one Friends of the Zoo trained as unpaid docents. He has remedial science kids from DeWitt Clinton High and even some Riker's Island recidivists working off guide sheets at the gibbon groves. The docents have a way of ticking off the veteran curators, whose empathy often ends at the animal pens. They don't sit too well with Sharfstein either; who is a stickler for streamlining things. Errol persists. It is hard to wake up with nothing but a sandwich to live for, he tells the curators; it is hard to block out the tinnitus that might chime from the nearing death knell. Were someone like Edith not here, she might find herself pastured with the lolling cadavers at a rest home, tottering openmouthed while a maniacally jovial volunteer plinks "High Hopes" on a freestanding synth. That is how it often ends; humans don't get euthanized without committing animal crimes.

He sips his coffee and sets to work. To a complainant from Mississauga, Ontario, he replies:

Dear Ms. Conifer,

I hope this letter finds you well. I was terribly troubled to hear your son was told that Wayne Gretzky "tossed a mean salad." We will rectify the situation and terminate that volunteer docent. Our vetting process cannot always account for surges in infarct dementia, or whatever neurocranial adversity might have precipitated the regrettable outburst. (It might just what she's like?) Rest assured, we are committed to making your zoo visit a happy and unmolested experience. I trust you will understand that this incident is the exception, not the rule, and that the problem has been handled expeditiously.

Sincerely,

Errol Condon

Director of Volunteer Docents

He will not fire Edith, of course. He will give her more hours. He will make her a mainstay of the apes. It's only a matter of keeping it all in house. Eric Sharfstein must not know, but he must pay. He must suffer. His operation must be subverted.

Errol would have lived a full and happy life not knowing Eric Sharfstein was a person; Sharfstein who somehow leapfrogged him in the space of no time to become Director of Primate Attractions; Sharfstein with his face of a hack sportscaster, his risible non-zoo creds. It does not escape Errol that, before his tenure here, Sharfstein sold lithium batteries out of a suitcase in Hempstead, Long Island, working under the guise of an Apple rep after flunking out of the Wharton School of Business. With such managerial prowess, it is no wonder Sharfstein has never set foot in the Congo and has no intention to.

Condon emails out another fast reply:

Dear Ms. Westfelt,

How do things find you in Libertyville? As a lifelong Bronx resident and erstwhile staffer at the Zoo, I've never been to Illinois, the birthplace of Lincoln. I hope you enjoyed your visit to New York. (Did you get to Arthur Avenue?) I want to express my deepest regret that your daughter was told what she was. No ten year-old should

*know that Connie Francis was raped at a Howard John-
son's. This is just not the kind of knowledge we at the
Congo Forest wish to impart. Our docent will be dealt
with forthrightly. Please let me offer you a free voucher
should you wish to return ...."*

There are many more emails to send. It will gobble up
the brunt of his morning. He hates emailing fiercely, but
it is a necessary trouble if Edith is to remain. These morn-
ings have been his second lease, his third act, his last-inning
grounder past the base. He still has to say it to believe it, a
bubonic mantra: Sharfstein is my superior. Sharfstein is my
boss. For months after his appointment Errol lumbered to
work, blandly managed his docent roster, his very gibbons a
reminder of being passed. Then one day Edith just turned
up and asked to join the docent course. Within a week of
passing, she came to him with revolutionizing notions the
zoo might improve. He nodded, disconcerted; then, after her
fourth unbidden tantrum when she told a woman she was
Reubenesque, "But not like the painting; like the sandwich",
Errol began to warm to her barreling displays. He would never
admonish her, never correct her; never interdict. He kind of
even liked her. Sometimes she has had "off-days", days where
she sticks to her docent pages, saying nothing of controversy,
and those days are very sad for Errol indeed.

Admittedly, he doesn't know much about Edith Frankel,
only what the bolts of invective let go piecemeal. He knows
she had a husband named Norman who keeled over in Boca
Raton while they were sitting by a pool reading their *Winds of
War*. From what all Errol can gather, he was an undermining
but faithful human being. She has a son named Martin who
doesn't visit enough and has some landholding boondoggles

drying in the sands of Arizona that have very nearly landed him in the klink. She was bad at math and couldn't teach math so she became a social worker; that was ages back, pre psychedelic US. She lives in a building near Mosholu that is now mostly Russians, of whom she has nothing very flattering to say. If her people had saints, she'd've put a shabbat candle under FDR's portrait. She wears a mock monogram-Vuitton handbag she copped off a Fordham Road vendor. She wears cloche caps.

He types.

"… I must apologize mucho, Senorita Villalobos, that your visit was so malo, but my docent's cabesa don't work muy good. Milton Berle's pinga certainly has no business being hablad aqui."

He hits Delete. He never learned Spanish, and knows he will have to auto translate this one.

Wonders of the modern world: auto translate. Megascreens. On the way in every day, he hauls ass past the 4D Colossus, there menacing the Birds of Prey.

A purist, it is hard for Errol to stomach Sharfstein's proto-digital whistles and bells; his penchant for CGI inducements when Man Small Beast Bigger as a wowing visual was already there for the asking if you only got your ass on the monorail. Sharfstein drip with new plans, though—voucher offers, more touchscreens; considerable rollbacks in primates.

"Animals are a nuisance for a zoo," he said upon his appointment, Errol getting the full douche ramble in his office. "The risk quotient is brutal. Do you fight screens? Screens win. The kids could have a reanimated Pteranodon thumping around in the ape corral like one foot in front of them and move to find the beast on the fucking Kindle. 'Hey ma, Pteranodon!'. Not like when you were a kid. Bogart sounded like some shortwave coming through underwater in monochrome, all black and white. You had to jack off your nut to a pursed lip kiss, am I right? That or a Botswanan tribeswoman's pendulous knockers bobbing over some rhino dung in a National Geographic your mom got so your brain would grow."

"I didn't watch Bogart growing up. I'm a little younger than that."

"A spring chicken you are not! Anyway, say sayonara to the quaint, Condon; pretty soon we'll all be shitcanned for a headset. We all know VR viewfinders are the coming wave. Kid'll strap on one and an ape will come barreling right up into his grille. They'll have to defibrillate the little pissant from the coronary. Rack it, babe. My thoughts are so rad they deserve time stamps."

It is little consolation that Sharfstein is feared but not respected. He drives a Lamborghini Diablo replica. The one time he parked it on the street vandals broke in, ripped the seats out and turned them upside down, pinning a note to the dashboard that read, "Whatcha gonna do? Call the replica police on us?" He is ascendant, though. growing; as colossal as the Le Pain de Quotidian croissant that sits captivating horse-flies on his work desk; for all its gadget gimmickry, modernity seems to be shot through with the animating principle of neglect.

Errol knows he should make way, clear out, pack south. Gregory Bullard from Marsupials owns a condo in the Yucatan that mostly survived the last named storm. But Errol has never had the wherewithal for that. He's always cursed darkness. It exacts less current from the grid.

A new email comes in, but it is not a complaint from a zoo-goer; it is Sharfstein.

The subject heading reads: "Heads up manana bubby tittie." Condon, sighing, clicks.

"So heads up manana as I said bubby tittie. Trakl and me are going to view the apes. Wants to see the docent. Stoop thinks your program rocks. Be there or be circle."

Errol quakes. Tomorrow. There will be little to no time to right the ship. He calls Edith, hoping to absent her, but she never answers her phone. He is never in any shape for Trakl but this is worse, *the* worst, a surefire axing. Trakl is a white-haired, rose-cheeked foundation donor whose dead wife is the posthumous christener of oncology wings, theater lobbies, zoo forests. He is a boorish man, but instrumental in repopulating the Congo's primate roster. No doubt he has come to look at what his funds have procured, to check in with Sharfstein, to smile unctuously as the latter eats his own tongue trying to express the worthy progress of the exhibit commensurate with the bounty he has got.

Errol tries Edith again. When the birdsong of her non-answer beats into his phone eight times, he considers his position, his years caressing his tenure in this kingdom. Have the years been worth it? He has communed with the natural tucked away in a cement mausoleum that has claimed his headiest of his High School friends, streets that have devolved into chain outlets, crack dens, rubble. At least some friends got out, through a northbound shuttlebus to the "pens", through dope; but what were Errol's options? A man schooled in the Passions, friend of Bronx boy iconoclasts who raided the aumbry at St. Clare's, he was told early by his mother Angie he was "wrong". Even though he never looked at women, was never caught concupiscent; even when Ed Solomon flashed that busty tomato nearly bursting out of her western house dress on the cover of *Hot Lead Trail*. It is just this kind of circumscription from a mother that makes a grown man scramble for revenge. Young Errol found his ecstasies in the cages, not the gospels. He grew full-hearted but single, a man habituated to unshared clutter. He has fostered and festered and fought. But an autopsy of Errol would show nothing but the accreted fats of his consolation meals, plaque from the maron glaces; no illicit substances, no marital heartache, just a curdling porridge of lukewarm payback. Just one old grousing yenta from Mosholu.

Maybe she's dead, he thinks, and that's why there's no answer. No, she has never answered her phone. Who would call? Her son? He sounds like the last one who would. Edith, not surprisingly, has no cellphone. He'll intercept her, tell her of an asbestos problem; a Congolese microbe that piggybacked the transatlantic journey on an ape. Something will work. He will stay and fight. What would his papa, Daddy Tangiers, do? Fight? Flee? Probably neither. The man liked bebop jazz and Cuban cocktails, dancing the rhumba in white bucks. By 1959 he was a beatnik without a cafe, a reciter of Bill W. love psalms, jittering around street corners, waving over cars with the windows near-down, sealing friendships with a demonstrative palm clap that passed on his intimate secrets as the Ramblers blazed off to the Webster bypass, their drivers giddy with his bagged grams, then he was gone. Young Errol only knew his father ended his captivity on Earth by deteriorating of peritonitis in a Tangiers jail, chained to two men under the mud dome that passed for the hall of justice. When the State Department called a year later and said they had his body, he and his mother were unaware he had even been out of the States.

When they shipped his coffin back his mother had him cremated and threw the ashes down the ventilation shaft, where pigeons fled the upswell of his triturated marrow, the powder of the name that would expire with his Errol's stunted drives.

Growing up across from the gate of the zoo, Errol could hear the lions in the morning, an urban reveille as routine as squab trills. He could hear those squabs too, confused, nativists inundated with strange Amazonian life; hotshots off cacophonous humidors like Madagascar, chiming from their palace The World of Birds. The pigeons would perch on the rooftops and wonder what these things were.

Errol knows he is a pigeon now, shrugging, grappling. Who are these new birds? Where does a man of his age go when the world is all 4D, replicated Italian snazz-jobs, polymer headsets overloading your neurons faster than his daddy's skin-pops; the world itself now a drug demanding full tolerance, a place so much bigger than it should be. Errol remembers his Edith:

Humans are the only animals to outlive their teeth.

She arrived early today. Errol intercepted her at the gate and told her asbestos was being cleared. She wasn't buying. He told her an ape was vomiting. She said "What else is new?" Errol, after imploring her multiple times to leave, getting bullheaded stares and rancorous mutters for his efforts, finally tried the honest truth: Be nice, he told her. Stick to the words on your docent pages. Pages, Edith, pages; no wandering off said script. She relented, unsure of what she had been doing wrong up till now, and took the packet. Errol spent the morning in the coffee room, drilling the words, testing the calcification of her memory, finding that, underneath the volatility, her mind was still robust.

Now she is standing by the triple-pane, a mandrill curled up in an unbothered slumber on the other side. A trickle of morning guests has very quickly become a torrent. Edith is wearing a cathouse's panoply of rouge and seems chipper to be promenading among the guests. The gorillas knuckle to and fro in the fern grove, nose out the smallest alterations in their habitat, pawing spiky cones and straw gewgaws on the bunched grass. Edith gives Errol a thumbs up. He gives her one back. He sips his coffee like a football coach watching a blue-chip prospect running tackle drills. The crowd lines up along the wall.

Sharfstein has come into the viewing area with R. Barry Trakl, Standing next to Trakle and clasping his chubby hand is a very tall drink of water, a vivid set of Cherokee angles for a face. In her lush Dior dress and white platforms, she makes her companion miniature.

Before Errol can say or do anything Edith steps forward, addressing the crowd that forms.

"Ladies and gentlemen, now that you're here," she says, "do you want to hear about these apes?"

Some use their native language to indicate assent, others grunt, and the crowd steps closer to Edith.

In tones that are strangely halting, like a local linebacker doing a cable spot, Edith points and says, "That is an Eastern Mountain Gorilla. It hails from the volcanic mountain rangers of Central Africa, namely, and not coincidentally, given where your visit has taken you, the Democratic Republic of Congo." She flings her arm out animatronically at the Congo sign. "This gorilla is a descendant of the very first hominoid primates of the Oligocene Period. Its average weight is upwards of four hundred and thirty some pounds. It is known to run up budding branches and forage grasslands for nutrients, hydrating carefully at the start of day. Hydration. That's water, people! And, our gorilla is diurnal. Which means it hunts and feeds during the day. A powerful animal, it uses signal displays to encourage its enemies to back off when *encountering* trouble in the vines. But, ladies and gentleman, do not let its posture fool you, it – is – no – slouch."

There are chuckles as perfunctory as the little scripted joke. Errol feels his heart steady now; the air fall under him like the cushion of bath beads. There are vague trepidations within those steady beats that keep Errol from believing what is in front of him: that this is really going off without a hitch.

He breathes in with Vinyasa-like ease.

Presently, Sharfstein motions for Errol to come over. Errol steps as though the floor panels will drop out from under him, but when he gets there Sharfstein is all smiles

"Errol, you remember R. Barry Trakl and his friend Oona Smalls."

"Yes. Right," says Errol, watching Edith buttonholing a Catalonian in the corner.

Trakl shakes Errol's hand, vicelike as one would expect.

"I was telling Barry about the docent program," says Sharfstein. "What a winner it is. *I told you, Errol!* I told you! Anyway Trakl here –"

"I'd like to meet your docent," says Trakl; his voice practiced in his voice practiced in the affect the powerful have of always just being along for the ride. "I admire it when the community gets involved."

Errol nods, notes a rising column of pressed air at the base of his skull. He should have walked before Sharfstein. He should've cleared out years ago. He'd have gone to Tangiers with his father, joined up with the merchant marines. He'd have cooked up a record label, been a Phil Spector who didn't shoot. He'd have had Hollywood stunners with the gams of Daddy Longlegs in a stretch Continental spread across the fatty reaches of his waist. The icebox of his loins might well have thawed then. But, looking at the pathetic figure of Sharfstein with his showroom smile, the smug taper of his jeans over his square-toed Payless loafers, the gleaming button-down left untucked of a fashion, that evil can be, that evil can be temporary, a snow job. He loves this place; its Benjamin Moore-scented offices, its landscape a dumping ground for history and he is glad to have picked through the smoking ruins the curators have left him in the form of these loyal simians. He has ample faith this place will keep him, that Edith is having one of her off days; that this last minute drilling of shtick will provide him cover. Why just look at how she nailed that rap. The Catalonian woman she is talking to looks thoroughly edified, smiling not queasily, but with gratitude.

"Edith," yells Errol, waves her over. She comes shuffling across, happy to be wanted.

"Hello, people," she says. "Hello Mister Sharfstein!" She waves at him as though he were standing a mile away.

"Edith, this is R. Barry Trakl, one of our chief patrons," says Errol. "And this is Oona, his friend."

"Fiancée, actually," says Trakl. Oona lowers her face demurely.

"Whoa," says Sharfstein, reeling back and clapping his hands together and pounding his chest gorillalike. "Mazeltovs in the casa."

Condon feels relieved that Sharfstein might be the one who needs restraints. In these kinds of rickety exchanges there is often a designated idiot and there is no rule that states it has to be the docent.

"Congratulations, Mr. Trakl; that's wonderful news," says Edith.

Edith's posture is reserved; she seems to have exerted command over the why-when-and-how of reality, the barest rudiments of equitable badinage. Yes, this is one of her off-days.

"You have a beautiful fiancée," she says, almost curtsying.

"Thank you," says Trakl. Oona, no doubt accustomed to such praise, fights a novel blush, receiving it from one so elderly.

"I'll bet I could cut glass with the shit-eating grin you must wake up with in the morning, looking over at *that,*" says Edith.

"Ah," says Trakl, his smile still wake-riding the previous compliment, with only a few scant flutters at the sides.

"Well Edith, we've got viewers," says Errol, putting a hand on her shoulder. "Very nice to see you all." Edith slaps his hand off.

"I'm talking," she says. "Don't you see I'm talking?!"

Sharfstein flicks his eyes to the donor; a rosaceous man, it is difficult to know when he is blushing, but he appears to be holding fast, unwilling to retreat from his admiration.

"You uh enjoy your work here at the zoo?" Trakl ventures.

"Oh yes. If I wasn't doing this I would be marooned, just out to lunch," says Edith. "I'm pretty much dead below the waist so I'm not going to be home getting my rocks off to some movie with Monty Clift in it. My bones are shit to the marrow and I can't afford Humira. I might as well become one of these poop-flingers with the sorry state of my hands being wrecked. People don't appreciate their basic blessings. This one standing here in the platform shoes, your betrothed, I'll bet you kiss the fucking toilet when she gets up. You *know* from blessings. You're so small they could bury you in your own ball sack, but here you've got this tree on your arm. No way this is your first rodeo with a wife."

"Edith, please," tries Errol.

"Mister Trakl's first wife passed away," says Sharfstein.

"Well I bet you're fuckin' glad about that!" says Edith, rapping a hand off Trakl's elbow and laughing. The man's flush is dramatic now, and Oona's readymade bonhomie has all but flown the coop. Trakl will be damned to cede his smile, but nods his head at a rate to suggest a new venue is dearly in the offing.

"You look Swedish," Edith says to Oona. "Are you Swedish?"

Oona shakes her head no.

"Why is it you Swedish women have such prominent teeth? Is it like something where you have to chew through the ice to get to the herring?"

"Is she always like this?" says Sharfstein to Errol, already helplessly miming "no".

"Oh I'm always very chummy with the apes," says Edith, reassuringly. "Mister Condon gives me good hours. He tells me I do wondrous. Every time I come in he might as well be handing me a flower bouquet. This place knocks me out; I want to come someday dressed like Jane from Tarzan, remember Maureen O'Sullivan, back with Weismuller and she wore that two piece? I'll have to rip off my cornpads but fuck it. I love the Congo. This is much better than the real Congo, with Belgian soldiers and AIDS. You know Reagan was a real asshole with that thing. He could've done something. AIDS took Gertrude Sobel's nephew Leeman who was very talented. He did a male-only fan-dancing number that Adele Blankfein found sick but I thought was very skillful. The music was unbearable, just clanging forks or some cockamamie xylophone contraption. But I adore our uncloseted humanity. We used to have a bonobo in, the ones that go gay when the mood hits. You know the redneck shitheels we get rolling in from south of the Dixon should get an eyeful of those fuckers going full-tilt, cornholing like world-beaters in this terrarium. Teach Ma and Pa

Clampett a lesson. I have this idea, my little brainstorm, that all the bisexual gibbons get planted in a nice field and then, to the right of these red-asses, you Astroturf in another field that is a foundry with a work gang of big bald Polish morons breaking rocks, as naked as the *miserable day they were born!* Then you have this cuckoo clock like the one in Vienna and when that strikes the hour the Polish guys all drop their pickaxes and bang each other in the ass till their eyes go cross. It'll show the descent of Man. But I never liked Reagan, his acting. He was in a movie with a monkey. Until I was here I didn't know from animals. Bernice Krumholtz the knockaround did. She once brought home this baby duck. Thought it was darling, but what shit she had going on with it. Quack you into an unhearing person. And the fuckin' thing had to be in the bath all the time! It was a mess. But Errol is like a son. *He's a gift!* He always says 'you're doing great'. And backs me up if someone doesn't get my answers. And that's important. It's like what my father who was a loser – should've gone into corrugated metal with his brother in law who became a mayor and a bigtime tomcat chasing after stage dancers in Piscataway, New Jersey, wouldn't you know he died on a chorus girl from Dickie Waldmere's Footlight Ensemble while he was juking her caboose from behind and he slumped right on her and she thought he was taking a breather but he wasn't he was *dead* – used to say: You can catch more flies with honey. Errol catches those flies with me."

Edith, as though to indicate a full stop, smiles primly. Errol feels the room air as a single blob of weighted molecules, the silence only pulling more atoms in.

"You wanna stay here for a minute?" says Sharfstein to Edith, finally.

Edith says. "Sure, Shitstain, I'll wait!"

"What?" says the latter.

"Ha! I know your name is Sharfstein but I like to call you Shitstain."

"I see."

"You know," says Edith to Trakl, "Sharfstein drives a Lamborghini that's about as real as your wife's tits."

Sharfstein leans over and is whispering in Trakl's ear but looking very squarely at Errol Condon. His eyes are very small and there is the shadow of a grin, the afterburn of a reckoning clear on his face: that of knowing the great squab of hope will die in roost before it even got the dry bread in its snapper. Errol looks at Sharfstein with a little smile and mimes a gun to his own head with his empty ring finger.

"Pow," he mouths.

Sharfstein nods, maybe even a little sadly.

Behind them, Edith has snuck away and is pressing her nose to the glass, meeting palms with a standing ape.

Errol bundles himself against November, but it is not so cold as that. He is going out to buy dulci off his remaining pension. He has few worries aside from time, which is more spacious now; a big skating rink for a man wearing flat-soled shoes. He can shuffle, though: No wife, no kids; some stories. He thinks of traveling, but there are no airports in the Bronx, and jetlag is alive in his bones. After the episode they checked his computer and found the emails. He was cooked before but that tore it. When he heard Edith had been made a ward of the state and sent up to a remote Brooklyn hospital, bored and fading, by all rights, he felt a little sad, but she has walls, he imagines; tapioca by the wagonload, a rec room with a TV that affords her the catharsis of a haranguing court judge, any number of these robed strutters fairly studding the daytime lineup. She can watch an assortment of malfunctioning backwash try to finagle easy money from the world, the ripe red future of the hominid, production values, meth mouth, and a wallet that fattens with the February sweeps. It is better to shelter in place, away from the noble battle that will fail. He flips his collar up, fights the cool wind, and wonders if the apes know what is missing.

Field Trip

"Deegan Expressway was a warzone," said Risky, watching the maples flame from the backseat of the Corvair as they rifled up Route-684. At the wheel Saigon Rydell spanked the dash, "Orchards! Orchards. Here we go," he said. Jamie Likes Me sang Ray Price in a coyote wail to the wheelman's dashboard antics and in dreamy synch to the feather tones on the dial. The lonely Price's voice sounded amiably manly, an unassailable western man towering over a dainty little thimble in a housedress, a man abiding and trusting his Shawnee scout, maybe laying roses upon the wife's bier when a smallpox outbreak claimed her. When the song came to an end, the western baritone of the DJ brayed out the letters-of-call: "1050, Dubya – H – N." Before Price, there had been songs by Glenn Campbell, Cystal Gayle, Anne Murray; Dolly Parton, this doddering cracker named Milsap.

"I want all red ones," said Risky. "Want to knock all the red ones off the trees."

"You still gotta pay," said Jamie.

"And I want the potato gun to fire spuds at the cardboard bullseye."

"I want to fuck the place up," said Jamie. "I want to sow dread."

"Pace yourself," said Saigon.

One time, stuck in traffic on the Willis Avenue Bridge, they had seen Timothy Leary gargling some nameless fluid while a blonde girl rubbed his shoulders. It was tough to say whether he was sleeping or awake. Leary was the enemy, but none of them could say why, except that Eldridge Cleaver had eighty-sixed him from his compound in Angola, said America your honky is one sad-ass ringmaster, a dipso: take him back. Ten years ago the blarney he was shitting could fill auditoriums; now he was passed out in a Listerine-green Monza on the dodgiest little drawbridge in New York. They laughed and hocked loogies at his window. He didn't see it and Risky said she was glad he didn't see. Saigon knew she didn't want to hurt the man's feelings. Jamie, for her part, wished they had.

That trip, gatecrashing a folk festival of Pete Seeger's, never panned out. The car broke down in Larchmont, the fan belt snapping on the Hutch. Using Risky's fishnet stockings as a stopgap proved untenable. Seeger would play unheckled, still hopeful, gypsy-picking his plywood as the Earth dropped off its space moorings, cruised inevitably toward the nuclear riot of the sun. Risky felt the trip was cursed the moment they hocked gobs at Leary. The directive this time: no spit.

On these trips, Viking raider sorties, three downtown rockers in studs ramming a plunger down the suburban esophagus of America, it was a kind of social burglary they were after, but the best thing—even though Jamie and Risky wouldn't admit it–was escaping the scene. Out of the City they could ditch being The Leatherettes. Their archangel pallor would scare here. "Punk", it seemed, had made the evening news. The band was Saigon's lark, mostly Jamie Likes Me's gum-chewing, Risky's faithful bar chords, Saigon's throwaway numbers ("Thank You For the Hard On, Crystal Gayle"). Risky and Jamie were believers; Saigon Rydell was not. You had to be shocked to shock, and the man was undumbfoundable: By now he'd known a jazzman who cut off two fingers on his left hand so he could play like Django Reinhart. He'd known a thrash band composed of coprophagic Hasidim that called themselves Scat Pogrom. He had lived with The Bloated Hausfrau.

Saigon switched the dial. They almost missed Nixon as constant news, three years past now, the old paranoid gone totally MIA. The New Seekers came on the radio, an ad spot, Saigon singing along, "I'd like to buy the world a Coke…" A message to Seeger and his friend, the granddaddy of all snot-gobbers Woody Guthrie: No six-string tune-machine could ever kill a fascist, but a Coke machine could sure put a dent in the blues.

"Gas station," said Saigon.

"Another Coke?" said Risky.

"She's smart," said Jamie.

"I'm pulling over."

He exited. The moment he opened the door the air hit him and it was as though he were burning alive: the thermal quickening of the season in his blood. He wanted to claw his way back into the car, but they expected him to walk, strut to the vending machine against the stone wall of the station in his ball-hugging pants of almost phosphorescent green leather. He didn't want to tell them how young he felt, or how old he felt a second later.

He was drinking a lot of Cokes now. He didn't know why. He needed them. When the chute sprung the can he held it, twirling it against his palm. He rubbed it on his forehead, the aluminum chill warming him, drawing his eyes to the browning maples. The can was as much a love affair as anything Risky presented. He knew that.

He swallowed the Coke and set the can on the stone wall in front of a tree, staring at it to make the warmth come back, but it had done its job and was done working. He got in the car, feeling he didn't know the other two inside anymore. He would drive until that feeling passed. Maybe the orchard would do it. The orchard would be his Coke can.

If they were going to make hell in the hayfields today they would require some snake spit in their guts. While Jamie ran into the liquor store, Saigon and Risky got the car washed. It was one of those places that drub you spotless with the octopus wipers, and while the Corvair got its laving ribbons, they undid their zippers and their flies. With Risky atop him in black, he had to imagine what he normally saw at home. Saigon had noted that if Risky was squalid, her sex was not. He figured unearthing her he'd greet the ash stains of a chimney, but youth kept her immune to the brack and grime.

It was a year since Saigon found her drumming on a trashcan lid in the park, a ring of novena candles she had shoplifted featuring the Angel de la Guarda lighting up her corrugated snare, her circle of itinerants mostly corroded human freight, a crush of long-gone Woodstockers, here or there a Village anarchist who'd known Valerie Solanis before her gun days.

She wouldn't talk at all about her family, until she was using and then would talk a lot. She had come from Delaware, from a small Irish clan that was not particularly mean, nor particularly kind, lost in the swarming rabble of sourpusses from Fermanagh who hemmed them in on all sides like rotting clover. They were not like the boisterous Italians who ran clotheslines across his fire escapes, or his own debacle of an Ozone Park clan; hostages to Bolognese and birdbaths, neo-Palladian touches to interior design. They were not like his dad who wacked his brother with a nub of a broom, simply bayoneted the poor shit above the brows. They were not like the whole brick tract of Calabrian housemaids who never recovered after Arthur Godfrey fired Julius LaRosa on the air.

Saigon had a mother from San Juan and that torqued the LaRosa types. She spoke Spanish; he didn't. Dad didn't and wouldn't. Brother couldn't. After a thunder whack of the broom across his brother's frontal bone, mother rapping her fists off dad and then bending over her second child, pronouncing him dead on the spot while his pulse raced and his head smacked the linoleum in faultless rhythm, Saigon going down to one knee telling his mother to shut up while dad backed against the wall and watched everything like it was too much for his senses, brother wouldn't speak at all.

Jamie came out from the liquor store, unzipped her leather jacket and pulled a Harvey's Bristol Cream from inside, passing it to Risky, who held the bottle up as though handling a dead squirrel.

"The whisky and the wine were too close to the register," said Jamie. "It's leaded, you know?"

"It's perfect," said Saigon.

"But not as good as Coke," said Risky.

The orchards stretched across Orange Moon and dropped off into hills. Risky vomited on the bottom of one while Jamie scoffed. They left their fat basket of Cortlands near the puke and headed up a grassy ledge, steeling for action.

Kids were rolling gourds in the pumpkin patch, tumbling heartlessly on top of each other's prone backs. The farmers who ran Orange Moon were bilious Germans, just barely holding in their worries about Westchester's potential litigants, their fear that the toddlers might cripple under a pumpkin's rolling weight, concuss under the recoil of the potato gun.

When the trio passed by these farmers, standing in a line and actually holding rakes. Jamie wanted to *sieg heil* and Saigon thought that wasn't too swift. They were a fat and miserable lot in bib denims, the son and daughter freckled lavishly, destined to inherit a farming life begun two Reichs back in the shires of Schleswig; they didn't need this Yankee scuzzball's acid razz.

In front of the cider stand, Risky began jumping up and down.

"Donuts, please," she said, standing a precocious inch from Saigon's face.

"Please, daddy, please, daddy," said Jamie, jumping up and down.

"Stop, you're not funny," said Risky.

Saigon got on line for the donuts. The younger families looked befuddled but pleasant. A little boy asked his mom about Saigon's earring and was duly shushed. An old couple, their mismatching polyesters somehow seeming austere, grimaced at the sight of him, shaking their heads.

"What?" said Saigon. "You never seen a wop before?"

"Excuse me?" said the old man.

"Are we not entitled to our autumn fruit?"

"Son, it's not my business to scold you. I'm just buying donuts."

"Let me."

"What?"

"It's on me."

"We've got money. You don't need to," said the wife.

"No no no, it's on me."

At the front of the line. Saigon said, "Gimme eight cinnamons, three of your powdered sugared, and two borings. That's 'plain' to you. And for these two here,"–he swung his arm back toward the old couple, turning around. "What do you want?"

"He's not paying for us," said the husband.

"It's my money. Tell you what," Saigon said the donut girl, a ruddy, nut-shaped teenager, her left eye endearingly lazy. "I'll take twenty of each for American Gothic here."

"We don't want them," said the wife. "We've got our own money."

"God, you two are really burning my ass," said Saigon. "You beg me to buy you sixty donuts all the way up to the front of the line, at last I blink, and now you act all noble before Cindy here. Is that your name?"

"Bess," said the donut girl.

"And poor Sissy who has one job to do which doesn't include dispensing Geritol or handing over fried rounds to welfare cases has to deal with an angry greaseball losing his shit among the fruit. Well that's it. The offer is retracted. Crissy, gimme my donuts."

Bess silently bagged the donuts with her head down. It was one bulging bag when she was finished, grease already feeding its way through the wax paper, like a science experiment.

"Thank you, Mindy," said Saigon.

The girl raised her eyes and with a stabbing little smile said, "Bess!"

"Put your hand out, Tess, on the table, palm up."

"Why?"

"Just do it."

The girl watched the line growing impatient and this seemed to release a little Lucifer in her. She put her hand down on the counter, palm up, thusly ordered. Saigon brought his down in one motion and Bess slid her hand away just in time. He smiled almost wistfully, cocking his head a bit.

"Sad," he said.

"Why?" she said, a hopeful little glint in her eyes.

"You failed the test."

"Failed? What test?"

"Only connect, baby," said Saigon. "Only connect."

Bess's cheeks cratered a little under the eyes and she just looked at him, waiting for a reversal. Saigon shrugged, turned, did a little pugilist dance for the oldsters, then copped his donuts, walking away from the stand without turning, Bess still watching him when the old man stepped up to claim his bag.

Saigon did not feel the way he'd hoped. Bess was nice. The warp spasm could not be summoned.

Risky and Jamie jumped into the hammock by the barn, rocking it ever so between a pair of lonely elms. Saigon noted with pleasure that women in a hammock together always became dreamy as fairy dust; the hardest Rosie the Riveter would go demure upon the netting with a friend, a little sway and their heads would gently click: bells.

Risky was, he noticed, still growing; her face even less plump than last week. The dirty trick, thought Saigon: What do you grow for but to kick off the downhill slalom. And your luminous labors won't save you. De Vinci was as dead as any strip miner in coal country. Let her earn her dour lines. Was it in those dour lines he had lost the warp spasms? He needed those spasms back. Nell had wanted him to have them; told him he was Cu Chailainn reborn and storming the adamantine pillars of unreasonable historical types. He could bring down the plutocratic state. What it took was Cu Chailainn's shock notions, his "warp spasms", and lunar tantrums to really put the scream in their guts.

She had salvaged him. If he was Cu Chailainn he would not be that Ozone Park kid taking collect calls from an upstate prison; listening blankly into the phone while his father front-loaded the calls with hurried questions, desperate and obsequious ones, seeking dispatches from a life he had sired and, now that that life was gone to him, had suddenly turned him frantic, desperate for a tunnel back into good graces. After a year, Saigon stopped accepting the charges.

When a year later his father came through the door, his hair brilliantined and the cross dangling from his neck four times bigger than the one he left with, Saigon ran away. He moved around, drove trucks, doctored motorcycles, tried commune life; got railed from commune life, his obstreperous ways were unsettling to the credulous longhairs. Back in New York, stumbling through Soho, thirty, he would encounter Bloated Hausfrau.

They had come to New York, beckoned by the ascotted Vaughn Spinnell. At his expo on Houston Street, Saigon watched their frontwoman Nell Farnsworth, the woman inserting what she called a "dowsing quill" into her anus and squatting over a paper runner on which aphorisms in Sanskrit were then dripped. Later on in the expo, she copulated with a man she'd picked at random from the crowd. The man had a ghoulish keloid running down his cratered jaw and it turned out he was a "plant", a London underworld figure turned outrage agent, a Situationist who had once done shakedowns on pornographic "loop" booth owners in his indelible East End cockney, now flavoring SoHo with the sight of his angry dick.

Saigon, plastered, introduced himself afterward. Nell asked him what he thought of the show.

His gorge rising, he stuck a finger down his throat and promptly threw up.

"Well," she said generally. "He gets it through and through."

She took him back to her hotel that night, and when the sun came up he thought he heard wedding bells clanging from the armory chapels. Nell must've seen something too; his mineshaft eyes, the Roman honker on his face vividly the forlorn boxer's. She would whittle him into being, like Warhol with his foundlings, making them superstars.

And he admired her. Nell ran from home not just in her body. A child of the Blitz, she saw her home spared but the district decimated by the V-2 rockets, those loud, ballistic falcons that squalled in after the Red Warning signals. She could hear the high whine and plunge of their suicidal courses down into bedrooms. In daylight she and her little friends would gallop the bomb-razed tracts, picking through charred dresser tables, roofless parlor rooms that looked like theater sets. It wasn't serious, only when a leg was discovered, or a pair of petrified fingers welded to a teakettle rim. How could she, seeing those bombsite kitchens, think a kitchen could ever be a *place*. Nothing could be what they told you it was, and, once you established who "they" were, you'd go full-on V-2 on their tails.

The gangster flew Saigon to London where "the boy" would put up at her place. Nights were slow and druggy. A coterie of pagans, college friends from Nell's limited spell at university, crashed on the carpet night and day. There, a faction of the Hausfrau played droning, medieval sounding music rendered squalid by Nell's effects. The neighbors were a young couple, strivers who abhorred the unending racket and rammed hands against the wall in rage. One night the gangster came over with a vibrasonic console one of the kids had designed. A twist of a knob and the machine would send thirty-herz infrasound currents through the plaster in inaudible range. The group would turn the machine on, leaving the building each evening while the couple communed in ostensible peace. By Whitsunday they noticed the husband's rhyming patterns, strange paranoid flights. He complained of agonizing bowel cramps not attributable to diet or nerve strain. The wife herself began riffing, pulling up slime phrases from her paraphasia, delivering supple beauties like. "Don't walk to me shat way, I am snot a wild, you get!" The sonic assault was working.

Saigon protested, said that their particular vandal band had, he thought, always worked off of decency; there was way too much anticapitalist cruelty out there for theirs to make a dent anyway, but the machine stayed on and the couple fled the flat, their neuroleptic remedies failing to relieve them of the idea that the building was a paranormal hive.

One night, Saigon smashed the console in front of the group and stormed off into the night. The next day he came home to an empty flat. He called the gangster who said Nell was at his place. The old man said he'd be better off not calling; the woman simply needed to "cool her heels."

But she never came back to her own apartment. Saigon cried for his brother all that month; the first time he had ever done so.

When he got back he found himself drinking a lot of Coca Cola. He would see a Coke sign on the wall of a pizzeria and sit there all day, eyes fixed. Staring long enough he thought he could see a shadow drinking, a male form in traces, like an afterimage of something known, and warm waves creased the cold where it lived in him.

The light was starting to fade. Risky was aiming the potato gun, resting it on her shoulder, nodding off ostentatiously while angling the barrel. Holding the launcher, there was nothing remotely "punk" about her now.

"Fuck me!" she yelled, hitting the spud off the wooden board. A mother covered her daughter's ears.

"Why why why why why why *why!*" said Risky, laughing until she was sobbing. Then she went down to the ground. Jamie laughed like a spastic mink. People began moving themselves away, making space. Saigon located a feeling he had not felt until now: embarrassment. And then he felt dread. They were doing all this for him. Risky thought these jackal theatrics would make him pleased as punch: a doting papa. He didn't want to tell her that, though vagabond mob art could have you running vibrasonic capers on a brain and bowel and that seductive warp torque would have you channeling the cutthroats of Irish lore while you copulated to frantic noise modules, life was still the ice cream truck in summer, Macy's lights on Christmas Day and Trick or Treat with mom on the side streets in autumn. It was the Halloween candy bucket little Sandro toted around with his bopping stride, and the prime number of his smile when the candy was unwrapped for him. Saigon had failed to protect him. Even now he did not know if he was dead or alive. And it didn't matter. There was nothing to preserve, nothing to renew or reclaim. It had all gotten away from him while he was running.

He got down on one knee and grabbed her by the shoulders.

"Stop it!" he yelled. "Stop it! Fucking stop!"

Jamie hit him on the back but he dragged Risky away, past the cider and the apples, through the orchard's pumpkin sprawl, not stopping until he had thrown Risky into the Corvair, snarled the engine, and drove away.

Crossing back over the Third Avenue Bridge and then turning south on the FDR he saw the towering neon Pepsi sign trapped among the jetties of Long Island City. It wasn't the right brand of cola, but it would have to do. One eye on the road and the other on the sign across the river, he examined the red light for shapes. He strained against the neon, looked for the trace of a person, a shadow crossing through the light, and saw there was nothing he could see.

S-Bahn 5:32

"The best thing about sunglasses," says Marina Slaninko, "is when you wear them, every guy thinks you're checking him out." On the pleather seat, the speed train beating tracks over Baden, she tilts her tinted squares at a passing man and goes on to bemoan the narcissism of all men, then goes on to enumerate the galumphing clods she has harpooned by the simple and opportune modeling of her stocking runs. The right thing, she says, is to find flaws and affix to the shortfalls. Develop an inmate's acumen.

"Pick a zit," she adds. "If it bleeds, they think they can have you."

Katie Lithwick checks herself in her compact mirror. She'll have to find something else.

"Nobody here today," she says. "We should try a different car."

But Marina knows odds are in their favor. Something male will always cop a squat. All they have to do is walk by the little cubbyhole that contains them and gander at the sunlit sparkles of their identical silver flats, their identical black sheer stockings, their matching skirts and matching bangs chestnut brown descending gracefully over their matching cat's-eye paint.

There is one now, slides the door wide and he peers in. Katie is amped; in a state to pat the vinyl space to the right of her, subtle as ox horns to the gonads, and the man would be stupid not to know that, for the duration of space between Baden and the Rastatt terminal where the fathomless rail line ends, he is going to be an Olympic swimmer wading into the kiddie pool.

"Namen?" he says.

"No. You first," says Marina across from him.

"Americans."

"Yes."

"Karlheinz. Your turn."

"Katie," says Katie, legs crossed but leaning toward him.

"*Kaethe.*"

"What?" says Katie.

"KAH-TAY," says the man.

"Oh. My German name."

"Quick," he says. "You're a quick one."

"If you only knew," says Marina, winking, perhaps at Katie, perhaps at the German man.

"I see she is wondering what we are saying," he says.

"Karl," says Marina. "You really have a beanpole quality, you do know that?" She does a quick bat of those cat lashes, smacks those lips, silver as the train they are riding. She is not pleased, however, with his patronizing intimations of "Kaethe"; these are notions that dispel something in her that she has labored to create in her friend. It burns her fuel, but stalls her engines. sShe needs to reclaim her victory, push.

"Katie is a photoessayist," she says. "She doesn't need words because words are for stupid people."

Katie thumps her chest: Tarzana.

"You think I'm stupid?" says Karl.

Marina winks at Kate, pounds her chest.

"And what are you studying?" the man says to Marina.

"Metropolisarchitecture."

"I beg your pardon?"

The door is locked. Thirty-nine minutes later, Karlheinz emerges through this small door, his gait ragged, no longer starched and cocky.

For sure it has been a monster summer break. They have won a Boar's Head write-in raffle that has taken them on a Lufthansa overseas. Following their sponsored (coach) travel, a train pass to some lederhosen zones. It was (and is) a joke by Marina, sending in the laminated stub. Katie is a skeptic when it's sent, but Marina says, "Boar's Head. *Have* to do it. It's a pop art coup de grace. You can burn the whole scum army with the win."

She is right, always is, and winning is winning is winning. Katie cannot say who "them all" would be, but her trust in Marina shines bright.

It's a minute's conundrum before they leave. Katie Lithwick has forbidden herself meat; even seitan she cannot abide, but she'll sop up the arbitrary remuneration of this greased pig company, pop a Klonopin to allay her flying fears, and live high on the *schwein* out of a carryon: She will gallows these dead-eyed scavengers by their own entrails. Then they will club around trendy Berlin bars in their black boots and shag innumerable happy denizens of the Po-Mo scene. The bier halls will expand as the urban glut grows nearer, the alpine waterheads will multiply as the towns get small. But the train turns out to be more appealing.

The Dada of Nike: *Just Do It*

In the railcar, they have Horst, his scanty black mop pressed forward across his perspiring forehead and the blue polyester of his nautical jumper clutching at his contours of his ribs. He says he is a DJ in Bonn, has your inevitable Dub-spinner's brash, wholly rolling joie de vivre; and certainly he's spun them suitably. Then the raffle brings them Geoffrey, a polyamorous laugher out of Baliol College with a habit of giving protracted hugs. It brings them Augie Carroll, a snaggle-toothed survivor of the "Maze" block prison, an Irish patriot with burned hands from mismanaging some volatile bomb jelly in a Provo "factory". Those hands – hands he's claimed passed over the expiring faces of men on the H-Block hunger strikes (…"feckin last rites, I gave em, and me the farthest from a papist …" – manages Katie in her Bremen bunk, then slings down like an opossum to bag snappy, uncorrallable Marina inside hers. A testament to how *new* this is: He can ring their bells even bobbing towards them with that wattled neck. But: He has the popped collar of a windblown, unregenerated revolutionary poet. He has the gothic wither and rag-shined, oxblood-colored Winklepickers (commemorating, perhaps, the high times he has missed while frittering away in his Ulster jail). He is like a child apologizing through rutting sounds. Or maybe he is adult apologizing to his young self; the useless car bomb bumbler.

Lying in the bunk, post sounds, he notices two sprung umbrellas, freestanding in this small space, like a dyad of black florets.

"You're trying fate," he says, "Them being wide like that."

"We know that," says Marina, her leg crossed over his, working out a flesh pretzel.

Above them, Katie Lithwick says, "We do."

"Couple of flies in the ointment, you two."

But his voice is different now, uneasy. What does he know of these umbrellas?

Of course, they do have to transfer, and the on-again-off-again shakes things. The destinations are nearly happenstance: On at Augsburg and west to Mainz, a little sightseeing ramble through the sloped streets of the miserly Old Town, a jaunt to the Roman gates and then back on the S-bahn west into Weisbaden (wash stop), then a bolt on the InterCity tricolor turbo wing to Saxony and Halle, after a scrub down in a nameless burg of Hesse, a breakneck lateral into Koblenz.

Yes. They scrub their perishable places in station bathrooms, but after a week nothing can hide the smell. The car is robust with body odor and odor in women means sex. That is how Marina sees it. Katie is slowly warming to the idea, seeing this part and parcel of their own premeditated nonchalance. Men, fractionally wincing, light up at the meaning of the fumes. The train is not crowded. They could sit anywhere but do they?

They sit here.

Katie is locked in her headphones, watching the cattle pens pass, the violent green swatches of unmutilated countryside blind to her love for the other traveler; she is stewing in Marina's rebelliousness. It is helpful when her thoughts are Marina's, for sure. Her friend, a more exotically cogitating animal, wields a Mont Blanc swivel-head and scribbles down the following sentiments on a ruled pad:

Heimat Slaves
Residential Minimum
Accumulated Train Tales
Irony-Fucking, Better *Mean* It

She majors in architecture in a small, grant-fattened city school, there, she will preserve her lynxish posture while hunching bored over an expensive drafting set. She is a theorist, but theories on paper seem coy, withholding; to make them palpable – that's what youth is for. She has been taken with the theories of Ludwig Hilberseimer, his railing against urban anomie, the punk manner in which he rails against the routinizing of all life that would put work *here,* house *there* – that seeks to divide and conquer. Shit where you eat, says Hilbersheimer. He wants a white out blizzard, big strikes, purity; it matters not if it is "ugly" all the same; it should jar the rabble clear of the commonplace. It wants Shock that cannot be shelved away from Function. Let there not be a moment of rest, a moment of peace in our towns, thinks Marina. Indeed she wants to blow through towns, arrive in Vienna soaking wet with the sweat of transmitted carnality working like thoroughbred racehorses through her pores. She wants to step on powerlines, a Japanese broadsword gleaming from a sluicing aperture in her chest. She wants to be Hilberseimer's vendetta, his naked wrath.

She looks out the window; dour at the spines of dusk sun slicing through the window, dour at the commuting German bores. The ride drains her from lack of change. She looks around. A spongy man in coveralls of olive drab nicks at his blackened cuticles across the aisle. Watching the man's dirty boils, his red beard shiny with grease stains from the *wurst,* Marina wants murder. Because his ugliness does not prompt her to act. She despises that, the beauty putsch; a reflex she needs shut of. What would her Ludwig say?

She tosses a chunk of balled-up rye bread at the *wurst* man, remembering that that was how Joe Stalin flirted. She bats her lashes. She cackles. He shakes his head, grumbling, and looks out through the glassed scroll of the fast-rolling country. Marina uncrosses her legs and yells, *"Achtung!"* He turns and she yanks her sheer panty an inch off its center to the left, then she rubs the little node and he turns away.

He must have a family. He must sink a tankard before speeding home and splotching his wife's enchanted mandible with a slime of wursty licks. Marina inserts herself next to him. He pushes himself up against the windowpane. Dare he glare back at those whopping hazels.

If he looks, she thinks, he defeats me. Keep looking at your country, poor man, your brittle alder groves, your exsanguinated Krupps-fed villages.

She licks his neck, cups her hand on his fly intrepidly. He can go no further. Yes sir, she senses a tensing bolus that makes his trousers flare. Ceding victory.

Marina looks at Katie, asleep or adrift, her head against the glass.

She kisses through warm waves of meaty breath. She grabs him where the proof is. Katie doesn't wake so she keeps pulling until there is no reason to. While she is noting the mechanized pleasure factor, she inspects the man's downturned face, his head against the glass, eyes red and teary because those wurst licks on his wife's mandible mean something altogether different now.

In the bathroom, Maria sees grease around her lips. She kisses the mirror. She has betrayed Katie, and swallows this thought. The wurst on her lips is a perfume. She smacks them.

The sadness flies up into the light.

Marina is feeling generous today, or guilty all over again. In their car, Katie seems pained, as though aware Marina has betrayed her. Still it could just be the motion of the train. The S-bahn whinnies.

The rail tracks scream, swine on a stockyard trolley, sometimes the sound is cattlelike and sometimes it is a distant choked whine that is unmistakably human in its timbre. Whatever it is, the chug and clack must make Katie's auditory canals go to snapping.

Marina crosses and sits, stroking her roommate's honey locks with the ease of a post-coital gibbon. Katie's eyes are still shut. She is not betrayed, contrary to Marina's hard concerns. Her earbuds create a vacuum inside which only the whir of Bach can be heard. J.S, who finished out as blind as Beethoven did deaf, is the soundtrack of echolocation, Marina has said. It is in those mincing plinks the clavichord makes that one hears the unseeing figure their way through the blackened routines, a crashed wineglass here, an oil fire by upended candelabra there; it is blind music that is purest because it is an act of will.

So: Katie, Bach-rapt, does not hear the soccer team from Dusseldorf, the players half-cocked on Warsteiners and passing the girl's room only to hammer at the washroom door. Finally, Marina slides open the portal. A nervous netminder, less biered-up than his midfielders, stands queued beside the lavatory. He shrugs, blinks, coy, and turns away. She admires him among the clutch of soccer strikers wailing *Wir Sind Die Fortuna* on the cleaner side of the bathroom door. She wants to take him, but Katie, apprenticing, immersing in J.S Bach, is still learning to be Marina, still learning to think anew.

The netminder is at the door again.

One betrayal is enough for one ride.

Marina lets him pass ….

…. Then enter Jay Guernsey, a country troubadour, walking lope-style with an Epiphone slung lazily over his western flannel. He sits right down and hikes his teju-lizard boots right up on the vinyl armrest that serves to gird Marina in her place. He strums a sweet nothing cowpoke song and then by golly he has got them hooked. He is on his way to Bremen, he tells a waking Katie, to play Dave Dudley trucker numbers for the latter man's North Oldenburg appreciation group. He tells them there is no load of compromising on the road to his horizon, ("'at's Campbell, not Duds"). He's happy to exit Earth broker than a hundred south Appalachian booze hounds. He has quoted a song from "before their time" and so laughter fails to back-score the locomotive repartee, but that won't hurt his cause. Katie, her legs stacked off to the side, a lonely, literate girl on a village green, does not remove her headphones and instead listens to Prelude in D, the fast clavichord powering her cerebral gallops. She sees Marina waving. She is on the floor with Marina, a successfully crash-landed airplane.

Marina spits on his penis. She asks him to grab her hair; her voice goes from surgical to imploring to surgical. But it's nothing pornographic even so; more an act of simple guidance, the way a mentor does their chummy part for Fate. They will give him a new song for his repertoire.

But Marina backs off now, rising. She goes to the door.

"Where are you going?" asks Katie.

"He's yours."

"Don't go," says Guernsey.

"We do it together," says Katie.

"It's *your* time."

"I'm not ready."

"You are," says Marina. "I know you are."

"She's not," says the wanton loper. "I uh, think she needs your help. You needs team up on me."

"*Pleeeeease,*" whines Katie. "Next time. Next time I'll do it alone."

Can Katie grow, thinks Marina? Find her own way, her own tastes? Because of Marina, Katie has stopped listening to

Demi Lovato, only the Françoise Hardy Marina likes so much. She knows only Marina's ethos. She knows to curse Dad and his vanilla-scented trash bag monopoly. She knows trash winds up knotting plankton strands, raining hell on the oceans. She knows that, like defecation, trash purifies, but much more vividly when it spumes up reimagined from burning piles. Katie has learned to be disgusting, having boned up on her mentor's Irving Klaw, those wide retrospective books of his photography. Now she has demonstrated Klaw's main jam by tearing runs into the webbing of her fishnet stockings, using the shutterbug as though his work was a coping manual.

Looking at her perfect slopes of her exposed breasts, Marina remembers Katie young. Katie was a sunny one in high school, before she was trying rage as a mission statement. It has been a process. For her spring project, she had projected the ravages of human sepsis across her thesis white wall. The one that most bridled the patrons was the layout called *The Zipline Girl.* She was an outdoorsy premed, an Alabama go-getter on a group trip to Cozumel. Above a gorge, the line had snapped and a river nasty had run a widening circuit through her inwards; now she was all livid cauterizations, a ghoulish warning to all uncomprehending daredevils: Disinfect, ye, no airborne horseplay over standing bogs if you know what is good for you. Katie had linked the clinical evidence as an oval on the wall (her raw materials scored easily from an online rag) and placed them side by side with a running video of a transvaginal colposcope. Dad, hands in his pockets, stood miffed; her mother Gladys undone, frankly unappreciative, given the work. Katie, for her part, had imagined a critique. Before the show, she had sat up at night inventing a kimono-wearing wag of the Warhol circuit who was now on the prowl for new blood:

"The off-green colorations play winningly against the rabid reds of the girl's done capillaries." So began the diary wag, whose name never got beyond Rene, but whose language Katie cribbed from journals content to let their smug flag fly. "The suppurations Lithwick traps in her primal conceit have a standard and identifiable texture, not unlike de Kooning's assiduous masterworks of scrape paint at the Janis exposition. I don't say 'going places' too often for fear of overextending my sense of propriety, but this one...."

She *had* doted on the colors. Working for color, this was pretty enough for Katie to secretly like it beyond the abstract ramifications of "art". But nobody, least of all Marina, shared her pleasure, and nobody was penning raves.

Marina was, in fact, infuriated. How fucking juvenile, she meant to say, mutilation as femininity? *A stab wound.* Dare to dream, Katie. Inside, though, Marina felt filched: a hotwired sports car in some trash banker's midlife crisis fantasy. She smacked Katie hard, felt the stubbornness of all-American cheekbone tight against her flattened hand. Katie's flush from the slap was post-coital. Marina had broken the seal on something larger, more encompassing than a selfhood philosophy, so she moved in and kissed her, her tongue a red millipede navigating a narrow lane of tonsils. It was a brash act but the remaining gallerians didn't fluster. (By the time of the kiss, Daddy Trashbag and Mumsy in her doll dress were much too benumbed by the images of spreading gangrene to bristle at anything Sapphic in their midst). The kiss was not shocking to the girls; they had tiptoed on Saturn's rings before, avoiding the galactic fireball of consummation ever since the heady days of preschool.

Now they would have to escalate:

They did a year of homecare for a blind man – having picked him from a menu of decaying candidates. They paced the room buff and brought him his humid bourguignons, wheeling the steaming trays in on meal casters. They pressed the soles of their feet together on the floor while they played braille Scrabble with the man, a cellist, his visual field shrunk to a buttonhole from retinitis. Presumably, he did not know they were naked and this was a hot balm to them. They enacted a French *belle dance* in his apartment, lacing their arms across one another's, their hands barely touching. Marina dangled her breasts over the cellist when she took his tray, close enough to fog her nipple with his breath.

"It's cruel," said Katie. "Why don't we just fuck him?"

Sex without anger is reproduction, Marina told Katie. With anger, though, it was a paroxysm of art. Marina did not want reproduction, which was the citywide anonymity of tower blocks in Joe Stalin's iron sinkhole; redistributed wheat grain making steel rise over the Volga, the masses foaming at the mouth for blini scraps.

It was compartmentalizing: death.

Marina had had sex only four times – and that her freshman year in college – before recruiting Katie into her auspices, even proctoring the moment Katie ceded her hymen to a man. Since the kiss they'd planted after the farrago of the Vagiscope, she had never let Katie from her clutches, and Katie had no desire to rut with anyone minus Marina. Marina now fears she will never break free, but she cannot deny she has a project in Katie, a child; a thing to love you always.

Katie looks at her imploringly, tears creeping around the edges of her eyes. Guernsey is a toothpick in a hairball, a non-person, and Katie is nodding. Please, her nod says, I need you. I am unready. Marina curses herself, unable to divest herself of feeling.

She heads back into the room.

The stout conductor, wobbling with the locomotive tilt as the train snakes a switchback at Amstetten, sees Marina approaching, hair mussed, and thinks: These girls are no same old same old. We've seen American Eurail travelers, their legs cocked high against the rubber frame of the wide windows, but behold, as we pass through the churning dells of Lutter, this carnivorous duo stuns us.

It is their world but are we living in it?

Periodically he has admonished them in tones that go a long way to establishing his libertine cred, painted a portrait of himself as the product of locomotion and so virtually, necessarily, blind to whatever passes in his wake. But as Marina approaches he must make talk.

"Please," he says, "I don't mind your having guests but we have had complaints. It is not me, you see, only my position."

Marina, though, would be bored to meet him halfway. The conductor is not prepared for the octane of rage he encounters. A stream of bawling cusses from the girl. *Fuck shit you slug suck my asshole eat me raw Heimat slave.* There is something unconscionably burning in there. It is not worth his time to pull it out, hold the burning devil-gem under the loupe that is beclouded by senescence anyway. He leaves with his ticket snapper and sighs into the next car of the train.

They are moving at speeds that make mincemeat of thriving cantons. The train smashes molecules, murdering untold scanty lifeforms as it motors westbound towards its mountain end. There are reindeer pummeled as well; add to the murder toll baby chamois, opossum, beech martens, mice, white rabbits, squirrels, porcine, and skunk. The spermatozoa of the country hack are likewise running reckless in Marina, the preseminal drop-ladder has flung in bugs, namely, the *C. trachomatis* red worm of venereal jeremiads known among the carnally "active" to make a hell out of your morning piss. Katie's host cells resist this particular insect, but the strummer, no novice wooing type, has stoked the yeast already dwelling peaceably within her friend, Marina. Thus the harmless "passenger" will soon be rising to a state of bread. This Katie Lithwick, apprentice provocateur on electropowered speed trains burning across the leafy German heartland, has no mantras, but, had she anything, it would be:

????

Katie, back in her earbud Sudetenland, slumbers. This Katie I have rendered, thinks Marina. I have invented a new naked, smacked the girl free from the fettering sentiments of the past. This new naked will do great damage in the world, and loves not knowing what it will do.

Mantras, take a backseat. This is real.

They are about to hit the alpine swell of Innsbruck, and the anodized speed demon gleams. Two lawyers hop into their car (the girls are unaware of their profession but figure it in the neighborhood of "stocks"). They are talking about the Right Wing of Austria, the absorption of the FPO ethno-craze into the sociopolitical mainstream, but Katie doesn't know that. Marina knows the acronyms and asks them if they speak English. Neither one is more handsome than the other but one stands a perfect foot taller than his mate, and that one is far more raring to wow her with the mastery of his sprechen sie. Marina finds a moment to interject and, feeling her oats, accuses both men of fascism, of a rank torpor "...in the face of ...". She accuses them of impurity; it is the compartmentalizing of life that they love; the flattening of ideals that is fed by money and a cycle of "necessity" born of, and aided by, the Law. She says the Nuremburg Laws and the Nuremburg Trials were continuous, not even a coin flipped over. They are splashing in the undertow of the Heimat in a country grown warped on Heimat principals, where the notion of associated farmlands notched up in little mountain shires is synonymous with the thrill of gentle liberty. She tells the lawyers they are heir to this slave mind: fat-skulled progeny of that segmented country manse.

There is a sudden swing in the power output, a slow shuddering of the carbody lights, and then the volts die, the train turns black, and Marina has no idea what is happening, who is where. On the other side of the outage, the upper cornice creeper lights blink back on in a single blush, and she sees that the tall man is laughing at her. The little man to his right is laughing too.

"What?" she says.

"Patty Hearst," the little one says.

"What?"

"The heiress," says the large one. "'Revolutionary intercourse' or some nonsense. Some garbage they fed her that machine-gunning the money types made you a better person"

"The Sym-bayo-neece Libowaytion Aaaahmy," says the little one, sounding it out from his nose.

"You better watch it," she says.

"Or what, you will speak to me of Heimat?" says the tall one, laughing.

The train hugs to the brittle mountains, steep declines open up on their left and grade down hard to elaborate waterways.

Marina sees the green drop away, the cold grey stones underneath the trestle bridges.

"You are Arts majors?" says the Tall One.

Marina nods.

"Art is what happens when the sick get tired of living," he says. "Art takes the world astray. It has made it grow demented. Stick to your foundations grants. Get small, stay small. You talk of Nuremburg? Well who were those men in the dock; bad scribblers, events planners, men who sold underwhelming champagnes to brittle bureaucrats, watercolorists of no skill. Hand them their insignia, and there is your present and past. You do nothing but desensitize. You make shams of the real around you. I could count your contributions all day and end at up dinner holding nothing but a pustule in my hand."

"What I do is a ton more palpable than what you do, more real," says Marina.

"Then rich people are realer than poor people?"

"No."

"Because I can only imagine your poverty. The one-room cabin you shared with five brothers and five sisters, in, where is it, the Ozark Plateau?"

"That's irrelevant. My money is irrelevant."

"The *only* thing relevant is your money. You don't exist but to rectify something you think is wrong. If I am money, then I am wrong. And if I am wrong, you need me. Take me away and you dissolve."

"You admit that you're wrong."

"No," said the Tall Man. "I think I'm right. But you still need me. It is not a likewise proposition. If you disappear, I keep going."

"Money is not a verity."

"Money is beyond a verity; it's the new water, and you drink too."

Marina notices Katie is biting her lip. She looks as though about to cry, or laugh; it is not clear.

"I don't speak in platitudes," says Marina. "So I don't want to listen to yours."

"Headphones," says the Little Man jauntily.

"I won't retreat either," says Marina, staring at the Little Man. "I pity anyone who thinks the world does not need change. And does not want to reinvent the mind so to change it."

"You need to stop. You need to gather yourself," says the Tall Man.

"Why?"

"You're going way up. High to a great mountain. You get colder there. Little cows who have imbecilic lives chew grasses on the hills and watch you rise on them. They are not dangerous animals but happy, and they watch you rise miserably to where you'll get cold, cold, and colder, until there's no choice but to get sick. And then you won't be human anymore."

"What are you talking about, Willie!" says the little man, laughing.

"First platitudes, then fables," says Marina, not laughing.

"If I must," says the Tall Man.

It is wowing. The tall man could say these things to Marina and still ring her bell, but he wears a wedding ring and has no interest in removing it. If she could tear his clothes off she could hammer him into frame, smother his very windpipe with the wad of his own stunned phallus, start new with these men in this car. She looks across at him and he is no longer laughing.

"Don't talk to me anymore," he says. "I'm speaking to my friend now. And by the way," he says with a disbelieving shake of his head, "it really smells in here."

But the men don't leave the car. They seem to feel entitled to their squatters rights until the ride concludes in Brenner.

Now there is a boiling détente, the two sides talking around each other. Katie and Marina reminisce (whispers). Tall Man and Short Man rattle on in hyper-speed. The cold mountain air sends its little emissary gusts in through the weather stripping. After heading south nine kilometers, the lawyer sighs, claims the attrition of guilt, and tells them he is riding the train into South Tyrol – his wife and his children are waiting. He apologizes, but again notes the humid smell. The man who is smaller, given to laughing fits, will depart in Austria, which is his provenance. It is where the girls will depart too. (They have no interest in Italy, with its pappardelle dicks and mopeded mama's boys gliding by the mummified tapestries. Nothing *Metropolis* there).

The wind has mapped routes through the mountain ranges, and the train is rocking a little heavy with the rush. Marina feels the brute force of untoward motion, barreling through her mind's own secret glades, the unmonitored superhighways that skirt the cordons of her occluded moral life. Katie is talking to herself, something Marina has never seen before. She seems to be trying to speak in new phonemes, mime the tall man's feather-ruffling, aristo-German cant.

The beanstalk, whose name they won't ever know, waves a foul ciao to the girls and shakes his friend's hand when all but he depart the railcar. The little man seems to know what he has in his pocket, his pheromone radar well-trained. They have taken all their luggage and their umbrellas.

He leads them to his flat, black and white and unlived in but for some balled-up bathing towels on the rug; they seem to have blown there like sage. They tell him to strip and then they strip too. Here his little Lucite Eden is now befouled by tannish flesh. He tells Marina the open umbrella is a no-no, so Marina closes it, and with that, presumably, her bad fortune. The man's torqued wand bobs up uncut, all membranes, and there is something about his intactness that signals the time is now. She stalks away towards the hall, winks at Katie and clicks the door shut. Katie smiles at the man. When she arrives at him she grabs him too hard and he flings back, tripping over a stereo console and into the A/C unit, groggy, trying to rise from his stomach. She grabs the closed umbrella, forcing it down below where his back meets his plumper curves. She feels his rectum give, hard soil into soft, and when she presses the button the umbrella spokes are responsive, contouring and then bursting him as she opens this jellyfish as far as its spokes will take it. The screaming does not draw the neighbors, who must not be home right now (the old teleological default nerve in Katie states this means it is meant to be). She bends erotically to him and blows him a laughter kiss. The man whimpers through an enveloping numbness, some major parts unusable should he survive to tell the tale. Katie sees that by turning the umbrella just so she can make his mouth twist up, make his mouth twist down. She can make *this* noise come out of him, something almost like laughter, and then *that* noise, a much more traditional emitting, a barnyard grumble, as from a swine. The Boars Head raffle: You wanted me.

Marina had suspected something different was happening so when she opens the door she screams. She finds it unbecoming to hit this rabid pitch, and that shame plus an instant nausea quiets her.

"What are you doing?" she says, though it's plain.

It should be obvious to Marina, Katie's intent: only the logical advance of a motion begun on a thesis wall, brought to maturity by a kiss, destined from the moment of the raffle.

The 17:32 S-Bahn is headed north to Germany, waiting in the station and the girls do board.

Receiving her train stub at the station kiosk, Katie looked at it, smiled at the ticket manager, and said, "5:32" She winked as he shrugged his shoulders. Katie won't have her keepsake since the umbrella could not go with them. The alpine spaciousness closes in on this little town that is only a few homes when one gets past the center *strasses*, no kind of nesting purview for a single man. They leave without a witness.

The hydraulic scolding of the door and the S-train heads off.

The girls have taken off their matching silver flats and are wearing separate shoes now. Marina is wearing jelly shoes which are like her feet but only blurrier. Katie has on a pair of au courrant white sandals with plastic straps that fasten by a pair of sliding buckles, a kind of futuristic variation on the shoes a tent nurse might wear in Colonial Africa. They flash their Eurail passes at the polizei, an old rail veteran from Eberswalde, near the Polish border, in Germany.

Marina skips sleep, or perhaps sleep skips her, and she sits not across from Katie but next to her, so she can stare ahead and only see a poster, a garish film comedy. A tiny blood speck has jumped like a flea onto one of Katie's shoe buckles. Marina eyes go back to the film.

The conductor hefts the Spezimatic railway watch that has kept him at peace with time's arrow. For years he was islanded from democracy, which gives him less of a sense of time. The watches are as unreliable as the Stasi were sharp. Now the time-piece gains minutes and he's given up all efforts to trap them in the watch. He sets it and expects the bum rush of the main-spring spindle towards its end. He sees the bespoke sirens in the car and perceives the eleven minutes his Spezimatic gains as a commentary on the ordinary pull of time. He sees black, which is a form of nothing but only what the living make it ….

.... When the train stops in the early dawn, the girls see a lakefront spotted with outsized doghouses, prudish cottages that only barely pass for human homes; above them, precipitous light pink dwellings tumble towards the rippleless alpine lake, the "town" framed scattershot around a tidy evangelical church spire. Arrested in this breezeless landscape, it is impossible to imagine battles could have ever caressed its sylvan face. It is impossible to see Hilberseimer's punk metropolis blooming as the crow flies to the west. Marina feels the air on her face, a scald of something speed has not the power to undo, though it had made it an inevitability from the start. Katie is staring at the mountains. They will board the train and head back to Berlin, which was where they were going in the first place.

Gorse

They picked up Wild Gorse at McCarran International and there he was, dragging a reptile skin embossed travel case. He wore a mackerel-colored seersucker meant to offset this spanking orange tan (he was less tanned than he was sulphured, really). There was something undeniably porcine about his face, his mandible unnaturally taut where it veered in; from the back, a bulldog's jetpack of loose flesh lunged from a space between his shoulders.

"Goddamn, there she is," said Hotchkiss, who was driving.

The younger one, in a red-striped motorcycle helmet, said, "I can't believe it. I can't believe he's here."

Gorse slid into the backseat. These were the men, his "escorts" to a valedictory on Paradise Road. He was there to receive a Lifetime Achievement Award, universal plaudits for his artistry from a weed-smoking panel at Adult Video News. There would be a lighted proscenium stage and vamping barely-legals there to ride him to the rostrum like Valkyries when the MC called his name.

For years, they'd assumed he was a funny topic. He was a louche German auteur of the hardest, most generous pornography from back in the heyday of the 1970s, a once-budding star of some gravely ambitious smut flicks that were bankrolled by his family's iron deutschmarks (they believed he was investing in a rabbit sanctuary near Encinitas). The films were omni-sexual spectaculars, nearly always pastorally set (a sylvan lake farm where nightingales chirped and fluted madrigals precipitated hedgerow buggery, a summertime idyll in Bled where the slinky commissars of Tito *might be watching!*). They were chiefly eponymous labors ("Wild Gorse is Wild Gorse in *Wild Gorse 6*"), premiering with neon marquees aggressively *de rigeur* for that glamour age. Gorse even purchased ad blitzes in the city press. At the height of his carnal fandom he'd been stricken with a pigment disease – Vitiligo – which stripped his skin of all color, and by the time *Wild Gorse VI* hit the Tenderloin its eponymous stud was whiter than an albino Iditarod. It drove him straight into recherché depression; it made his flamboyant pretensions sad. It somehow accentuated his German accent. It made him write letters in which he adopted the style of George Sand.

It was funny.

AIDS was not, but he was circling the punchline like a peregrine hoping against hope that a laugh would rear its head. The protease was making tracks with flanking maneuvers towards his inner Berlin. The Prezista and the Sustiva tanked. He was becoming a collage of mouth sores, manifold indignities of the immuno-suppressed. A bad bout of oral hairy Leukoplakia was chased out with radio ions and a shit ton of multidirectional bowel spills. He attempted other cocktails. He fetched up with quacks, denialists. He avoided cat litter and the niacin hazards of birdcages. The hits kept coming. Enteritis. Thrush. Cryptosporidium: Amazonian bung-insects as shocked to be thriving in the northern latitudes as Wild Gorse was to be hosting them. Strasser, his ID man at the Olgahospital, said, "You've met your resistance, friend. Thirty eight T-helpers. Better get the manor shipshape."

He was not ready for his close up, Mister DeMille. (Or did this mean he was?)

"We thought you were on a cocktail," said Junior Boyce, who belonged to the helmet, looking at the foundering German.

"They hit walls," said Gorse. "And then you switch to another and that one runs out and soon there is just this flea circus. Happier topics, please."

The limo was no automotive centipede tricked out for the rap stars whose music went right by him, but it wasn't any K-car either. It was an '01 Eldorado stretch, the upholstery a bit stained. They approached the airport exit. They would have two and a half hours to pretty up in the hotel room and then get themselves down to the Hard Rock where a mic'd host would await the clack-clack of his merry Vera Wangs on the runner. He would submit to a red carpet interview.

America.

What a run of months he'd been having. He'd been living with his mother in Stuttgart, devouring his family assets on a skein of Ankaran kept men, sinewy, hair-trigger catamites who'd had their fill of his dogged kindnesses, his maudlin mothering, and eventually cased his digs. Ran off with his mantle clock; a great piece some Schwartzwalder filigreed with little birds, terns on some gunwale in Danzig. He'd prized his attic trunkful of Reichs field articles (SS trumpet banners, flieger-uhrs, an Armanen rune belt buckle perfect for S&M, a nice Kreuz cutlass): gone. Those Ottoman hyenas cleaned him out, pointed his own jugend at his chest; the gadgets hauled straight to the Latvian marketplace. He would never see such aestheticizing of the End Days again. Because what could be expected of a terminal case? He despised Nazism but admired the Fuhrer's grasp of kitsch. If only they hadn't localized things, just killed everybody, gassed all creeds, *all* man; spared none with the Walpurgis lightshow …

But dear those Turks. Some elected to beat him when he didn't ask for it. He was a hit on two continents. He'd pined for the Valley, leading with his chin against the boot heel of the dreaming west, the ghosts of fatal Grand Dames who ran scribes out of Art Deco dream palaces. *"You can never write a script for me; you will never know love, young man! True love. My love!"* Would that he could be one of these. And now, finally, he was back. Now he would be wearing kimonos on a roof deck and using the high summer smog for a kind of dissolution-convalescence, a la Kenneth Tynan in the 1970s.

A la the parties. Garden champers with Angelica, Warren and Jack, *Rolling Stone* fledglings in miniskirts saying don't mind if I do to some speedball bonbons on a tray. He'd missed out on that, Bay-marooned, perceived amoral and underserving. Now they were old, Warren: hitched, Jack, moribund. Angelica the proud owner of a gullet. Nothing to blame but Father Time.

The exit signs to Vegas proper stood ahead. They were leaving the airport.

He daubed some blush on from a silver compact monogrammed with the initials W.G., tilting his head toward the rearview mirror. He saw his face: It was like staring down something mythic that stalked sheep in the Outer Hebrides. For assurance, he asked:

"How do I look?"

"You look a million," Hotchkiss said.

"You are a lazy liar."

"It is what it is, brother."

"I think you are a lazy liar."

Hotchkiss keyed the GPS to find where the Hard Rock was. It was taking too long for a man with a hurryup disease.

Gorse sparked up a slender Gauloises and dragged slow like a Stasi interrogator, "*Andale* to the American picaresque," he said. "I aim to buy snapshots of Waffle Houses and to have that Peyton Manning in this backseat. I want to saddle burros on a famous western butte and ride the arid pastures like the iconic gunslingers in the immortal Wayne 'flicks'."

"This guy's a fucking mouthful," said Hotchkiss to the man in the passenger seat. "Is this some kind of dementia?"

"John Wayne?" said Junior Boyce, turning to Gorse. "You grew up in Germany."

"We have screens. Germany has screens."

"What's it like," said Boyce, "over there?"

"I'm not over there; I'm here," said Gorse. "And I never wanted to be from anywhere."

"Well," said Hotchkiss into the windshield. "Nobody gets that wish."

"Quite," said Gorse.

"And if I was you, I would douse that cigarette," the driver said. "That packed tar don't do your breathing any favors."

The car headed off onto the boulevard.

Before Paradise Road there were many others and they were evidence that Man was here; substantially and irrefutably present, but a few hours earlier Gorse had seen all this as the tiniest white splotch on a miserable and oceanic sand sweep as the jetliner circled the airspace for a landing. He was a splotch and he had splotches.

They passed by a giant Popeye's chicken bucket atilt over used cars, overpasses, underpasses, hot pink arrows indicating proximity to the Flamingo Hotel. Bronze-painted minarets loomed high over neon wedding chapels. A factory-distressed brauhaus announced with pride it was the House of Veiss. What had Gorse missed of this America? Terrible reports: Around the set, there were coke rails next to condom wrappers. The gaffers put a foil over the ranch windowpanes and ate leftover Russell Stover chocolates. The male talent got their revs up by doing pull-ups on the uneven bars when the fluff boys were held up in the automotive cluster on the 101. They were entrepreneurs now, "crowdfunding" gangbangs. Words like "heteronormative" emerged.

"I'm going to call you the Fukashima Meltdown," Gorse said to the man in the helmet.

"Why?"

"That helmet looks like something on a Japanese firefighter."

"But I'm American," said Junior Boyce. "It's a look I'm doing."

Boyce was a gay porn actor, he told Gorse. He was starring in a movie about a man who takes a 1950s robot for a concubine. The movie was called *Pumping Iron* and it was due out on a website in February (Boyce's PlayStation handle: FanBoy. Hotchkiss was one who had drifted from different pleasures into that of being a "handler" and, at the request of the AVN Hall of Fame Committee, was to temper his antigay stance while chaperoning his new porn friends. He had been a deacon near Barstow once

Gorse listened to Boyce telling him of his future and found it was nothing at all like his past. What would he tell any of these people? What of his Von Stroheim fantasies? Striding the Chatsworth backlot with a croc-skin horsewhip stashed in his studded waist holster, firing a buck ringer from the Castro for blowing his glans out before the "take", quoting the maestro himself when he did it. He had once wanted to open a kennel for canine microbreeds using all the fine clear lines of Walter Gropius in the building plans. He was going to call it Bow House and make it a spectacle, a little meeting space for the pup-enthused on the planks of Sausalito. He was going to hold houseboat salons, end the nights by lighting candles on the casting deck and doing his imagined variations on Marlena's Weimar revues. Who in his present company would understand this?

He wondered if hanging on wasn't worse than dying.

Coming from where he did, he knew there was nothing more terrible than winding up on the wrong side of history. His friends from the dream days, the Bay martyrs, knew where they stood. He did not know this land or its ranges.

At the hotel, Gorse napped while Hotchkiss and Meltdown spoke in whispers. The two had set up a gaming system and all around the rug a rising tide of coaxials and toggle panels threatened to submerge the little space. Gorse fled to the high ground.

Waxy-eyed, he now emerged with what appeared to be an ancient stereophonic amplifier in a garrote of shiny black cords, setting it down on a nightstand and jacking it into the wall socket where it immediately began whirring like a Martian spacecraft. With his eyes closed, he pursed his lips, and his mouth seemed to water.

"Wild Gorse?" said the younger one with the meltdown helmet.

"You are wondering what is this thing, what is this contraption," he said. "It is a PERL-M machine, designed for heal me in lieu of meds."

"What does it do?"

"The machine uses argon plasma tubes," said Gorse, woozy from his catnap but still rallying. "Integrated light, gratis chronometer; a 230 VAC power pack. And this: Remote touchpad

I can hand-click to get even more healing frequencies from the transmitter. It snuffs the dirty pathogens using electro-magnetic resonances generated from a carrier wave. Imagine you are trapped in a sonic boom; echo power would decelerate your heartbeat and snap your bones. This pearl of a magnetron wreaks similar grief on AIDS cells."

"Does it work?"

Gorse wrapped a cuff around his wrist.

"Not yet."

"Not yet?" Meltdown looked hurt.

Gorse let the cuff build in pressure and raised his arm, holding it out, as though a sailor sighting the mainland through a mist. In the next room, Hotchkiss yelled into the telephone.

"We need nonalc, Jerry, virgin gin. Cranberry and lemon wedge thing. Maybe an Aid Kit and I dunno, an adrenalizer. We got a goddamn cadaver here!"

The PERL-M Resonator blinked off.

"Scheisse," said Gorse

They were getting closer to Paradise Road. Gorse noted the toasted almond sun that was different than the chicken-fried sun of hours earlier. There were back in the Caddy, possibly running late.

Hotchkiss slammed the horn; a slow-going pickup from a lumberyard nearly spilled its plywood cords onto their front end when the blitzkrieg of honking stunned the driver. It was a crawl. They were getting near the barrel-vault canopy on Freemont Street, even from blocks away, the colossal megawatt floor lasers set down on their block swivels were silently projecting John Wayne and his Appaloosa against the manmade curve of sky.

"Holy jeepers, it's the Duke," said Boyce.

Hotchkiss, through a mouthful of Rold Gold minis, said, "It's his birthday. They do that."

Since the windows were closed and they hadn't yet cranked *Stagecoach* from the loudspeakers, the effect was something like a meteor shower.

Boyce turned to Gorse. "Did you know that? John *Wayne,* Gorse!"

Gorse was silent, his eyes closed and he seemed asleep. They passed the cowpoke by in the stretch, the hood nearly whipped by his blinking lasso as they moved ever closer to the Strip.

But he was thinking. He was dreaming. Gorse possessed the Euro-tendency to view death as the final arabesque in the choreography of a maestro powerless to stop the flow of art into anything and everything in existence. He saw no flower as beautiful as his KS spots; convoluted reds and bursting violets like thermonuclear summer skies, the quartz whites of his dried skin rashes after the maculopapules seared his trunk were a miracle of modern pointillism. Immune deficient, he was as beautiful as the mod-banged honey traps he saw gallivanting around raver warehouses. Death (and what it was seemed bigger than one word) would be an outsider art coup de grace. The many dear ones who'd gone before him, those biker morsels at the I-Beam in Haight hiding their cherry sarcomas under chinstrap beards, the Ailey school fan-dancers strutting bare-assed from the scalloping of the taffeta curtains, bony as all get from the pulmonary Antietams they had claimed were merely chest colds, were too young to fathom that. They were too stubborn, wedded too vainly to their coils. The price of having good taste in an ugly world, he thought, was that one *appreciated* everything too richly; you looked so spanking grand it was unfathomable the road would not rise to meet you. He found this hard to swallow when he thought of the tyrannosaurs that thumped the Mesozoic plains only the wind up fueling rattletraps through Shell nozzles. Time was invisible but it sure did tick. Young people were only old people who didn't know it yet.

It would be so easy to not live. But he'd worked so hard at it. He'd had psychotherapy for his life, Adlerian thieves; sumptuous thinkers with fantastic probing minds running transcranial currents across his jellied noodle. R.D Laing. What for? They were contract killers, there to murder instinct with kindness, coddle his best thought before thudding it with a psychotropic cudgel. Death, a nullity, could not talk you into itself, and these witches, who thrived on the occidental promise of improvement, would prolong his gruesome existence out of nothing more than pride.

But was he not complicit? A man on the gibbet, about to ditch the somatic spin cycle, still fires some snake spit when the neck snaps and his undies reveals slippery, contraindicative substance. It never ends. Because, really, this is how it always begins.

Hotchkiss cranked the parking break. The valet sprung the door.

On the carpet in his seersucker, his bony pontoons troubled by the makeshift runner (neuropathy) he doubled over and phlegmy air from his throat hit the room air and people noticed. A bottle-black, nose-studded "alt chick", moved away with a burning scowl, her meanness was her calling card; she could do this. There were unenviable specimens from adjacent businesses all around; shadowy men, fired film technicians, un-sexed fanzine traders –agoraphobes who had nourished malign ideas about the softer gender now in love with all who passed by, men who didn't chew well.

Gorse was supposed to talk to a loudmouth trans pro-ducer who was working the red carpet for this gig. A few gra-cious nothings, some bon mots flung offhand and in his usual smoking manner, and move on, but it wasn't going that way. Right away the trans man buttonholed him, busting out of his chiffon, but Boyce and Hotchkiss pushed Gorse on through, backstage to the waiting area.

Gorse wobbled, the blur in his eyes clearing up. The juicy gaggles were there and saw death. The men in tight-ribbed tank tops, the girls-next-door projecting the image of the girls next door, the MMA fighting baldies with proprietary clamps on these girls. Who were they? Whither my loves? My passions. My mantle clock.

The man was the face to the name on the program, the fabulist of rut-spectaculars in loose costume, rank and natty. He leaned against a speaker near the curtain, feeling the blur of the kliegs, the hideous sporidium rising. A girl approached; but for her six-inch scarlet platforms, she might have been the host of a midnight omnibus horror show, circa 67', the comprehensive scream queen ensemble right down to the ace of spades hair. She had slathered thick mascara into loose, violet ovals around the sweetest and weakest blue eyes Gorse had seen from this distance in a while. She had been daddy's little muse in Edina once, or an Akron, Ohio telemarketer who saw life speeding by and said "Who, me stand athwart it?" Maybe her hubby, a hydroponic weed dealer, got pinched, and she'd flat-back a little under the Ariflex lens to make his bail. Then it became a life; usurped her. It had usurped everyone. The curtain of

Gorse's mind pulled up and revealed the welling of ambush tears, because the unanimity he was feeling could not be taken away from any of them; he needed them, these new ones, bound to maroon on the sick side of life when the sex stopped. It wasn't a sudden prudishness that made him fear for them. It was that they had so much ahead. They were too immersed now to know how much their lives would become preventative maintenance; how impulse would fade into second-guessing, second-guessing into no guessing at all, into a calcified screen over your very who-ness; a grime of oral thrush over everything you. He had been building to a valedictory of sorts well before Hotchkiss gathered him from the airport drive and if there was a grace to be found at the rostrum, it would be in the memory rush; a bracing frisson of all the good things lived through that would make the hellish ones worth the ride. It was a life's suspended notion brought low with secret knowledge: Memory is not enough.

And now he backed into a pipe on the wall. It burned him but no one saw it. The burn was real, and corrective. He began sobbing into his hand, because, like the gallows dick spasm, this was not the end; this was only the end of the beginning. This was the night of his charity, the showing of his mercy to *them.* The sweet muscle oafs, the chiffoned naiveté of these headstrong prima donnas; his very own Charon, young Meltdown. He wanted them saved: *Vater* Flannagan, he, Patron Saint of Bavarian Crème loads, Bugger Barker of Life's Big Circus Tent: wrap its sailcloth around these sad souls, hold them, bid them away: Tell them to run if they can.

"They're calling you, Mister Gorse. You're up next!" said Boyce, all peepers.

"Next?"

"Congrats to you and we love you," said the Alt Girl Scream Queen. He knew she didn't love him at all; but oh dear, how he did love her.

He could feel her hands on his shoulders. She was shaking his very bones. Boyce was giving him the thumbs up. Thirty eight T-cells. The neck snaps. Life clings to your last turtleneck. Don't be so young as to break down. Summon the reddest of your spots: Look them in the eye with your extinction.

Go.

Skaters

The light was hurting from up there. Dom Moore and Cameron Glover, watching the Swede's pelvis swing as she unlatched her motel door, wondered about the whereabouts of Roddy Villemeure. Glover a little more than his friend Dom, who was preoccupied by the lady as she turned the latch. Her factual motion which disclosed nothing even remotely performative in her limbs: They were natural as flowers, as sky. *I am me,* said the moves. Need I ever be anything more? Those jeans of hers debauched into sheepskin mukluks, cosmo chic of the bumpkin-citified, an urban goddess in rural gear. Moore thought of the factual capacities of all girls suddenly. Myla Rain Sweetwater, Carla Kunulu the homeroom girl (homeroom was every room here. Everyone crammed into a long wood room; spit and you were in the papers). Now the Swede put the key in the door, hip out as she cranked it; factual. I am fourteen, Moore thought. Could my future include such swinging? To go out and grab it, to steal a worm before the birds woke, to just shit on the dog's lunch this crumb of a musher's life insists on.

"Where's Villemeure," said Glover. "I'm scared."

"What?" The jeans didn't hide her shape; they were not those kinds of jeans.

"Scares me, you know. The other boys," he said, a little iffy in the larynx, his voice changing.

"Nah. Don't quit now. They was from other side of the Bay."

"I can't ever see Roddy just not showing." It had been two hours.

"Give him time," said Dom.

"How much more, till Christmas?"

Roddy was supposed to show up because the boys had managed to bootleg in a little suds from the Angry Métis, Cole Pickering, Nations man surly out the hydro works, worked at the Dene substation. Cole must've horded big sums in his aluminum trailer. He was gone driving most days; big, elaborate gambles in his flatbed Sierra winding into Roundeye zones where he would slyly procure his suds, get them the liquor octane they wanted though the town was dry. Enough belts of the stuff if you were watching the turning lights of the borealis, your mind raking things straight out of your own homemade folklore.

Dom looked up at the sky, grabbed an eyeful of dynamo stirring. It was a closer, low-lying phosphorous tangle under the moon's rays. He watched the Swede turn, her lush mane feathering out from the creamy divide of her center part; she watched the sky churning in the same greens he was watching.

"I'm worried," said Glover.

"Why would you be?" said Dom, watching one more hip sway as the door shut behind her. "Nothing to worry about at all."

Glover shook his head and went inside to the Propane shop and used the phone. Even a tard like Villemeure had worried parents.

Bill Sharpentier read in bed, *The Dene Trader*, all about no progress on the boys: the ice statues.

"Bloody number thirteen," he said to the woman stretching her arms on the edge of the battered bed.

"Confuses my heart," she said.

"I read it, my hair comes out."

"It's good hair."

"Am I laughing?"

A year of lumbering nowhere, meanwhile enough stone-deads on the frozen lake you could pull off a full squad with line changes. Now the gristmill was saying Swedes were here, landed yesterday, via planes, a miracle the telemetry braved the lights. Combing the lake ruins for fodder, the Swedes, or did they think they could help? Could they find the boys? Thirteen gone missing in the white over four years and nine months, their mukluks gone into the whirly scatter under murmuring light. The aurora had been stunning above the flat snows, its ions were caught shimmering in the other towns near James Bay; cars lost navigation, transcontinental air travel was rerouted away to southern points to escape the hypnotic hum. The electrons were blamed for mood swings, strange patters of otherwise reliable sled dogs in Inuit-inhabited plank houses. There was circadian upset, battery. The first seven boys were Inuit, tokers off the Census roll, and freezing to death was not uncommon, so "probes," such as they were, remained sparse. Once unfrozen, some boys were found with liquor in their gut—and liquor was arduous to come by, so anyone with a bootlegging past was given a once-over till the lawmen said All Clear.

But the pace was new this month: three boys gone in as many weeks. The boys had been jolly, carefree as they trundled out to practice skating strides, but then, unexplainably, they would want to go alone. No shinny on the lake or ice racing games among schoolmates. Hours later, after searches, after the rescue dogs had exhausted their trailing skills, they would find them. The grief was the only thing standard: Ernestine Muzzen went to her knees and hugged Luke Muzzen, the boy frozen in the cocked-leg pose of a right-wing taking a howitzer slapshot. Ten days later, Connor Blier was found bearing down clutching his whittled Koho, locked in a wrister mid-release. One had only to wait eleven days and Devlin Akiak was found: A fisher awoke in his bobhouse one-hundred yards out onto the ice to find Akiak feet away in a spraddle, hands on the nub and shaft of his Feather-lite, a pro stance the fisher remembered from so many promotional yearbook shots. The old Sahtu hauled the body across the ice on his back, crying tears that froze instantly at his lower lashes. On the banks, the victim put back down in his poster boy best, his extended clan of Tlingit singing under the phosphorous that blinked like silent heat lightning through the clouds.

"Keep on freezing, by god's lights, and you'd think, some progress," Bill said, flapping the paper to make the words maul her. The woman whose hair was only a little grey, and a fetching grey at that because she was younger than most who had it, came out of the bathroom clad in a dowdy robe. A ruby jewel in a wet shoebox.

"Scares the daylights," she said. "I ought to be getting home."

"Big cold."

She crossed the room and peeked out the curtains, like a jail-breaker in a road motel, the alerted troopers patrolling nearby. "Light is really humming out there. I doubt the street-lights should even be on. Put the hydropower alternators to the test. Shops should all be shuttered anyway."

"I got Marla at the shop," said Bill. "I want the night business."

"From who?" She started dressing now.

"Dunno," he said. "Got to be takers."

"See you wanna close up. Flip that sign over at six. Get the world thinking batteries they can't get, hair combs they can't get. Then they'll flood you in numbers." She hiked her jeans up, did some lively blouse-buttoning.

"Conveniences should be there till late hours." He smack-flipped the pages of his paper.

"I ought to be getting home. Roddy. Dinner on the table."

"Don't, sweetie."

"What?"

"I don't like mentions of kids' names."

"Because of what's in the paper?"

"No," he said, raising the covers and showing her his shrivel. "Not the paper."

"It makes you small."

"That's just the start of it."

"I shouldn't mention him."

"And I won't mention mine either."

"Can I say Denny?"

"Say him all you want; he come in roaring Wednesday last, big stinking huff about tire chains, what I gulled him because it wasn't the tensioner kind, says to me I misrepresented my chain stock, that I don't know my stock, or something like that. I think he was drunk."

"He doesn't drink. No one can, right?"

"Must'd got ahold of it somehow."

"A Nations. A Cree. Bootlegger." She stood up and faced him at the foot of the bed. The light through the drapes lit her left half and sunk the rest in darkness—a space that begged filling in, but he didn't speak, wouldn't. "You trashed my husband," she said. "So you say your kid's name. You have to."

"Carmen," he said.

It did hurt Orla hearing it, but somehow they were crossing a needed threshold; behind it something unknown would either save them or leave them brutalized, and the careening mess of it all put her in a place out of time, out of the asphyxiating certainty often waiting at the first sight of grey hairs.

Carmen.

Bill thought how easy it was to say his girl's name once he had taken the leap. Maybe it was too easy. When the ice thing on Madigan happened, he imagined Carmen and her friends forming a ring on the ice, a circle of them in mauve leotards for skating ballet, linked at the hands and jumping till they went in.

They looked at each other, Orla having stepped out from the shielding black. They looked at each other until they had to look down; the names had claws after all.

"Get going, grayhead," he said, smacking her chummy on the rear with the paper in his hand. "I gotta check on that Marla."

Orla tied up her grey hair. He could always get worked up seeing grey; it was "womanly." When a person wore the age well, it was somehow tragic in a way that felt of a purpose, as though handmade to your betterment buried in you: a carnal enrichment that gainsaid a fuller life because every grey breath of it was lived. Bill didn't want Grey Orla to start working in him, but that was what was happening.

She leaned in like a fist, kissed him; there was a fine dust in the air, caught in the light though the window.

Roddy had set out of his home holding a pair of Tackaberries by a tied string over his shoulder; these were promising new skates he'd got off secondhand from Charley Langmore's

Repo-to-Return Outlet, and he was hotfooting through the wavy drifts to try them out. He had his Bauer composite APX2 lumber ready to stickhandle in his left hand, and a bag full of his dad's binned regulation hockey pucks in his right, pucks collected from around the league and, as he hefted the antique puck—the one great Orr side-armed with enviable finesse into the stands in '72— he wondered if his dad would miss it. He'd only raided the garage once before when his pet guinea pig had stopped being Bobby Orr, but that time he chickened, and did not act. Of course, it wouldn't stay Bobby Orr permanently; maybe till school was done and he had to "man up" (dad's agenda) at Bay Hydropower, like dad. But strange little thing, to one day, just barely, not be Orr. No graceful rushes through stymied squads to the enemy net, blonde locks waving as he doodled with the vulcanized rubber. It stopped in the weeks after the night his sheets stuck to him; first they were wet, and then they stuck. The boy still was consumed by hockey, but it wasn't the same since the dream, and the guinea must've sensed it, bowed out of being Orr. The churning Northerns were saying "Play" outside the window above the cage where the little rodent flatly refused to be the estimable Bobby, stubborn rat. The mint-green in the sky said anything could be what you did with it: the boy saw the phosphorous churning, hefted the not-Orr guinea, remembering the little maul dad kept. It chirped a little, as much as daring him to call it Bobby, since it knew it wasn't. He set it down on the bench vise, a whim, but he couldn't give it a slow death, so he raised the maul and braved a nice downswing, swift as a skate stop that sprayed a goalman. He felt wetness on his coat. He grabbed the Tacks, flurried into the carport, scrounged the puck. He was marching out to the ice, through the weighted maples; the haranguing fist of the cold moon was blunted by the dynamo beam. He was going to play Orr's game: no pig necessary. He wasn't going to be a man and that was that.

The one with the Coleman lantern, deep behind a birch wall along Madigan Lake, thought: My head goes to the dogs. All the same, he was touting himself in his head: I am a good sort, was his thought, with mainly noncriminal inner workings, outside of the one that smarts. And it only smarts because *their* law has contaminated what is natural to say, you sir, this is out of the question. So what that my brain is a bust gasket; I've only begun to realize my wherewithal in Art. No more lineman's purgatory at the hydroworks; I've manned that dumb substation and sent watts into the Klondike snows, fed the First Nation's brain-glazes from back when the linemen spoke Innu and sent out horsepower currents into the valley, powered the plankhouse Diocese that fed workmen that long, caressing line of Magi bunk.

He looked at the lantern light, then closed his eyes, immersed in the blinking afterimage. He saw a trail of his life melding into the long white and, in a sense, he felt righteous. The man with the lantern was point-Oh-thirty-two Northern Cree but claimed a three-quarters' lineage. There were more than enough Cree to go around here but Cole, an Acadian French, wanted in; he thought it would explain the dawning spaces in his life, the slag he felt plumping in him that flooded over opportunity. So he claimed to be Cree waterman's one-fuck mongrel in the name of owning righteous complaint. Became is one-use human man, "supplies" the inevitable firewater. Bootleg as a French and you're a perv; you do it First Nations and you are folklore. He could be anything if he made

.032 his destiny; knowing a Cigar Store Brave is nobler than Frogs any day; consider their history lost a war in less time than it takes a moon to turn new and afterward went lickspittle on the winners. So he fudged, and they called him the Angry Métis, and to be that he became angrier (or, as angry as he was meant to be). But he had other reasons than the grievance of a Nations Man to be angry, and because he made that grievance the reason, he couldn't summon the other ones from where they hid. In hiding, they washed over him without him knowing it, and made him something else. Or was that the reason?

Where had it all gone, opportunity? Another word for "youth"? Probably. The Dancy girl took up three years with that marriage; had her in the altogether twice, but got sick looking at her one night and even though it was something he ate, it stuck around for whenever he saw her from then on.

But she didn't eat all the years, the "opportunity" or all the nonperverted thoughts that might have bloomed. Did she? There was so much she or anything could explain, like what had drawn him here.

Then something breaks this thoughts, or rather, completes them: Here comes the trudging laddie Villemeure and his skates on over the hill, thought the Lantern man as he watched him. Snug as a bug in his Macintosh, the little swisher tame as gumballs in windproof earflaps. Another one who'll try to break even in a world that was orphaning him before.

Watch him lace up those skates. Fit on those Tackaberries, little musher man. Tight.

Gunnar was already in her bed.

"I think some boys were watching me," said Britt, just shutting the door behind her. "And not even shy about it." Gunnar Gronstrand did not give the impression of being dressed under her bedclothes.

"We won't even need unnatural light to see each other. Just part the drapes. I like it controlling us. Galvanizes the limbs, if you like."

"Charming reader. You're a magician without a top hat, Gronstrand."

Gunnar raised the sheets: divestiture of imagination.

"I've barely checked in," said Britt.

She was tired but awake, and that was enough.

She wasn't surprised he'd beaten her here. The Scandinavian men always arrived as a team: Gunnar an aurora folklorist and Erland a neuroscientist of good repute. They didn't have families. Gronstrand had called her, told he had booked the place: Nagy's Road Inn, in three rooms though only two were really needed. Britt was there to bridge something, she wasn't sure what; it may have been just kicks. The men had done previous collaborations, attempts to chart the dynamo's major effects on the human mind, all failing to produce a salient outcome; the "data" they amassed seeming folderol to any of the legitimate quarterlies, easy pickings for the killjoys of peer review, but when they read about the petrified skaters it was only a matter of who would call the other one first. Britt, a criminal profiler in Uppsala, had arrived almost simultaneously, eschewing the electromagnetic delirium notion and, rather predictably, believing the boys had been called out to the water by a perp. Erland would fear her, Gunnar crave. She would marshal her wares: poll, assist; travel. Gamely, do the things one did, reminding herself that she had things to offer the commonsense types, the rural famous for lording jealously over their woodland sinecures, because didn't she have these things to offer? Gunnar and Erland were manageable; she had weathered flirtations with both men, Erland less so (it pained her, but the latter had the strange, vivid tripod shape of a storybook mammal that put her off). Beyond that, his attempts were uncertain. Once he had simply peeked over his notebook and told her, "I see you spearing fish in a pelt of your making, marooned," but she couldn't pin it down to a flirt; it might have merely have been observation. For her part, she despised the domestic cornering of Home. Like Gunnar, she found monogamy unsettling, not quite unnatural, but then neither were uranium mines. If everything was so ultimately rejiggered, reengineered and recombined, what did "natural" mean?

Her husband was a furniture magnate, her son cute— fiendishly lassoing a runaway heart she wished she could make run faster. Sometimes he seemed to belong to the jungle, but she knew he would refine until the wrinkles came. Then he would assume the drear anxiety that was rapidly transforming her from within. The "cycle" (nervily, it called itself that) would endure. The sun would fuck the grass the rain made drunk above the coffins, the terrestrial horseabout of mortals, born of natural sex.

But it was not theoretical that boys were dying. She saw a mortal instigator behind the deaths, but romanced the spirit notions—and where the lines blurred between what she knew was *right* and the carnal notions that myth would gamely tolerate, she reached and saw folklore as a compass through the fog.

So: Erland saw suicide, Gunnar saw myth. Which of these striving gadflies would she go to bed with? Gunnar, good Gunnar, had raised his hand.

With so many boys dying, it was nice not to have surprises.

Erland set up his C-pap machine, found his converter for the outlet. His bed did a fine thing and creaked ascetically. Through the window, muted light; the drapes were solid: of a hard cloth repellent to the electrons that banged against the reinforced glass. He could think here. He set out his books: Keenan Searle's *Climatic Variances* and a Clive Cussler airport purchase. He loved bare rooms, places where he could touch thoughts, no obstructing bookcases or women's frills to riddle. Gunnar would accompany Britt like an orphaned puppy on the plodding heels of a wifeless Italian pensioner. That was fine. He had scuttled romance, which was only something in *The Blue Lagoon.* Better to be a movie, a flick himself, where his big teeth gleaming— the fangs emblematic of his supremacy on the Pontic steppes— would make him a man to reckon with. His long neck and minimal shoulders: flexi-coiled, made to peer over fences or crawl though the bent wires of fences. He was *real* under the Northern Lights. Upon checking in, these Nagys were certainly askance. Britt wasn't making any apologies for being Britt, that's for sure. And Gunnar: a stye in the eye of good practice.

Erland peered out, flung the drapes. To horror fans, the most magical thinkers (Gunnar): an oblong sailing blob that stalked after winsome puck-handlers. Erland was unsure whether science could exist without magic, but knew that the opposite was true. On the north fjords there had been cases of herdsmen tracking after the plasmoid wind, wandering beatifically across grids of snow; the men were found hypothermic and smiling on the veldt after barely a brief wave to their dear ones, their goosedowns and auger gear nowhere in sight. Erland had once flown into Lofoten. Normally the lake saw skating boys, the slips of these gleeful skaters across its frozen top. On the day the neuroscientist was summoned, it saw a peacoated Laplander on its underside, smiling, hands pressed against the lid of his translucent coffin. Erland had stood there. The wind blew the collars of the boys, their eyes screaming saucers that saw wraiths. But that, of course, was not his business.

There was a knock at the door: Miles Nagy.

"You got to come out and see some folks."

"Okay," said Erland Rennberg. "What about the others?"

"I knock but they don't come."

"Did you knock persistently?" said Erland.

The man looked at Erland, and Erland couldn't figure out if he was dumb or angry. Erland pounded on the others' doors but got no answer. He could only assume they were out, separately or as two.

"I'll get my coat," he told Nagy. Nagy, a packed mound of gums and jowl, smiled in callisthenic fashion.

The boy did a kind of four-in-hand with the moth-eaten laces of his Tack skates.

"You how old?" said the man.

"Fourteen."

"How you like it?"

"Good."

He wrote words down in his head; sometimes he saw the letter curls get a nice imprint above the birches in the low sky, carved inside the dynamo trails, and he noted them there: dabs he would consult from his own head's palette.

"Those skates?"

"Tacks, my dad's Tacks."

"I was born with dimples."

"What?" The boy shifted slightly; he chunked a little bad ice with his blade, almost like he was prepping to skate away.

"When a baby has them," said the Métis with the Coleman, "they think maybe big things'll happen cause the little tyke is cute."

"You, um, were a cute baby?"

"Tell me why those skates."

"Dad's skates."

"What's he like?"

"Well, he's like dad."

The lantern man shook his head: Got a lot of work to do with this one.

In Nagy's Inn, Britt used the tip of her big toe to caress Gunnar's penis, making it bob up and down. When she did this, he raised his head and exhaled in an almost-paranormal bellow from deep within his abdominal core; doubtless, "loving" was really quite silly, thought Britt. A little pleasing friction against the arch of her foot and he would holler like a wounded boar and slingshot a week's worth of tepid nectar across her leg. This very projection had happened an hour before: a first-rate mood slayer. She looked out the window while he bobbed and saw an icicle's meltwater running down in sluices across the panes. She swore a sigh could be heard from somewhere out there, a metallic sort of cawing, like the high whine of a skate blade on ice.

Gunnar didn't hear it. Welling, fending off another projection, he had taken his glans off her arch and put her foot to his lips. Again he was brimming, in visible torment because he couldn't eat her foot, but he was really trying. Even if it had not all been risible, she knew she'd be distracted. She missed her son, who chewed everything there was to chew. He spent every second being as guileless as she felt when she made these searching trips and thought longingly of the dead men in the snow. Guileless because years pressed her advantage; he knew nothing, and she knew everything, and so it could never really be love between them. It would be guilt, condescension, and then resentment when the parity of maturation damned them to look back in shame. And now, watching this voracious manboy teethe her instep, she wondered what brought her out here, away from the real boy, whose patronage she needed: guilt she needed to hammer out. She didn't remember boarding the little Piper Lance on the runway at Iqualuit or even the moments getting off it. What call was she answering?

The night felt urgent, anyway, and it was.

In the Villemeure kitchen, Erland gulped an alkaline mouthful of rosehips from a little teacup, Officers Tyne and Richard sitting next to him, rapping their wedding-ringed hands off the table.

"Has Roddy shown any penchant for these kinds of night outings?" Erland asked the parents.

Mum and dad shook their heads no.

"Uneven temper?" No again, said their heads. Erland noticed that the father couldn't shake a sneer.

"He's been experimenting?" The officers cocked their eyes at Erland—a sideswipe, this, eh?

"As in what are you talking?" said Denny Villemeure, leaning forward on his elbows. The sneer was a kind of sagging cleft.

"Sexual explorations. Drug tries?" said Erland. "I knew around here there is drugs."

This made Denny raise a finger. "Now you gonna *listen...*"

Officer Tyne craned in: "That wouldn't be a thing here, see; very, very tough a man'd get his hands on the liquor."

"But it gets in," said Erland.

"Very, very tough, hands on the liquor."

"We're dry," said Orla Fitzsimmons.

"But there is an epidemic," said Erland, "And if one can't get that, what do they get? They improvise."

Denny Villemeure needed coolant; the officers knew they were wise to be here.

Richard, untested by the grim routines that dogged his superior, Tyne, put a hand on Denny's wrist and looked at Erland. "Not with Roddy. I can't begin to speak for the other boys, but with Roddy—"

"He's a little different," said Orla Fitzsimmons. "I mean. It's."

"Could we say Roddy likes things and not at all in the way you or I do? We could say that, right?" said Officer Richard.

Orla nodded.

"How so?" said Erland.

"He's got some imagination," said Denny (contributing), his eyes no cozier, though. "He's a bit what my mum calls a dreamer. Don't let Orla say no tard here."

"Denny." Orla.

"Dreamers have wishes," said Erland. "Dreamers can go to places where the only thing to do is medicate."

Orla said, "We should go. We ought to really go! He doesn't think."

"Hasn't been…"

"…Denny…"

"…much time. Much time at all."

"Denny thinks the boy's just a boy," said Orla, looking at Erland. "Like any boy."

"Yez just don't know me, mum, not at all," said Denny. And after too long a time for it to count, to register anything, he pounded the table—baring his teeth but no one saw it.

Detective Richard looked towards the pantry off the kitchen and saw minute dots of red leading out. He got up from the table.

"Where you off to?" said Tyne. "Hot date?"

"Mind if I?" said Richard to Denny and Orla, who shook their heads.

In the pantry the dots got smaller, but something shook Richard by the neck, a flicker of wind through the window, a nearly percussive blink. He unlatched the door to the garage and the dots became bigger again, broadening into a continuous stripe that eased into a feral vermillion and stopped at a row of paint cans; under the petrified strings of acrylic spillover, a bright metal sliver could be seen, the light from outside sp_king in.

"*Jeeesu,*" said Richard, in a whisper.

"It is only one muscle ring," said Gunnar across the table, tilting his wineglass that did not have wine in it but a kind of unleaded apple sputum Britt's way. "It dilates expeditiously with the right oils. It isn't like you go just shove it in."

"Borji tried. Once."

"Not a propitious evening?"

"Disastrous." (Sip). "And it isn't supposed to go there."

"One man's trash is another man's treasure."

The Inuit innkeepers were sipping milk at a table on the left side of the parlor, away from the fire; they shared a leathery, almost Austrian reserve.

"I'm here to profile," said Britt.

"Start with me."

"Sick bastard."

"The mice will play."

"The mice don't always."

"They'll play," he said, gazing through the snow globe of rising pulp in his wine flute at the delicious specimen across the round divide. "I should've pocketed one of those little airplane bottles. Now there is nothing but vegetal shit."

"I need to be pliant," she said.

"Especially where I'm going!" he said.

"Sick bastard. No need to expand on my diagnosis."

He thought: I have gone too far, and, as he was wont to do, blamed it on the light.

They parked on the Nanisivik Road, which had a small trail through the birch woods to the lake. Tyne had gone back on Erland's request to fetch the remaining Swedes at Nagy's and would meet up with them later on the rim. Orla saw a weather-beaten plank house crouched on the muddy lip of the frozen water, green, termited plywood nailed in place of the windowpanes.

"Used'd be little Dene guy who throat-sung kind of thing from in there," said Richard. "Loon sound. Only sound a mile out. That elder'd sing out and your boat'd near flip if you was pulling bass from the water."

Richard was young, and chatted in bright rhythms, like a mind just flickering awake.

"He got a son who burned him down, blowed off some Wyman's floor cleaner. A chef, you know? Man burned clear so his skull was bared."

"I've got the willies already; I don't need more," said Orla.

"Sorry, ma'am."

The Swede blanched. Erland himself was a risk to be infelicitous. He was here to be clinical, after all. Nothing he would ask her would be the right thing. It was a matter of sugaring his approaches; perhaps affect the opposite of the Socratic interrogation. If he made statements, overbearing comments on fear, tragedy, she would align with him.

"Children these days…" he said, louder than he wanted. That was a start. But when he looked up, she had moved twenty paces ahead, once again next to Richard.

They parted some alder branches, and now they were on the main beach side. Richard shone his four beamer, examining the lake ice with even spray. He yelled out for Roddy; the padding of winter snowfall killed the echo fast. Orla feared negation, total negation, on these shores.

Where was Bill Sharpentier, who got things done? But, wait, that was blasphemous, nearly. Hadn't they laid the moral manure that led to Roddy going off? Officer Richard sprayed the beam, working in subzero to smoke out what any other person would deem a halfwit. He was *her* halfwit, though, and shouldn't it come down to that? Whatever she'd done with Sharpentier, she was entitled to her possessions. She should not feel pained watching the foursquare Richard and his noble beam.

"Roddy admires the Northern Lights. Don't the young respond to bright things?" said Erland on her tail. It nearly jolted the life out of her.

"Yes. I dunno. Yes."

"When they glow, he is more apt to display a sense of wonder."

"Yes, I suppose. Can we do this another time?"

"No."

"*No?*"

"This is pertinent."

"Jesus *Christ.*"

Officer Richard stopped spraying the beam. He put a hand up in a hushing gesture. Then he shook his head.

"What?" said Orla Fitzsimmons.

"You sometimes hear the sound of pucks, kind of clap on the ice."

"But it's not that."

"No," he said, "It's the sound of an old tree falling."

The lantern in his hands, running on white gas, might be running down. He conveyed this probability to the lone boy, gesturing to the rod-like mantles that ran orange glow into the lidded beaker he was holding.

"Maybe you don't need it," said the boy.

"Name some players," said the man, turning down the lantern until there was nothing but the aurora for good light. He was squatting, as though an elder over a ceremonial fire. The boy was rocked back kneading his shinbones with his forearms, his butt going numb over packed snow.

"I like Bobby."

The man nodded. "How about David Backes?"

"I don't know."

"You don't know."

"I like Bobby.

"You get the Russians too. Fast. They go fast. You like them when they go fast?"

Now the boy nodded.

"Bobby went fast."

"More," said the man. "Gotta give me more."

"I dunno. I like Bobby."

"Which Bobby? Bobby Orr? Bobby Hull? Bobby Clarke? You got Bobbies out your asshole in this game."

"Orr."

Now the man got mad: "Well, goddamnit, shithead, there's more than one fucking hockey player out there in the goddamn world!"

"*I don't want you to be mad!*"

"Then don't *make* me mad!"

"I don't know!"

The man laughed and this hurt the boy, although the boy didn't know why he should be hurt or why the lantern man should find himself laughing. The laughter was of a kind that seemed ripe with what it thought could come in the future; not a past-looking laugh as he saw in his father; *that* was a chuckle at the sight of a falling brick, the last silvery sip of backwash in the Labatt's can.

"Taste, you," said the man.

"What?" said the boy.

"You got some kind of taste in hockey players. Bobby Fuckin Orr. Go all the way back to the cavemen why don't you?"

Roddy shook his head: "The others weren't my guinea pig. My guinea pig was Orr. He told me."

The man smiled now, chuckled distantly, and shook his head.

"Man, I sure know," he said, "how to pick em."

Gunnar had her like so: her belly down on the bed and her hands clasped together behind her back, as though handcuffed. He was on top of her, one big hand keeping hers bound at the palms and the other pulling her up towards his chest by the hair as though he were raising a heavy anchor; with each inch the back of her head rose to his chest, he was further in towards her intestines. It really was one little barrier of sinew—a matter of relinquishment, thought Britt—and, as the act shed its mystery and the adrenaline surge fled away, she really was his anchor going up, and her shoulder blades began to burn her. There was a kind of synovial popping, pure fright. She began interrogating the haphazard chandelier of condensed hydrogen droplets outside the window, the small ice strands decorating the overhang of Nagy's.

There was a sighing out across on the ice. It was a sigh familiar, a little trill her son made when she had been salving his backside, a tragic protest under the invading lasers of bathroom light. Did the sky here make sound? She wanted to bolt up but couldn't, and the words spilled.

"It's happening," she screamed.

"What? Are you hurt?" said Gunnar.

"I don't know!"

He was climaxing. She could tell from the flickering pressure, a sharp run along the hem of her side.

"Something's wrong," she said.

Gunnar was panting, receding out of her even as he was right on top, tracing her limbs with his own, as though trying to hide her with his body.

"Everything is right," Gunnar said, noting the sleek, almost radiographic scatter that breached the drapes. He was folkloric on his belly, a bullish cairn they were making, runic under the splinters of unnatural light. He couldn't impregnate her from here, and he thought the Japanese would frown. They propagated under the auspices of the dynamo, their inheritors made magnetic by the blue emissions. The Finnish Samis saw the lights as an arctic fox, a kind of ethereal vulpine that slung lasers from Orion's Belt, tracing the luminous patterns with the tip of its tail. Other Finns saw games of football on high. Gunnar would have perished had he stopped and thought "heat levels," "radiation belts," "substorms," "small intestine." So: Light poured out through holes in the sky, foxes scrawled light: and that was that. Britt moaned heavenly and he pushed more. The cairn wobbled. He could see those Labrador mushers, nudging a soccer skull across a cirrus plain, telling the live ones left earthbound to rein in their bereavement, and play.

Everything is right.

There wasn't even blood on the bedspread.

The boys' view of the Swedes was blocked by the Nagy's drapes, and now they were too bored not to think with a little bit of fear that Villeameure was still a wrench in their game plan.

"We ought to trek, or something, for him," said Glover.

Moore was shivering. He had his hands in his pockets. He worked his blood up enough to shrug so his friend could see it.

"What?"

"Why we care so much?"

"He's good, Dom."

"…fucking got a gasket bust. Brain is all over his damn coat sleeves, you sure know it?"

"The Métis guy don't work out. Bet he's gone west on some other booze runs. Bet some guy in Great Slave'd pay a little more handsome for his shit."

"I had this night worked in my mind: Roddy Tard shows, we got the Métis's blend, and maybe I crank one into the snow. Get this Viking bitch out of my system."

"You don't think he's at the lake?"

"Damn is no way I'm trudging over to the lake."

"Find Roddy?"

"Damn is no way I'm trudging over to the lake, find that Roddy Tard there."

"Get some idea where he's gone to?"

"Damn is no way, Glover, I'm trudging out to the Madigan and not cranking this Swedish bitch out of my balls, once and for all, in a snowpile. And you can go trudging to where you are content, and like, seeing the mysterious spirits born, because your whole brain is froze out."

"Fine."

"I'm going back to my Sega. Then I'll jerk off."

"It fixed?"

"You bet so."

"*Minecraft?*"

"Yes."

"*Diablo?*"

"Hey dink-head: Jerk off, yah?"

"We didn't finish *Diablo*."

"We will. We got scores to settle. But I gotta jerk off, yah?"

"I'm stuck in a Dungeon Level I want out of."

"Not to mention there's the *EA Hockey* I got too."

He was shoveling.

The traction soles of his pac boots sanded bald by gathering winter rock salt. Slipped on a patch now and his bum smarted. A tailbone slammer: The final insult was never the final one. Denny had a head full of gunpowder: Rise up, you limp dick, and dust off. The lights hovered like a cloudbank over the crosstown moguls, making a perfect spotlight over Sharpentier's place.

What he would do with that shovel. Walk maybe on over there with *that.*

He had watched Orla head off, presumably with the cops and the Swedish guy—the nerve this quiff had worked up that she would now see fit to follow through like you saw in a proper mother. On the other hand, could he blame her?

Denny Villemeure stared at the lights and thought: I collided with Life the moment it reversed engines on the womb and the docs barked me down that mother tunnel. His lips had been mangled in strange ways by the forceps landing, never to look like other mouths. He would slur like a tippler without drinking booze. Barry took the nefarious haymakers of common sleaze like a class act and swallowed; who could blame anyone for slinking around behind his back? Say one took Denny on his face: He'd been handed the crown jewels on Ellesmere, foreman at a generating station, there to draw 7357 kilowatts to James Bay from the stone dams in the Eastmain tributaries. Denny the morose, now Captain Morose and his delegation of Red Nations trapeze men shimmying up the transmit wires and sucking the last good terawatts from the spillway. Keep the drilling rigs in full drive twenty-four-seven, keep a working force of Baker Lake glue-guzzlers chuffed as little songbirds on the wellheads, keep the town lights blinking, fire the turbines. Harness! But he was a chump at the core in his duties. The inborn sneer did not intimidate. They thought he was inebriated constantly. "They undermine me!" he would tell Orla, throwing things. And on the other end, the bosses: They had him browbeating tribal elders whose only offense was hounding after a day's wage without snogging to damn boot heels of the Hydropower.

He made foreman one week before Moses Doig hit the alternating current off his hardhat, misjudging a four-way grid, and his face was just gone with the buzzing. Smashed onto his back a hundred feet riverward, and Denny chucked his guts. A more stark sonofagun'd say a prayer and call the men into the trailer. Denny vomited, passed out, and was an intruder forever after that.

Then there was Roddy. *Off.* You had to be strong to be a father. What was the point? They were young and you weren't. You were no longer young anymore, and there was no sense in heaven's name pretending young could ever be the thing you were again. The thing was to get down on their level, scrap with them among the Tonka trucks. But if you were to get down on their level, you would *all* die. Most kids are trees: Cut em open by the year, and the rings of what you made them become clear to you. Roddy cut would have no rings, be the same and you'd never know the good you'd done him. Denny remembered health adversities, the doctors who said the kid would have trouble with "coordinative" things, a small kidney, bad eyes on the drift to different sight fields so a yoyo among braintrusts was what he looked like. He tied to teach him games; Orla did the motherlies, but that was only out of fright. Denny worked this kid, his sweet yoyo Roddy, and now he wasn't only thick, he was out the door: probably going horndog but who would lay him, and he'd never understand sex beyond what his friends would say, a foreign language. The hurt was too great to go chasing. *Off.* Only buddies is Dom Moore and that quarter-Dene sick fuck Glover. They'll show him the light of the bootleg jug: a life dipping into Porto-Sans with model glue. They'll rebaste my little turkey.

I am not going to the lake. Let Bill the storeowner squire the runaround wifey to the lake. They'll go and find the boy. Bill's certainly got his fair share of augers. Some real good tools on him.

"My bros, they got me the hard stuff and it's waiting."

"I know your bros; they'll drop some back without you."

"You're looking at the ice?"

"You'd think a man knows his sculptures. I'm trying to get a world of my own. Ice is where my work is."

"I shouldn't of used my papa's maul—"

"Ice, brother. The unknown world can happen on it."

"What are you doing with my legs?"

"Stay right here."

"I shouldn't have—"

"Don't move."

"I shouldn't've killed that pig."

"Let's get your stick like that."

"I can't stay this way."

"I'm losing the body, and so I'm going to turn the lantern up."

Gunnar, Britt and Erland sat under the kipper waves of Lt. Tyne's campfire, ducking the lake wind. Richard sent a four-beam current into the birch wall, but the dynamo's descending radiance scooped the ray. It had taken some time to link up, but they were now a "party," taking shifts to look and listen, to hug to the rim of the lake and hope they would sight the boy. Orla had decomposed in anxious waves and was sitting in Lt. Tyne's green cruiser, running through the hideous probabilities, listening to the CB static overplay Tyne's contemporary Nashville tapes, alienating. She was past and future but not present.

Britt saw the firelight under Gunnar render the man ghoulish; he had done an impaling thing, made her tummy a shaken vial of air and gut flora. Had she taken this far enough?

The sap popped in the angled kindling and Britt observed her search team: Tyne had an infant's roundness, and in this ring of men, she—the only emissary of femaledom—was able to see with certain clarity: They were boys. They are all boys. The clothes are enhanced for aging, the features have begun to capsize, the vigor of their dermis breaking down, but the charm of them—if there is any—is that their world is still a contest. It is games that are the gills from which they breathe. If I were not here, they'd all be happier; I matter but not as flesh: I must be elusive to them. That is why a little touch hurts so bittersweetly when they get it: When I go the whole hog with them and their wincing ensues: no campfires, so jungle Jim. The gills are all verdigris.

They were having a high old time. Erland and Gunnar, dissimilar but identical patrons of these contests. Tyne was greedy; inside him lived a teenybopper leaping over the red ropes for a hip-swiveling man of song. Richard had his role: unsullied, thin, but really, did he mean it—this flashlight waving, the effortful minesweeper's stare? She watched as he sat back down, rubbed his hands together, and dug in to a sandwich as heartily as a winger after a day of skating drills.

There was silence, a lack of game; hours had passed, signs of the boy were unpromising, and after some silence Gunnar said, "Hell."

"What?" said Erland.

The men began to talk. Tyne chimed in. Britt lightened. The fire cracked. The search team began talking about what would become of you if your own misfortune landed you in Hell. It was that subject, and could have been anything in the white space.

"You bale hay," said Gunnar. "But the hay is all packed tumors, giant malign squares that have teeth growing in their sides. Fat men whip you while you stack the clotted cancer."

"You have only small dreams," said Erland. "Your shoes are small, but your feet want to clomp sturdy mountains. You see rain in clear weather and songbirds have a bat's visage. It's all vaguely warped and topspin-like, as a slice you get sometimes on a golf ball."

"That ain't Hell," said Tyne.

"What is Hell, then?"

"Hell?" Tyne jabbed the fire with a loose stick. "Put you in a lobster tank with all the lobsters you ever ate."

Villemeure had this thought on the lake ice, the lantern man down by his Custom Tacks: He's got me in a good pose now. Orr Mouse, I see it in his sadness, his sad face of a mouse creature. I trust that I should not have did what I did; I apologize to Orr Mouse for blowing my stack and sleeping papa gone mauling won't have the mauler if he needs. But I'm hopeful for the first time since my garage knife that Orr Mouse is not dead. He could be the Angry Métis.

He could see a campfire on the other bank, say, not a hundred feet from his position. There was some lively types it seemed, people, trading stories—you-speak-I-speak—like people in the world did do. They were near but also faraway like Dom Moore and Glover; you could not get *inside* them. The pose Orr Mouse had him in was something he would like to show them, but they wouldn't begin to understand.

Don't call out to them. Don't spoil it.

Lantern Man pulled the other leg high.

"Hell is always on its menses," said Gunnar. "In Hell, there is always catches: You get to fuck Jean Seberg on a live bear rug. You have orgies with couture chicks, but your mother is always watching."

"…they jam you in a small refrigerator," said Britt. "Unplug the refrigerator, and put you in there with a bagpiper who exhales funereal hymnals for like twenty-four hours a day."

"Hell don't got hours," said Tyne. "Hell isn't measured in time."

"Right," said Erland. "Terminal eternity. Beyond lunisolar. No mortal mind conceives time on the present terms down in there with that demon colony."

"Anyway," said Tyne, sipping eggshell coffee. "Hell don't got hours."

"Ring saws," said Gunnar, after a palled pause and the crackle of the little fire. "Ring Saw Frisbee."

"No, no, no; no blood," said Erland. "A mucus toucan squawks from a snot-rock waterfall. You have to shower eternally under the raining snot."

Richard shone his flashlight at their faces, and they all heaved back, a flurry of protest titters.

"Clam up," he said.

"I should remind you," said Tyne, "of my seniority."

Richard walked deeper into the woods.

"You get down there," said Gunnar. "And they conjoin your balls to a trailer hitch and pull you down a flaming highway. And this ride takes forty-thousand years."

"And that's just in the first five minutes," said Tyne.

"Pack forty-thousand years in five minutes? Prorated time?" said Britt.

"No time under the auspices of Satan, remember," said Erland.

The fire cracked.

"You share a jail cell with a reggaeton mammoth," stabbed Gunnar.

"What in the hell is a reggaeton mammoth?" asked Tyne.

"It is a mammoth that bellows reggaeton, extremely disagreeable substrain."

"Mammoths is extinct," said Tyne.

"Not in Hell," said Erland.

Orla had crept away. The fire had been burning, and the Swedes and the officers were very much taken with that. Mulish laughter protected them, fastened them groupwise to the rim. No chance Roddy would be sighted here; even Richard, noble Richard, was untrustable. The lake was a winding specimen and the black night would not yield Roddy because Roddy had been gone since he came. How many years? Denny had been counting and she had been out on Bill's bedspread gathering wool.

She wrapped her frock tight to her chest and sloshed in her mukluks through the trail; the frosted bramble crunched on her soles and she tripped over some downed branches licked with hiding ice. She didn't look down, only ahead, until the packed trail ice became road and road followed the lights across town. She could trace the years in her carriage, in the creak of her footfalls. There had been an immensity of lost days: diaper changes, the primitive dumb show of routinized care: nourishing his sad Orr fantasies. The seizures when she couldn't hold him hard enough: how the effort was paining because that's what it was: effort, not nature. If he had been a stud show horse, would she have suffered beyond lamenting all the waste? Denny was soothing to the thick boy because he cared, and she was jealous of that. Her life had been momentum, nothing more. The afternoons with Sharpentier were a cleave down the middle of all that, but all it had felt like was fun: a little devilry that would not put the brakes on her wrinkles. To turn back, head to the lake, would be to rot with Denny and what he'd faced, go cockeyed with Denny and his hydro-Denes. She did not stop walking until she saw the clock radio gleaming through the window by the sleeping man's double bed: It read 3:30 AM. She was pleased to see his chest rise and fall.

"Bill," she said when he came to the window. She had thrown a little ice chink.

"Orla," he said, as though completing a sentence. She looked like a little girl in her frock, the halo of fading aurora making her face green as algae.

"My grayhead," he said, after raising the window and taking in the cold that strafed in off the lake a mile away, nestling in the ice of her fur collar. "I've been waiting for you longer than you'll ever know."

The light, at this moment, did not seem like a stranger to her face.

The white landracers would gather at the high drifts of dense snow packed in the shadow of the massifs, the clarity of the overlook that gave the dogs their sway over the creaking lake ice, the snarl of the meltwater under it. Whatever ore had been scoured from the washes, whatever southland Robber Barons had clobbered the iron mines, ripped gold from under the braided moss banks and blinking rosebay of the paleo-arctic terrain, the dogs had had no part in it. They howled and stayed limber on the snowbanks and steered clear from noisy kayakers, the crack of the hunter's guns. They looked up, not down, and saw the glimmering lodestar, the lux currents that drove them to the lip of the known world, the glacier conclaves that stirred below. They would raise their muzzles and howl into the light.

From their promontory above the frozen lake, the dogs could recognize human figures; a man and a woman, up against a tree. The woman's hair had a pleasing windblown texture, messy how the man would like it, and he was crouched down behind her, his head in a place the dogs knew. The dogs liked this place, but when his tongue made the sloshing noise the dogs knew from their metal bowls, the woman said,

"Ease off. Jesus."

It embarrassed Gunnar, but he kept up. Britt had her hands on separate tree branches, balancing. She worried about the camp; it was light now, and the boredom that had carried them to this node only yards from where Tyne had set camp was now subject to worried revision, examination; it was Gunnar's idea and she hadn't demurred. "Like we're running a thermal test." He could've said anything—in this white space, out of time—jetlag and runaway failure—she would be hard-pressed to find anything a radical act.

They had slipped off when Tyne was dozing, Erland consumed, Richard in the cruiser with Villemeure (son of a choirmaster, consoling). When she had found some solid footing, Britt wriggled out of her pants, yanked down her thermal lining in a thick patch, and Gunnar went slavish on his haunches.

The night was so cold they warmed up, but now it was morning, and as the light thickened through the sagged trees, Britt, on her tiptoes, wiggled away from Gunnar's clutch, the braising of his teeth. Something peripheral had troubled her: an object, striking as an unfamiliar car in a neighbor's driveway. She hiked her jeans up, chastely, not urgently, thumped some snow off a hanging branch and saw the lake as a proscenium under an electronic vault of sky.

And she didn't know it, but it was a photograph of Bobby Orr, the one taken when he clinched the Cup for Boston in

1970. In the shot she didn't know, Orr has just tapped in a pass from behind the goal net and, upon sealing the win by a simple shovel of the runt disc past the reeling minder, is tripped by the stick of a defenseman for St. Louis. Orr hurls into the air, horizontal over the rink's surface, his stick perfectly vertical in his right hand while his left punches out to brace against the inevitable fall. His face is giddy but assured: For some, flight is simple.

When Britt waved aside the alder branches, she saw this expression on the boy's face. The positioner could not hope to recreate the famous shot, but his proximal best was worthy.

Britt padded a little further out and saw the face was white, the body scaled with ice, mist pellets that froze into barnacles on contact with the insulated corpse. Gunnar walked a little behind her, wanting to rest his head on her shoulder. Britt looked back. The cruiser was parked through the trees, the fire faint but still burning. The flux of the aurora was visible above the lake, muted at the edges and in the center, a whirring heartbeat of searching light.

The Clinch

To get to Amagansset there was no way to skirt a one-lane road except to take another one-lane road; bumper to bumper on a five-mile run. Gabe looked at Yael in the passenger seat, the stack of hatboxes and travel bags behind her. She had packed with her usual Prussian rigor, and though idle, looked equally determined now.

"Kai will have to reheat his basmati casserole by the time we arrive," she said.

"I dread that casserole," said Gabe. "You can bet Carl will be belching that long into the night. A summer tradition."

The sun smacked off the dashboard blindingly, but he began to feel a spike in his mood, imagining Julia and Carl clearing Happauge on the broad back of the eastbound Jitney, Julia staring longingly the roadside stands while Carl thought only of the gallery. It pleased Gabe to think Carl's laborious scrape jobs would lie there like calcified manure for the gallerist to sell. He knew all would be fine at Sandy's. His oak of a houseman Kai Boone, awhirl in his vermillion day robe, would have caipirinhas and tiger prawns to greet them under a heady flight of gulls. Julia would drink those caipirinhas, liberated.

He would just have to weather the ride. He and Yael had tussled all the way out on Route 27; the Audi was warmer than on most drives, the A/C compressor on the blink. Near Center Moriches, a stray bird struck the windscreen. Yael screamed and Gabe got mad with fear. A severed wing lodged in the wiper blade. An eyeball slid its way down the glass at a lulling tempo, strangely sentient.

"I wonder what kind of bird it was," Yael said an hour later.

"A red-crested asshole," said Gabe. "I see a crack."

"Where?"

"There." He pointed.

"I don't see it."

"You don't wanna see it. That is why you don't see it."

"Well I don't see that crack but I sure see a fissure in my mood."

He would let her have her fissure. He could focus. He had resolved that back when they were packing, perhaps well before they were packing; this would be the year to see it through. Sandy, wonderful Sandy, had introduced him to Julia their first summer out. Sandy had known Yael and Julia's husband Carl from their days at Exeter, when he taught them American Literature, having kept up with alumni quite frequently. To the manor born, he rusticated separately in two waterfront homes – one on a lake near Woodstock and one on the beach on Long Island, and loved having this foursome out to play. He was an original Stonewall rioter, bound to a motorized wheelchair after a surgical mishap, but he was never caught frowning. Gabe sometimes thought they were all on hand to supply dramatics; their hetero-travails bearing all of the sweet tang of a sentimental Catholicism Sandy had always thought pretty in his youth.

Julia was a yearly promise, somehow miraculously fixated on Gabe. To see her he'd have put up with Carl, her hulking lover-son who batted out unwieldy paint sprawls on giant scrolls of flashspun paper, Tyvec home coating mainly–something "recontextual", or so it went – but Carl was a limited obstacle compared to the mercurial heavens. Gabe was left probing the subconscious roots of his anemic lust; was he secretly ambivalent, or was Julia? Whatever the reason, the two could never quite get it done.

There was '06 in Woodstock to begin with. While Carl and Yael discussed the Ashcan school in Sandy's farmhouse kitchen, Gabe and Julia waded into the backyard creek and lurched to begin necking. They were really getting at it when Gabe took a header on some sphagnum and hit rock. The pain was unreal. He couldn't express it for the noise that would travel, and Julia, feverish, anxious, stunned at the unmanly rictus in front of her, turned tail and gusted off into the house without a word. Gabe toddled from the rock floor bitter, blushing, variously and throbbingly contused. They spent the rest of the weekend talking around each other, finding distance at the table, Gabe explaining his wounds to Yael by barely lying.

"I fell on the sphagnum," he said.

"What's sphagnum?" said Yael.

"Moss," said Julia.

"How does one fall on moss?"

"It's moss in the water, like, fur," said Gabe. "I was going for a dip."

"Fur isn't slick," said Yael.

"You want me to show you the sphagnum? It's there. On rock. You can slip on it."

"Sphagnum," said Carl, spitting crème fraiche through pursed lips.

"What?" said Gabe.

"That's a funny word!"

"Enough, Carl," said Julia. "And fur *can* be slick."

Yael said: "If you say so."

"I do."

A summer later at Amagansett, as they scooped up their forkfuls of fusili on the ocean deck (unshellacked, in duck's egg blue), Gabe passed her a note stating his wish to meet on the sprawl, in secret.

Leaving the table, he whispered to Julia:

"The cedar gazebo. Eleven sharp. Meet me."

"There are two."

"The one on the left."

"From which direction?"

"The house."

"Oh god, Gabe."

The night was not winning; it was dark, and somehow Gabe, Julia maybe – no one could say exactly since both were dead reckoning without a flashlight – ended up in the wrong gazebo. They waited an hour and left, assuming the other had ditched the plan.

Gabe looked over at Yael now, her eyes rolling. He knew she needed a cigarette but he wasn't going to stop.

"We'll get there," he said. "It's always a glut up in these parts."

It was. Gunmetal Benzes, Jaguars and Audis sleeker than polished stones, all bumping fractionally towards the rears of their luxury brethren. A stray orange Bronco from the 60s began butting its way in from the shoulder. Gabe waved this stunner into the gap. In its sun-peeled front seat sat a veritable Norseman, his passenger a dream in biker boots, cutoff Levis, her V-neck Haines T plunging to reveal sweat-glossed and lissome arcs of breast. When she stood up on tiptoes to get a view of the traffic, her shirt flared up like a mainsail, exposing her midriff. It was easy to forget the longhair's tailpipe purring smoke into the hairline fissure of Gabe's windscreen, until Yael lurched forward and put her finger on the spot.

"I see it," she said. "I wonder if it's dangerous."

The Norseman did not wave thanks when he nosed in. Gabe noted that. After a minute in front of them, the Bronco pulled off to the shoulder and sped ahead into the dust.

Pulling up to the house, Gabe found Sandy waiting in his wheelchair, the machine humming on the broken shells: the rich man's driveway gravel. Kai's enormous shadow padded about the kitchen through the drapes.

Julia emerged from the house and looked so smashing Gabe about buckled to his knees. Her Joan of Arc hair had grown out, undomesticated after a fashion. She had had her teeth bonded. They seemed smaller but more vivid, the surrounding dimples more explosively alert. He was so busy chasing her all these years he hadn't noticed that her eyes were shaped like minnows.

But there was something platonic in her cheer, something less charged; more at peace with itself. Had Carl remediated? Or was there …

No. Well. Of course, it could certainly be. Gabe had stumbled, procrastinated, really, perhaps to stoke the fire even more, but the starved wouldn't remain that way forever. Julia had to act. Had she? The dimples, the anodized tuskwork, that gaze …

She hugged Gabe like a cousin. He thought he would spool out right there. He told himself she was acting, dissembling the connection. That would get him through lunch. After lunch, if he made it through the medley of marinated crabmeats without lashing out in the glossolalia of a psychotic break, he would ask her, face the doom he wasn't ready for.

Julia clutched Carl's arm as Kai, towering, sandaled in enormous Birkenstocks, led them up to the roof deck. There the shelled shrimp were waiting, the fresh-squeezed Svedka-loaded lemonade. They sat and Gabe passed significant glances at Julia. The glance was not returned. He bit a shrimp in half without dipping it in cocktail sauce. Some kind of subaqueous discharge splashed on his chin and he wiped off the whey with his shirt sleeve, defiantly.

"You all right, Gabe?" said Yael.

"The drive winded me," he said. "I'm a little nuts."

Carl, who had a whole midden of prawns on his plate, wearing his napkin like a bib, his mouth full, said, "We took a bus."

"The Jitney," said Julia.

"Straight shot," he said. "They even gave you water."

"That must've been a whole new world for you," said Gabe.

"*Gabe,*" said Sandy. "You are on the warpath."

"Yeah Gabe, *have a drink, will ya?*" said Julia, mock attaboy.

"Oh huh huh huh huh huh," said Gabe.

Three drinks later, he had corked up the gumption and clutched Julia's hand under the table. He met no resistance but noted that she didn't squeeze either. He closed his eyes; he opened his eyes.

He said, "Who do I have to fuck to get a *nap* around here?!"

"*Take* one, then," said Julia.

"Kai has the beds all ready," said Sandy. "Your sheets just like you like them."

"Rubber. With fire engines," said Yael.

The evening culminated in a seeming parade of board games. One was called *Apples to Apples* and was less invigorating than the outbound drive. Throughout it, Yael laughed aggressively and Carl massaged his wife's shoulders. They were supple bones, the kind of dancerly clavicles Gabe did not see on his wife. He was bothered to find he was bothered by this, the precise iniquity of it all, but there it was. He watched Carl's hands smooth out Julia's goosebumps; the hands were buniony, wide, wedges of crude flesh, mugging her exquisite collarbones. When set against his brawny grabbers, his face was small, rodentlike, obscene.

Presently Kai emerged from the kitchen with compote of berries and rum. There was always too much liquor here. Sandy, diminutive, chock full of snapped wires, somehow had the constitution to handle it. Carl and Kai could absorb anything within their hulking chasses, but Gabe felt the dizzies from the start.

He began shinning Julia under the table. She flicked him away with her hand. He shinned her harder, pinning her leg against the sofa. She sighed. This made Gabe sigh louder, and all heads volleyed.

"Are you bored, Gabe?" asked Sandy.

"Not even a little bit. This compote is bitchin'."

The room nearly burned up in laughter. The laughs were like a hot iron on his neck.

"'Bitchin', is it," said Sandy. "Are we at the *mall?* Is it '86 again?"

"Would that it were," said Kai.

Outside, the ocean became louder and they all stopped and listened.

"I miss water," said Carl.

"Go to the tap," said Julia.

"I don't mean the tap, like drinking it. I miss the proximity."

"I always make sure I'm near it all the time," said Sandy. "I don't miss a chance. Maybe the Sioux could make a game of being inland, or the Wisconsinites."

"They got twenty-thousand lakes," said Carl.

"Minnesota," said Gabe.

"Lakes are haunted by boring ghosts," said Kai. "Some kid who got diced up by an outboard waterskiing in 1970, terrorizing the prepubescents in their bunks. No offense, Sandy, I like Woodstock. But in oceans you have those whale hunters, those peg-legged bosuns on the mizzenmast, and lest we forget the Wreck of the Marie Celeste."

"We're all haunted by boring ghosts," said Gabe. Yael looked over at him sharply, her head turning quickly.

"Sometimes I think I paint so the ghosts are less boring," said Carl.

"Or more boring," said Julia, smiling through a sip.

"You can save your water," said Yael, drawling, looking at Gabe. "Religion is the most boring ghost. You know. In our park. There's this, we have these Watchtower hawkers. Jehovah's Witnesses. Old white-haired man, very natty in his Baltic way, and this zaftig black sort of throwback maidservant who seems so thoroughly content to just sit. They *sit* there, little lawn chairs. Just a sort of a resignation of nonsuccess on their face. I mean the Hari Krishnas at least do chants. They give you intriguing material. But these — how can they stand to just sit? Youth is going by on skateboards. They are seeing lesbians with the hair of some redneck samurai doing all but the full beast in front of them. They see a blur of nanotechnology rising on the streets above their heads. And then there's Byron Doumanian's wife the yogi. He did Eastern meditation. Eastern meditation didn't save him from a neural disease. Some might say it gave him a 'roadmap' through the final tunnel, all the Buddha blarney armed and ready like a Thanatopic navigation technique. But there she goes, still pushing the sadhana to the wives." She took another belt of her drink, wincing through an acid swallow. "I had this vision growing up that once something is disproven the world adjusts. But we're staring the untenable in the face, and it's mother may I have another. We don't ever want to cut and run. I mean, I mean, if you take love, even when there's still some pulse in the body, it isn't always right. It won't *do* you. I am sorry. You will be damned sure to get submarined when abiding by your own true love, whatever that means anymore. People wonder why war, why religion, why marriage. We don't want to spoil the momentum. Ninety percent of the world is just rote."

"They *make* them sit there," Julia said, stanching the cigarette she was holding, her head down.

"What?" Yael said crossly.

"The Jehovah's people. They have to. They make them."

"Same difference," said Sandy.

Yael looked daggers at Julia.

"Band Aids," said Kai. "Yael wants to *rip the Band Aid.*"

"Off what?" said Gabe. But he regretted asking, worried she might get specific.

"Everything," said Yael. "I want to find a new planet."

"Terraforming," said Carl, speaking confidently from his trance.

Gabe noticed himself running a finger up and down Julia's back. His hand didn't seem attached to him. What was better: Julia wasn't doing anything to stop it, but it might just be she was drunk and wasn't sure whose hand it was. No, of course, Carl was almost a spotlit presence in his barrel chair bounded by plushy armrests. She couldn't think it was him. He kept up the finger stroking, his heart restored, his groin throbbing. All of a sudden Julia rose with an ostentatious yawn.

"That Jitney. I hate to be a drag but I think I'm crashing."

"You're kidding," said Sandy. "You'll miss the disquisitions."

Gabe felt slapped, nauseated. Carl just sat there, arms on his recliner like a bloated kingpin.

Gabe told Julia, "You should sleep."

"Thanks, Gabe," said Julia, cocking her head in mock surprise, doing a little southern curtsey thing with her dress. "I'm glad you care."

Gabe gave her a full-on salute.

"What about our de Kooning here?" said Sandy, pointing at Carl.

Julia tapped him but he didn't stir, just smiled. She waved him off and began a slow and rhythmic climb of the stairs, which creaked under her. A few seconds passed and there was the sound of a door shutting.

While Yael stayed outside in a sling chair smoking, Gabe collapsed down on his bed, his face digging into the covers. He drooled on the fabric, drowning a little stitched tern as his mind turned loose on his sorrow. He felt suddenly old but unfurnished; what was he beyond a guy with a sinecure at his brother's ad firm, a halfhearted husband to his wife. It didn't mean much that he had stuck it out; his parents seemed happier, on opposite sides of the same small city but close enough to lob mortars across the mall-studded valley in between. He wasn't sure what he was good for. The world is a prism, he thought, more forgivingly, but he'd never learned to narrowcast whatever wares he'd had onto the kind of lucid surface that would more accurately refract his given light. Sandy was a genius at knowing his skillset, teaching "not the student" he always said, "but the child they were." Well, fine. To edify these pustuled dweebs he applied his southern bearing. And they respected him; found the ontological solutions they could convince themselves were not merely anecdotes dressed up in spiraled clauses as he ran on about Emerson from his chair. Most paraplegics' feet pigeon in, like toddlers'. Sandy's remained straight, as if ready to spring up for a round of croquet. What of the others in his midst? What were they born for? He couldn't imagine it. It only struck him now how Yael's beguiling snark only fell away around children. Children were as much habit as marriage, he thought; but they must have lay at the bottom of her "disquisition." He had prevaricated about them until it was no longer a subject. He had given Yael no alternatives but to love him and bear him; assuming the averages it was either him or the Peace Corps; him or a Bank Street kitchenette where she would noodle over the acrostic puzzle while the young clearing out from the bars below backed against her building eating face: a thought he resisted with a flinch of his shoulders, a stanching of eyeball pain, as his thoughts became cloudy, and then black.

He woke with Yael sleeping next to him. So she hadn't walked off unto the breach. He was pleased to find her there; he felt warmed, as by a house. He leaned over and kissed her on the shoulder but she didn't move. He kissed it again and pressed a finger into the palm of her hand. She issued a pleasant sigh, smiling and fingering his palm back, still sleeping. It could almost make him forget her little speech.

He heart was racing, the booze doing voodoo. He went downstairs. The wooden smell of a house uninhabited nine months out of the year was palpable, the ocean quieter. He drank water, knowing it wouldn't halt the onrush of the poison one whit. Upstairs there was a pensive creak of a door, then footsteps, not clomping but careful. He knew Yael's rhythms and ruled her out. Carl's strides were unnuanced, so something of a promise was in those feet.

He closed his eyes, waited for stairs to stop creaking, let the moment meet his wish, and opened his eyes again. Julia stood in the doorway. She walked right up to him and put a finger on his lips. It was not a dream.

"This can't happen," she said. "That's a disappointment to you. Well, you'll deal with it."

He brushed her finger away.

"Why?"

"It's not fair. We're getting on in years, Gabe. I will be forty in three of them. You will be forty in one. Carl and Yael are already there. None of us have any children. And that part is crucial."

"Kids?"

"When we married who did we adopt but each other. Carl is my child and I am his. Yael is yours. Don't deny it."

"That would make me your stepchild?"

"Glibness now." She zagged those minnow eyes. "I took the winter thinking about this, knowing we would converge." He liked that she used the word "converge" – aside from having all the archness of a daytime drama, it suggested hurricane forces, moon-sprung thunder, Category Five solar winds. "This recklessness," she said. "It will kill our children. You have to think poor Carl. You'd better begin to think poor Yael. That whaduyacallit after charades that she gave. And they were the ones who brought us together."

Gabe could have jumped ten feet in the air. He didn't know what to do with the unchanneled rush, so he rested his head against the refrigerator. He could turn around and look her in the eyes and see himself, not another, not a replacement; he would not have to stare down a reinvigorated passion for her lummox Carl and his sprawling easels. She was a penitent here, he saw, and this produced in him a pathetic smile. He found women's indignation charming. They stood screaming at you while you were only a mask. If you could ride it out, they would soon realize they were the ones wearing it. Once they knew that, they would never admit they were wrong – not in words; it would all come out as indulgence.

"I think you're right about this," he said. "Now if you'll just take a walk with me."

The first kiss was deeper and more burrowing than the one they had tried upstate. There was no falling because his feet were anchored perfectly in the sand. She held his hair and pulled at strands of it and plinked out a little minuet on his navel, pecking in small spit pools around his lips and then going in with more insistence. He felt overwhelmed but a match for it, and pulled her nightgown up over her and tossed it to a damned torpedo. She went at his belt while he threw his shirt off to the same place. She saw him stark and bobbing and took that by the hand and led him into the water, a natural place, where they collapsed. The waves were gently pulling, and they carried out to where the two were submerged to the waist. They had to resume the necking where it was on the shore; it was a moment to revisit, to trail out, and now in the water they could see each other by a more caressing frame of moonlight.

"It's not so cold," she said.

His mouth made bubbles in the water. "I don't feel cold at all."

He did think of his room fifty yards away, what was sleeping there, but that didn't retract him any; nor did the thought of

Carl waiting on shore rubbing his knuckles undo him either. There was life and childhood, Yael's spectral kids, long unifying chains of mourning, the geriatric undertow of the commitment that would riddle them in future days, and then there was this, and this would have to do right now if any of the other things mattered. She lowered her head down to his waist and there was no doubt he was in new country; then – wisely – she let off, rose, pushed him lower by the shoulder and fell forward into a stooped embrace, looking at him as though about to impart something rueful but horribly, terminally true. Now she fit him in and his amazement was immediate, the surge of his glands too stark and he tempered his motions. She seemed to be halfway to climax when he went in and Gabe knew he had to turn his ears off; let her run her course and wait for the second bout – and oh let there be one – for any kind of simultaneity to occur. Better to enjoy this, notate it from afar, and he continued in detached, rhythmic thrusts. He counted thrusts the way people count sheep, and in the mechanics of this counting a buried worry broke free: I've done it. This is what we call being "untrue". This cracking of a little radius, by flesh that feels like an eyelid. But there was no escaping the twinge that something changed, a little scratch in the Rolls Royce Silver Shadow that saw generations caress its leather seats and fawn over its perfect upkeep. You could replace the door, but it wouldn't be the same car.

Soon Julia was climbing him, shaking, biting his back. He felt a decisive uteran clench and she was draped on him as he was bigger than ever in spite of himself.

"Your turn," she said, her voice fuller than ever, relaxed, lower, laughing.

So now he had permission. He began a thrust backward but felt no give. He tried again. It was a funny thing, as though the clench had numbed him down there.

"You can move, you know," she said. "It's kind of a part of it."

"I'm trying," he said. "It won't budge."

"That's impossible."

"Feels tight." He wriggled. "Really … intractable."

He pulled backward but this time felt it in his groin.

"I don't like this as jokes go," she said.

"Who's joking? It won't," he said, through clenched teeth, *"move."*

Suddenly, it all seemed possible. If snogging this limber wonder under a summer moon on a sheet of eternal water where the only missing thing might be an animated kestrel flinging a stardust trail across their brave nude forms was suddenly within the realm of thinking, his penis being fox-trapped in Julia's very plumbing was no far leap.

"Oh shit," he said. "I've heard of this."

"What?"

"The climax in the water; it's a vacuum."

"Does it last?"

Gabe closed his eyes and nodded.

"Well god! How do you get out?"

"They use a shot. Relaxes the muscles."

She began swiveling her head quickly, as if looking for a lifeboat, or a passing schooner light beyond the breakwater.

"Can you at least, like, wedge your fingers in there?" she said.

He used the smallest finger he had, which he remembered was his pinky, and positioned it as a pry bar, wiggling in to where they were stuck fast; he felt nothing but a sharp pinching. He was retracting. And although he thought he only thought it, he said it: "I'm retracting."

"Well that's good, isn't it?" said Julia.

"I dunno. I don't think so." He pulled and no go.

"Can we get out of the water," said Julia. "Maybe that will ease the suction."

The thought of movement was stultifying; his primal lever gasping in a noose. With the retraction of each new coil, a kind of electroshock sent his dumb tongue stabbing over the barrier of his bottom lip; it was almost Pavlovian. The fourth or fifth time it happened, she stared at him agog and said, "Boy, you're really feeling this." He would have cussed her for crimes of inhumanity but there was something else: He was beginning to plump. The pain was new too; where it would go and how far each time the coils drew back was the Sixty-Four Thousand Dollar Question.

"Hardening," he wheezed out through clenched teeth.

"What?"

"I need to be engorged here. It hurts retracting. Talk me up." His voice was husky now, like a tribal elder.

"Jesus."

She tried a few blunt phrasings but she was no real pro at dirty talk. Yael could be, and it had always made him bristle. He'd felt exploited, almost scandalized by this intruder in his bed. Now he was begging for it.

She bit his ear. That was better. He said, "More. More." But when she lurched upward to really chomp on his lobe a sharp stab where it counted nearly dashed him. She adjusted, licking his face in a perfect circle.

He wondered if under better circumstances this could manage to not be disgusting. She saw him wince and stopped.

He had now to enact the inverse of mining the unappetizing slide reel in order to keep himself effectively in play (no baseball, no sir). Of course, if he was too successful, he'd be back where he began, but there was very little chance of that happening. He was referencing anything; a menu of past conquests; the acrobatic couple from Yael's perennially mothballed

Kamasutra guide, Charlotte Rampling. He asked Julia politely to cup his testes. He remembered that once a girl had done this and the name of the girl that did.

Julia did as asked.

"Just keep your hand like that. Suggestive, suggestive. Talk," said Gabe.

She rolled her eyes.

"Your balls feel good, leaden," she said in a randy whisper. "They're so leaden they could crush me."

He saw his testicles rolling Mothra-like over a Japan. He must've smirked because Julia yanked herself back and he had to stanch a scream.

"I don't do this on command," she said crossly.

He looked at the moon, how it seemed to have found a finer, yellower cast, and panic shot through him. There was no given time before a rescuer – or fate – might arrive to make the essential winching. Even rotating movement here wouldn't help make the snarled blood get flowing to the place it was needed. He suddenly remembered the term: *Penis captivus.* The last Roman you'd ever want to meet. The name made it serious, of course, real. It was a *condition.* How long before the fifth limb would meet its somatic expiry? To get away from that thought, he let his mind shift to the more logistical permutations of the dawn: Yael deciding to walk off her hangover. Or Carl wanting to paint the sunrise.

Gabe said, "What if Carl wants to paint the sunrise?"

Julia didn't register the implication right away.

"You know?" said Gabe. "What if he comes *down?*"

"Oh god, *right,* like painters just paint anything. Besides" she said, "he would sooner clobber me than you."

"He's violent?" Gabe thought that would suit his image just fine.

"I don't think he's ever squashed a bug," she said. "But that kind of heartache could make him do anything."

Gabe had the thought that if Yael didn't immediately kill herself she would be happy to separate their loins with pruning shears. If the thought of such discovery were not enough, Gabe could sense the water getting higher. They could count their luckies the tide hadn't turn to rips thus far, pulling them out by intervals. (A Block Island trawler would find them, prompting the skipper to pour forth in silver-tongued eulogy: "Till death do us part my *ass*.") He looked up at Sandy's; the ignorant little breadbox on a bluff. If Kai found them, or Sandy for that matter, they could engineer something, some kind of accommodation. Gabe knew Sandy had an ambient liking for Yael and Carl but beyond that ambience was probably not too favoring of the pair. He would be willing to minimize the hurt, to dissemble and conspire, if for nothing other than to mine it for a little more gossip. But all that would be moot for the racket they might make.

"We can't go to the house," said Gabe.

"Where to then?" said Julia, shivering a little now.

He remembered.

"There's the other one. A little higher on the bluff." He pointed to the left of the breadbox to a cedar house, where a small square of dimmed light shone in back.

"People leave their doors unlocked when they're here," said Gabe. "If we can get in there–"

"That's Gutstein's, Gabe."

"What?"

"Leonard Gutstein. The painter. Carl loves him."

Now Gabe remembered vaguely, some years back, the dolt marching over with a kind of pioneer vigor to break bread with this mystery guy and being effectively sent packing the other way, spending the rest of the weekend staring and shifting about uneasily, as though concealing a diagnosis.

"You think he's there?" said Gabe. "The place looks condemned." He realized that didn't tell you much of anything when it came to artists.

"He doesn't get on too well with Sandy, I think," she said.

"He might go the extra mile for us," said Gabe. "Lie just to keep him in the dark." Julia nodded.

They began a squatting foxtrot to the shore. The pain was unearthly. He held onto her shoulders to truss her right, and she onto his. He heard her groan; he hadn't thought this might start to smart for her. All that trying to relax her contracted muscles against his rising chub might just be a continuing source of agony; these parts unsuited for this sort of high-impact flex. Had they only progressed to a new pose, he thought; had only the suction gripped them when he was at her from behind. Then she could tow him easy, a long uphill asana of double-decked "dog".

They made inching progress toward the dunes, where the sand would harden and help them and then soften higher up and then not. The undertow made halfhearted clutches at their ankles, just robust enough to have them bear down, which slowed their advance. But here they were, by steps, and the sand met them. Anciently nude, they dredged their bones from the water and clutched each other's buttocks. Stars blinked down volleying off a stray plane nine miles high above the Moriches, the last mortals fleeing the Milky Way. Gabe felt like they were only people on Earth.

They began up the beach.

They could thank the moon for lighting them through the drifts, helping them avoid sudden steep falls which could make this a separating event. He saw himself fishing around the dunes for his very package. Upon retrieving it, he would rise in demented triumph holding the dong up to mighty Polaris, bawling in almost Visigothic phonates while his crotch looked like a lensless SLR.

"I can't feel my legs," said Julia. "We have to switch. Roll."

"Right."

It wasn't sex, Gabe thought, but it was teamwork; the Pensacola cracker and the Harlem black going full-on homoerotic on a Mekong trail. Gabe went down and rolled Julia carefully on top of him. Now they commenced the slight grade up the sands, the jelly-textured seagrass bunched like little nests of Dr. Seuss hair beneath them; small spikes of driftwood, hermit crabs. Suddenly, Gabe felt a twinge from the webbing of his glands, the first renal whispers of an angry god. He stopped mid-roll.

"Shit."

"What?" said Julia.

"I have to … you know."

"Oh no you don't," she said. "Not here, not now. This is sick, Gabe, *sick!*"

He tensed further. He knew it was a bad enough doing this logroll pasted at the nexus of tender "spots" that one shouldn't have to be rendered a human toilet. He owed that to her, at least.

They rolled further, getting closer to the bluff. World War II had hinged on such topography, Gabe remembered. They would have to resume their tandem squat. They managed the transition to half-standing, negotiating the rise-to-knee hike in a grind with their trunks flush to each other. Julia this time took the first step and Gabe followed. There was no strength, only the drubbing of his testes, the hyperextended wrenching of his knees. After a good ten or eleven of these arachnoid stutter steps Julia wobbled on her cold soles, sighing.

He couldn't see her eyes, her bright little ovals which always betrayed nothing but the present. She was here with Gabe and she would stay, had to stay, but a shroud of resentment would fall on each of their encounters from now on if they ever dared to rendezvous again. What were the odds that would happen? The relaxant in the needle would vault them instantaneously to separate hemispheres. They would need to forget this, and thus, each other. He did wonder about that needle. What if it didn't take? Would they pry his dangler loose with a pair of forceps? He would be another baby of hers then: Eat that, Carl.

Back on the climb and higher, the air felt slightly different, the wind more textural. Now bunched spikes and parched grass were popping through the leisurely sand. A curling xylophone of demarcating fence wound towards them and stopped at the point where some windblown beach pines fell. The dry locks of saltbush were more satiny on their feet. Gabe wondered about the tableau from above: an attraction at a bacchanal, or a modish installation wrenched into an alcove of one of Carl's group shows. "Those are The Sandworms," the curator would say louchely, holding his Shiraz atilt.

They were cresting the hill. Julia's heel struck a rock and she bent into him, her head smacking his jaw and their footing wobbled, the moment in cascade: an event. They fell over each other, clutching, punching, then landing. Once stopped, the dread markers of progress fell away, and there was a house, a corrugated cedar "shake" ranch resting on a flat plot of weather-beaten sand. There was the rear bug zapper, the muted gleam they had seen from the water, fritzing the nuisances like a charm. Gabe couldn't tell if the house was vacant; there was only a rusted Dodge Power Wagon notched into a trace near the bluff to suggest that life was there. In the quiet here Gabe began to notice things: He was numb; he could only hope with adrenaline. There were nameless insects flickering in the dry reeds around them. The tide was louder now.

"I don't see lights," said Julia.

"What?"

"At Sandy's," she said, looking eastward. "I think everyone's still sleeping."

They rounded the house in a barrel roll and saw through the window that a light was on. No way to get at the knob lying down. It was time to stand, one last genital finesse and they'd be able to hit the bell. But they were spent, their bones without joints, their tibias arbitrary filaments in the cloudy suspension fluid of their legs.

"One more," said Gabe. Julia planted a hand on his shoulder to hoist herself up and Gabe jerked his rump up, rising against Julia; her breasts were piquant but mostly forgotten against the sand clods caked on his sternum. Now they were standing and here was the door: white wood, screened, with a dirty window behind which a sooty old voile curtain draped. Gabe jerked the screen door, releasing some carmelized midges as it sprung open, unlocked already. He grabbed the doorknob with his hand, cranking hard; but the old bolt and spindle deal was solid.

It struck Gabe now there might be a burglar alarm. The rusty pickup notwithstanding, there was no telling what was inside this place that may have been worth safeguarding with the latest in sonic watchdoggery. They had to get inside; somehow indoors there could be instruments, mid-century first aid kits, an old Trinitron to watch while their genitals turned a thrombotic blue.

"Can you break the window on the door?" said Julia.

"The noise could travel-"

"Break it!" she said. "Break the window."

Something seemed to have aligned for her and her voice came out full and commanding. Gabe had no choice but to trust it, use what little leverage he could summon from this contorted half-stance to get it all over in one bashing.

He brought his arm forward. The glass crashed everywhere, and though his elbow was a cherry-rhubarb spectacular, he could sense that nothing very vital had been clipped. There were no simulated sirens or digitized avian hubbub, not even a teacup poodle to come snuffling out its feeble remonstrance, just the wind through the dirty curtain, slapping him in the face. He looped his bloody arm in and turned the bolt, then the knob. He opened the door forward and on an intrepid step promptly tripped over a raise in the threshold, spilling to the floor with Julia's weight on top of him. He found himself uttering the rattles of a dying man, almost delusional with pain and relief under Julia's diaphragmatic holler. Had he finally jolted her irreparably in that place? He jerked his head out from under her and saw that she was staring ahead.

"It's *like* a kind of knocking," said the man sitting at the kitchen table, a coffee cup in his hand and a large, artless sandwich in front of him on a plate.

He seemed to have been already speaking to them when they crashed in, as though picking up a conversation whose tenor was already set.

"We're so sorry, Mr. Gutstein," said Julia. "We didn't mean to break in. We crawled all the way from the water."

"We're stuck," said Gabe. "We need you to drive us to the hospital."

"The hospital?" Gutstein said. "Well. It's not open."

"Of course it is," said Gabe. "They're always open."

"If you say so," said Gutstein. "But you don't know from me. I could be anyone."

"We know who you are," said Julia.

Gabe looked at Gutstein, the picture of a shtick outré that inevitably turned real at some point, the humus smell of seclusion emanating from his Carhart pants, his silvery hair slicked back to the neck by a month of collected grease; the hawkish profile, once handsome, cratered. When he spoke his accent would shift mid-sentence from phlegmatic Bronx labor chief to that of an Etonian fop; it was difficult to say which one was more affected.

"You're part of Sandy's coterie," said Gutstein. "Sandy and I are not close. Bridges too far." He rose to his feet and poured coffee into his cup from a decanter. Next to it was a mason jar of liquid: alkaline yellow. He held the cup to his chest with the faint aspiring smile of a trial lawyer ramping up to an opening gambit.

"That jar, it's piss," he said. "John backs up. Between the Bayside commodes I was raised with, my time dating around Croatian port towns, going down as far south as Ancona and living with those choice little *domesticas* hauling human slag down from the promontory dwellings to the bay, I have never had the blessing of a proper crapper."

Gutstein now looked down at them, as though for the first time realizing the state they were in.

"Fusion?!" he said. "Why are you doing this on my floor? Why did you come in here to do this?"

"We're stuck. We told you," said Julia.

"Why don't Sandy's people take you where you need to go?" said Gutstein.

"They can't know," said Gabe.

"Why?"

"We're married," said Gabe.

"To people next door," said Julia. "People who are sleeping next door."

"Ah," said Gutstein. "You bring intrigue into my kitchen?" Suddenly he didn't seem mad anymore. "Fazio's on Amsterdam," he said. "Memory lane. My first infidelity, Benita Sandoval,

'63. Met at that butcher's like it was the church steps every Wednesday. I do miss when we would fuck of an evening."

"Is your car working?" said Gabe, trying to shift Gutstein off his path.

But Gutstein turned his face straight ahead to the window over their heads, as though addressing his words to a lighthouse. "I remember our first assignation, like the first time I ate *traif,* Like yesterday I can see going down afterward to an upscale market and buying coffees for Benita. This was back in the untamed Upper West before a skein a sham gourmets obliterated the original Jewish ambiance. Here I again evoke *traif.* A wonderful store I came into. How those poetesses at the cashier's were onto me, beatniks. Raw. Human matte. Talcum white faces. Nothing like the mieskeits of PS 9. They knew I had breached a portcullis of sorts; left schlub Lenny thrown out in a forgotten land, staring up at the wallwalk where a new me strode hung as a murdering lion among the parapets. I would be in the game. I was in the castle. I have dearly liked fish since then."

"What?" said Gabe.

"There was fish in the store." Gutstein sipped his coffee and bit a chunk off of his tuna melt. "It hung there and it was also in the case."

"Ah," said Gabe.

"Sir," said Julia, in an urgent but tinny voice. "We need your assistance by way of a phone. If you won't drive us you can at least let us use your phone."

Gutstein took another bite of his sandwich and another healthy sip of his coffee. He gulped.

"That's good," he said.

Gabe and Julia looked at each other.

"You know you guys astound me," Gutstein said, suddenly rising. "Not a single fucking question about my art! Fuck you!

Fuck you and the very horse you rode in on! I'm going to get some for you now."

Gutstein fled the room and ran to wherever his output was.

"This is worse than being out there," said Julia.

"We can turn him," said Gabe. "We're going to."

The pain was coming back.

"How?"

Gabe had a dire, delirious notion that if they let him paint them, he would deliver them to the hospital, no questions asked.

Gutstein returned holding a giant laminated square of sheet metal, holding it up for them. Gabe knew that this frazzle of dumb blunt angles would, if its progenitor chose to unleash it, fetch bounties of airheaded currency from the lamoes south of Broome Street: an army of Carls and their agents.

"This is what I do," he said. "*Torch*. I use a blowtorch. The metal in sheets and flame on the metal so blow me. Got me some T and A fierce: 'Mr. Gutstein, can you teach me? Can I live with you?' Bushy tails are virtually tripping over the rosebushes with accolades. They had foldout stories on me because the droves thought the torchwork was 'neat'. But it is not that and only that. You must know why I do this, see the gist wherein lies the pattern. So have ears pricked, oh newcomers. Have ears pricked."

He paused, let an imaginary hush fall on the room, then spoke again.

"Geometry. *That,* is what I do."

"Geometry," said Julia.

"I subvert geometric ideas. Math preaches this crap as a feature of its solid and unassailable place. It's understandable; astronomers couldn't rocket their steel whaleships up the uncharted galaxy knowing they hadn't mastered Borsuk's plans and earlier tackled Euclidean Space."

Gabe looked at it again: a tossing of black lines into a blotchy riddle of acetylene char.

"So what does my geometry do?" continued Gutstein. He put his finger into the center of the sheet. "See this polygon center in the gauge." Indeed where Gutstein pointed Gabe saw Star of David shapes and bent triangles all slapped into a graveled Z shape – if one could call it that. The char of the torch made all things a matter of squinting. "Do you see these hexagonal wraiths?" said Gutstein.

Julia nodded at the little stars. Gabe, sure his penis could care less, followed suit.

"I knew you would," said Gutstein. "They're submerged; they are buried. I do this not unconsciously. I have full command and am never left dry by my Innazon 1 chef's torches which have served me well without fail since Reagan's days. I overdid the pentagon, sure, by applying my acetylene portable and now there's char. As a standard I'm fine with a 24 by 24 gauge plain aluminum as my go-to aluminum sheet and usually you won't see this scattered burning. But you must understand what I'm at here in a geometrical plain of thought. Now I'm going to get a little obscure now."

Gabe burst out laughing and Julia smacked his head angrily. So there were limits to teamwork. Yael would have laughed, he thought.

"I misled you, and that's by design," said Gutstein, oblivious. "The Earth is not a polygon. The sun is not one either. But in the run of things the Earth contains all the properties of geometric lines and these imperishable delineation points take Man to the spatial and equilateral spirit of everything that is dear to us. Now look at the painting once more."

He let the sheet take light from the musty chandelier. Gabe's eyes were burning.

"Note, if you will, the triangle," said Gutstein.

"I see it," said Julia. Gabe was sure she was lying. Gutstein must have thought that too.

"Where?" he said, gruffly.

"It's the whole sheet," she said. "More or less."

He chewed his lip and nodded.

Gabe narrowed his gaze and halfway made out at the edges of the metal something of a burned-in trace: an isosceles, with the blurring bevels one sees in early drawings from a child. "The Earth, my friends, is a triangle. All the stargazers are wrong."

He bent down to them, on one knee, the painting held up with its lower edge to the floor but barely touching. Gabe began to feel faint. He needed water. He was getting black dots in his vision, a whirling lagoon of thoughts slithering over his mind's sandbars. The dots could be the spit of cuttlefish, his brain said. His brain might say anything.

"A triangle," continued Gutstein. "Which means we are all equilaterally fucking one another for better or worse. You *had* to show up here. You came to see the painting. I complete your triangle."

"We came because we're stuck," said Gabe, the words coming watery from his maw.

Gutstein shook his head: "You came to see the painting."

He pointed again to the sheet, fingering the space between the triangle and the mottle of squares and stars and overlapping circle shapes.

"You came to see it. Because if it is a polygon there is an incircle, and these circles are where, boys and girls, we refract and reflect each other." He pointed again to the circles in the middle and, when he pulled the sheet up to the light, there seemed to be a shift in the painting's dimensions for only a blip of a moment that Gabe held his eyes on it, and, in that crease in time the charred mess in the middle blinked off into a coil of repeating circles, which did not seem to flee the visual field; instead falling in a vitreous image to the sides of Gabe's eyes before regathering and making a swift curl back, like the swarm of a million Slinkies, creating from the flat frame a prism in which, like parallel rooms in a manifold world, things that had not happened, and some that had, were visible. Byron Doumanian hadn't been deuced by his melted cerebellum and Yael was driving and did not have her hands at ten and two, instead she'd flexed one in a glove of peerless Milan leather onto the wheel at twelve o'clock; she was smiling, because she was young. There were families, not least Sandy and his brood of broodless couples. Gabe could hug Carl near the slapping water and Julia, dread Julia, wouldn't blush. Nobody detached themselves into a simmering quiet by the patio in a race towards premature death. This would include dad and mom, old pets and brother; a many worlds carnival in which divorces were annulled by a toddler's fiat. He spied down on himself in a hammock, his arms reaching out for someone to take …

Gutstein stood up, grabbed the metal painting, turned it to face the cabinet. He crossed his arms on his chest and shook his head, looking down at them.

"I don't see any kind of refraction here. Your incircles are all jammed up with sand. We got to get you the fuck out of Dodge. In a Dodge. To a hospital. Let's go."

Gabe couldn't believe it. Gutstein slapped on an old plaid hunting jacket, stained variously, and directed them out the front door.

"I can't move," said Gabe.

"My God, you look green, Gabe," said Julia: all of her wheatgerm shakes, those treadmilling hours at the health club, lording over him.

Gutstein, six-foot five in his battered work boots, took all four feet in his grubbers, subtle as a logger with a branch. Gabe was once again, perhaps mercifully, insensate below the waist but his head hit every rock and rut on the way to the vehicle. Before Gutstein would let them near the Power Wagon, he wanted to hose them off.

"Thank you, though, we don't need this," said Julia.

"It's not for you, it's for the car," he said; his accent was now the thickest Brooklyn.

He left them on the ground shivering after aiming the large hose nozzle at them for a long time, then crossed to a shed where he produced three large towels, mildewed and stone-stiff, laying them on the backseat of the Wagon. In one heaving motion he piled Gabe and Julia into the seat, then climbed into the driver's seat.

The truck took a few turns to start, making asthmatic rumbles and then high, percussive sounds; the nostalgic smell of carbureted fuel-air filling the cabin with each turn the engine made. Finally the machine got the balance right and Gutstein sat there while it breathed.

"Let it warm up," he said. "This bitch stalls."

Gabe wondered if the engine sputters would wake the whole house up. He needed the thing to move and Julia put voice to his thought.

"We should go," she said.

Gutstein didn't say anything, just sat still while the engine sputtered. Then, with a nod, he pulled the shift back and the truck went back with it and they were off.

On the road, the occasional bumps on the ocean highway were gentle under them, and Gabe looked ahead as Gutstein drove on silently. He bent his eyes over to Julia, who wasn't crying, did not at all seem sad; just impassive, staring at the seat leather in front of her. He liked the sound of the pre-fuel injection roar in front of the steering column, which crowded out the ocean rolling by, and he could think a little more solidly by the sound of the piston snaps. It was probably a delirium that, he suspected, made some kind of epiphany out of those burned-in circles, and he could not bring himself to the degree of sentimental dreaming to believe that anything more cosmic was at play. As they drove on and the bumps burst and rippled through the backseat he remembered that he had to pee, but, fastened as he was to Julia and with everything they'd surmounted that night he would not for all the world let it go in her; and he was very sure that his wife, with any luck still slumbering in style seven miles back, would have let him turn it loose in a second. He was feeling the air through the truck's window splinter his dried brows and felt the tickle of Julia's salt-coarsened hairs against his skin. There was a lot of story in this night and he could not deny it contained shame and that losses would accrue across years in instances he would not control because if one didn't believe in resolution, then nothing or anyone was saved. But it was also hard to deny that the night had been rich, and though the slapstick massacre of its long unraveling lie made any kind of sharing impossible, if there was a person he'd pick for a rainy day to know he had survived these concatenations, and to give them their due grimness in the form of a laugh, there was not a person in the world he would've wanted it to be more than Yael.

The truck continued to mow the road, heading where the lights were on in greater number. The engine was gracefully ticking.

Acknowledgments

I would like to thank the following for their guidance and encouragement, for this book and for more: Christopher Breyer, Nancy Brown, Rivka Galchen, Graeme Gillis, Rebecca Godfrey, J. Holtham, Len Jenkin, Sam Lipsyte, Ben Marcus, Stevan V. Nikolic, William Rosenthal, Elissa Schappell, Ira Silverberg, Bettijane Sills-Garson, Scott Sowers The Great, Lloyd Suh, and the Ucross Foundation.

Publishing History

"Gorse" and "The Wolves" were published by *Adelaide* in 2018, "S-Bahn 5:32" appeared in *Faultline* in 2018. "A Friend of the Zoo" appeared in *The Potomac Review* in 2018. "Field Trip" was published in *THAT Literary Review* in 2019. "Skaters" appeared in *Rivet* in 2019.

About the Author

Ben Rosenthal's stories have appeared in *Adelaide, Faultline, The Potomac Review*, and elsewhere. He is a graduate of Columbia University and The New School for Social Research. His work has received grants from The Alfred P. Sloane Foundation and the National Endowment for the Arts. He lives in New York. This is his first book.